EMBER IN TIME SERIES

RECOVER OR Yield

BOOK TWO

Also by Kim Malaj

Castle of Teskom
Book One
Ember in Time Series

EMBER IN TIME SERIES

RECOVER OR *Yield*

BOOK TWO

KIM MALAJ

Recover or Yield

To my littles

Imagine a greatness just out of your grasp and reach.

That stretch will change, mold, and unfold the secrets to happiness.

Never settle and always keep your truth.

1

"Leon, we won't stay at the Castle of Teskom forever," Danae says, arching her back. "I'm not giving birth here, that's for sure." She shifts from side to side and looks past him. The Castle of Teskom rises at the far side of the clearing, the top hidden in the clouds descending from the night sky.

Leon nods and turns away from her towards the archways. "I won't leave my wife as a stone statue for eternity!" He kicks a small rock across the clearing. "Hell no!"

Danae winces. "How are we supposed to defend the castle and the goddess Ember?" The ember amulet around her neck shifts and vibrates. She presses her palm to still the object.

Leon watches her face change from startled to calm. "What is it?"

"It's vibrating," she explains, lifting the amulet out from under her shirt to look at it more closely.

Leon moves closer and reaches to touch it.

"Wait!" Danae steps out of his reach. "When Itra tried to touch it and he was propelled back. I'm not sure what it will do to you if it did that to my husband."

Leon raises his hand in surrender. He calls his long wooden staff, a gift from Ember. The glow from the top creates a halo of light over them.

"Should we wait out here or in the castle?" he asks.

She turns in a circle, looking at the clearing, the archways, and back to the castle. "I hesitate to stay out in the open after watching the battle this morning. Castle?"

Leon responds by turning towards the castle, but he pauses after a step. He glances once over his shoulder to the archway where Kaly remains. Danae loops her arm through his. She feels his tension slowly release with a long, ragged exhale.

"We'll try everything we can to bring her back," she whispers.

He swallows hard before taking the first step towards the castle. They walk quietly on the worn path up to the enormous steps. He bounds up the first and extends his hand to her. She takes his offered hand, and they climb up the next three giant steps together. Standing at the top, they look back out over the clearing to the five archways.

The night surrounds them with a quiet unease. A cool breeze slithers a wave of chills down her spine. Danae rubs her forearms. She notices a slight shiver run through Leon as well.

She abruptly turns back towards the castle, longing for the warmth of the conservatory just past the foyer. She stumbles to a stop. "Leon!"

Leon whirls, double tapping his staff, transforming it from an ember glow to a long, shimmering scythe.

"What's wrong?" he asks, scanning the entry for intruders.

"The blue and gold waves on the mosaic tiles are gone." Danae kneels to examine the entry floor.

Leon taps his staff back to an ember glow and lowers the light towards the floor. "It's a mural of us standing here and now," he states, stepping back.

"But how?" asks Danae.

"It's a reflection," Teuta says, appearing in the archway leading to the conservatory. Danae and Leon startle at her sudden appearance. She stands barely half as tall as Danae and a third of Leon's height.

"Hmm," Leon mocks with a scowl. "And what else does the great and mighty castle messenger bring us?" Leon rolls to his toes. "More bad news? Or are you sending another loved one away with a single word?"

"Teuta, where is Itra?" Danae asks, placing a hand on Leon's arm.

"Itra is with Elis and Anton." Teuta twirls to enter the conservatory but pauses, tossing two light stones towards Leon and Danae. They catch them and activate them by tapping the center. The light hovers just above their heads, illuminating the entry.

"Come along, we have much to discuss." Teuta dances forward past the first row of plants.

Leon growls. He has not forgiven Teuta for blocking his exit when he attempted to locate his missing wife.

The warm air lifts the chill Danae had been feeling moments before. She nudges Leon along as they follow her towards the dining hall door, always hidden behind climbing vines and rows of plants in the lush conservatory.

Teuta holds open the door. Danae and Leon enter but hesitate a few steps in. The warm yellow walls of the hall are now a vibrant purple and the glass dome, dark by the night sky, has a few new panels of shapes that are currently shifting in various patterns.

"Whoa?" Danae whispers.

"How?" Leon asks.

"Ember." Teuta states. "When a new bloodline is assigned to the castle, the old traces are removed."

"Itra's line is essentially erased?" Danae asks.

"Yes, precisely," Teuta says.

Danae scans the hall. The long table and chairs appear nearly the same, minus the carving on the back of the chairs. A swirl pattern compared to the bird of Mui's crest. The floor's design across the mosaic tiles reflects the castle as it was originally built surrounded by a valley of trees and the mountains to the east. All six doors remain, three on the wall opposite to the conservatory, and each adjacent wall has a single door.

Teuta skips across the hall towards a door opposite of the door they entered. She opens the door with ease. Danae remembers Itra had previously tried to open this door during their first visit. It had been locked.

Teuta walks through the door. The light above her expands.

Danae follows her, but then stops.

"Where are you taking us?" Leon asks, running into Danae.

"To your living quarters and war room," Teuta sings.

"Our what room?" Danae stammers.

Danae and Leon step inside the door. Teuta dances in a large hall draped in ruby red silks with bold purple accents on the walls.

Leon and Danae take in the large ancient marble furniture and the contrast of color on the walls. It's pristine, no dust or cobwebs. The glass dome above has several painted figures of Greek Gods. Zeus, Athena, and a few others they don't recognize.

"What in the—" Leon whispers.

"This is the family war room for Zeus and his descendants," Teuta gleefully sings. "Preserved only for your return."

Danae sighs and shakes her head. "Teuta, we can't stay."

Her smile falls when she faces Leon and Danae. "You two must stay and find the Medusa Shield to protect the Castle of Teskom."

"How?" Danae asks.

"Using this," Teuta says. She holds up the gold cube that the blogger, Unis Beard, had used to transport to the clearing outside of the archways before he died. "Leon said the blogger saw Medusa bring a shield back to the bunker before she sent him to the clearing."

"Yes, but—" Leon says, shaking his head, "why us?"

4

"It is the duty of your bloodline to protect and serve," Teuta says.

"That didn't exactly work out for my sister-in-law," Danae snaps.

"We tried to save Iana," Teuta says.

"But you didn't succeed!" Danae exclaims. "Elis is without his loving mother. I refuse to risk any more of my family, especially Leon, who just lost Kaly." Leon winces. Danae turns for the door. "Figure something else out, we're done."

The door to the dining hall slams shut before she reaches the threshold. Leon double taps his staff and swings the scythe towards Teuta. She vanishes before the arc of his flaming blade can make contact. She appears on the opposite side of the room, unphased and smiling.

"As a descendant of Zeus, you will protect and serve," Teuta sings and waves her hand. "Read and learn."

Two books appear on the large marble table before she vanishes again.

"Son of a—" Leon shouts. His voice echoes back.

Danae curses and kicks the door. She walks over to the table and picks up a book. She looks at the cover. It reads 'OPEN.' She picks up the second book and holds it up so Leon can read the cover.

Leon squints and says, "Medusa Shield."

"The other book booted me out through a protection portal when Itra and I found the castle."

"Great! Try that one first," Leon says. "What chapter was it?"

"Chapter nine," Danae mumbles, bracing for the stomach drop sensation of transporting as she cracks open the book. Nothing happens. She feels an overwhelming compulsion to sit and read.

"Danae, what is it?" Leon asks, watching her eyes narrow. She lowers herself into the chair.

She doesn't hear Leon's question.

"Danae!"

Danae looks up and blinks.

"Sit," she states in a monotone command. "Read. We don't have time."

Leon gapes at her expression and response. He follows her instructions and releases the staff. He rubs his forearm where the new staff tattoo holds the essence of his gift from Ember. He plops in the chair next to Danae and opens the other book on the Medusa Shield.

2

After two hours, Danae and Leon switch books and start the process over again. Leon's stomach growls.

Danae looks up and frowns. "When is the last time you ate anything?"

"With you and Itra before the battle at dawn," Leon answers without looking up from the page. The sound of a tray landing on the table and the tinkle of china breaks his attention from the book. He glances up to find two plates with a burger and fries on each and a foam topped beer. He shoves the book aside, grabbing and draining the beer in one long gulp. Before he sets the empty glass down, another beer appears.

"Easy brother!" Danae scolds. "Food with the beer this time."

Leon snorts, tossing a few fries in his mouth. Danae joins him, starting with her burger.

"Do you think we can recover this shield?" she asks between bites.

He nods and wipes the corner of his mouth. "Turn a few more pages." He motions her to stop on a page with bold cursive writing.

"To seek the lost, you must find, a heart's desire to draw the line." She follows the drawing of a line through the illustration of a maze. The line stops in the center of the maze and then vanishes from the page. She turns the page and turns it back, and the entire image of the maze is gone. "What in the sorcery is this?"

"Magic." He grins. "Did you read chapter seven yet?" He turns the titled "OPEN" book towards her. "It says we can armor ourselves with Ember when on a mission to retrieve or recover an item. Does that mean she rides piggyback on our mission or is this physical armor?"

Danae nearly chokes on her last bite. She clears her throat and takes a sip of her water before she responds. "Turn the page, you goon."

Leon sticks out his tongue and crosses his eyes. He turns the page. An illustration of a cloak with large wings is drawn in the same red and purple decorating the war room. "Whoa!" Danae laughs at his wide grin. "Wings? Dude, does that mean we can fly?"

"No idea," she says, "but I have a feeling we might find out soon enough." She tilts her head toward a wardrobe in the corner of the room that has just appeared.

Leon stands and bolts across the room. He impatiently fumbles with the latch and it finally releases. The doors open, revealing four red and purple cloaks with large wings.

"Freaking cool!" He runs a hand over the feathers.

"I see you found your wings," Teuta says from the door near the dining hall. They scowl at her entrance.

"Lock us in a room one more time," Danae says, pointing in her direction. "And I'll leave you locked in a box next time."

Teuta's smile doesn't fall. "It wasn't you that rescued me. It was Ember."

Danae rolls her eyes. "What are we supposed to do with the cloaks?"

"The ember archways are protected so descendants don't crossover to other dimensions minus the future and past portals," Teuta explains. "The cloaks provide safe passage through the other dimensions."

8

"But Mui's line knew stuff about the other dimensions," Leon argues.

"True, but it's because it's all documented here in the library and the archives." Teuta states, but Danae raises a hand to interrupt. Teuta shakes her head. "If you try to walk under the Ottoman or revolutionary archways, you don't actually travel to that dimension, you remain in the communist dimension. The cloaks are the key to opening the archway to another dimension where you don't belong."

Danae's mouth opens, but no words escape.

Teuta holds up the gold cube for them to see. She taps a corner of the cube the sides fold in. It makes a small square. A string of text hovers above the surface. "The cube contains a record of the jumps the user made." Teuta uses her finger to scroll through the text and highlights the second line. "The coordinates indicate the bunker is at a lake-level path in the Mokset hills."

"That doesn't exactly narrow it down. There are several bunkers near the lake," Danae says, but stops as Teuta holds her hand up.

"In your dimension, yes."

"What dimension is the shield in?"

"It is in the Ottoman dimension," Teuta says, too casually. Danae raises an eyebrow. "Only three bunkers were built on the lake's edge in that dimension, buried deep underground and heavily guarded."

"If they are guarded," Leon says, stepping closer to Danae, "how did Medusa and Poseidon move freely in and out?"

"They likely stoned their way in," Teuta giggles. "You may even find a few statues of soldiers along the way."

"How could you possibly think that is funny?" Leon charges towards her. Danae pulls on his arm to stop a swinging fist.

"Oh, my!" Teuta flutters backwards. "I meant no disrespect towards Kaly." She takes a few more steps away from him before continuing. "That is simply my assumption about how they entered."

9

"If we have the coordinates," Danae says, stepping in front of her brother and points to the hovering text. "Does that mean the cube can drop us in to the exact location?"

"Possibly, the last jump we know of was the dead blogger." Teuta points to the top. "The next one is the assumed location of the shield. Because the next three are all locations here in the castle."

Leon looks over Danae's shoulder. "How do we activate that location and one back here?"

Teuta highlights the third line with her finger. "This is the present cavern." She hands Danae the square. "When you press two sides in, it will transform back to a cube. There is a three second delay. Those connected to the cube will be transported. Leon, take Danae's hand." He complies but is still frowning. "Now press and wait."

"Now?" Danae asks. Teuta nods.

Danae presses a side with her thumb and pointer finger. It pops back up to a cube. She tightens her grip around the cube as the floor falls out from under her.

Danae's feet find the floor, and she looks around the space. The open cavern wall with the sheer drop to the lake, the crumpled box in the corner near the edge, and a new statue of a half-veiled woman makes her take a few steps back, releasing Leon's hand.

"Ugh," Leon groans. He bends at the waist, attempting to breathe normally. "This will never feel normal." He straightens and finds the statue of the Medusa. He calls his staff and double taps for the scythe.

"Careful!" Danae mutters. "You could do some serious damage with that thing."

He sighs and taps the staff back to the ember glow. He steps closer to the opening but doesn't look directly down.

"It looks peaceful without a fleet of enemy ships," Leon says, watching moonlight dance in the small ripples of the lake. "How many sunk during the battle?"

10

Danae shakes off a chill. She turns towards the interior wall. "Show me Itra."

An image flickers to life. The light catches Leon's attention. Itra has a sleeping Elis draped over his lap on the sofa in the living room of Anton and Iana's city apartment. Anton is behind him, talking on the phone and pacing.

"Itra, can you hear me?" Danae asks. Elis stirs at her call. Itra looks up. "It's me and Leon."

"I can hear you," Itra whispers. "Are you ok? What's happening?"

"I'm fine," Danae responds, but hesitates to divulge the task Teuta has placed upon her and Leon. "We're being orientated as the new descendants. I hope to be home soon. How are Elis and Anton? And how are you?"

"We need your help." Itra frowns. "Elis's memory of Iana's passing won't stick. It's like the memory wipe erased any recall of how or why Iana is gone. Anton is forgetting as well. And I don't know how long I'll remember."

"Teuta," Danae calls loudly.

"Yes," Teuta says, arriving at Danae's side, nearly making her fall into Leon with alarm.

Danae repeats Itra's concern. Teuta shakes her head before responding. "It is true, soon they won't remember the castle, the battle, the ember archways or anything related to the goddess Ember. However, I can make another scenario stick for all three."

"Itra, are you going to be ok forgetting the truth?" Danae's voice cracks on the last word.

"If it means I don't have to break my nephew's heart over and over again, then yes." A single tear falls down his cheek, landing in Elis's wavy brown hair.

"Done," Teuta sings. The image fades as she vanishes.

3

Itra lays Elis back in his bed and joins Anton in the hall.

"Have you heard from Danae?" Anton whispers.

Itra feels a tingle run up his spine. A scene unfolds like a vivid nightmare. Iana is carrying Elis upstairs from the car. She slips on the top step, falls back, and hits her head on a step. He releases a breath.

Itra shakes his head, trying to process Anton's question. "I think my lack of sleep has caught up with me. What was your question?"

Anton rubs a hand through his hair, and his brows crease. "Have you heard from Danae?"

"Danae—is with Leon." Itra tries to recall the last time he spoke with her. "I'll call my Uncle Vincent and he'll help contact the family on my dad's side. And my cousin, Nada, on my mom's side." Itra pours a glass of water and drains it one gulp. "Did the funeral director say when we can—"

"Yes, in two days." Anton looks at his phone. "My parents are coming by in a few minutes so we can get some rest. They'll care for Elis if he gets up. You can take the guest room. I'll be on the couch in the office."

"Why the couch?"

"The thought of lying in there," Anton whispers, pointing to the master bedroom door, "without—I just can't."

Itra shakes his head. "I'll take the office. I need to use the phone in there to make my calls. Please, I insist, take your guest room. I really don't mind the couch."

Itra hangs up the phone with Nada. She cried more than she spoke, but she agreed to call her side of the family. He wipes his tears away before picking up the phone to dial his uncle. Memories of their last visit with Uncle Vincent come flooding back. Iana's laugh when she declared victory over Leon at dominos. Iana's smile and tears at the announcement of Danae's pregnancy. Itra stands to pace the room. *How will I ever be able to enjoy another family gathering without her?*

Ring, ring

He fumbles with the receiver but manages not to drop it on the desk before answering. "Hello?"

"Anton, is that you?" a male voice asks.

"No, this is Itra. Who is this?"

"Vincent."

"Oh, I was just about to call you."

"Good, can you tell me where Duke is?"

Itra sits down, confused, and unable to respond for a full five seconds.

"Itra, are you there?"

"Yes, sorry. Your dog is missing?"

"Well, no, not missing," Vincent sighs. "Kaly had her neighbors watch Duke, and I can't get a hold of Kaly."

"You may want to leave Duke with the neighbors until you return home again."

"Return? Why would I leave again? I just got home."

"Iana—she's—there was an accident."

"Did you say accident?"

"Yes, Iana's gone." He winces, waiting for his uncle's reaction.

"*Gone where?*"

"Iana's gone—she died."

The shuffle of footsteps and a door slamming are the only sounds Itra can hear in response.

"Hello, are you there?"

"On my way," Vincent mumbles. "I'll call again from the airport when I have a flight number." The line disconnects without another word.

Itra freezes, with the phone receiver still pressed to his ear. He only snaps out of it once the dial tone returns. Itra hangs up the receiver and eyes the couch. He feels the weight of this new reality sinking in between each rib. He staggers to the couch and buries his face in the cushion to quiet his sobs until he finally falls asleep.

4

"Show me, Itra!" Danae shouts at the wall.

Nothing happens. She tries three more times before Leon releases his staff and swallows her in a protective hug. She cries softly into his shoulder.

Eventually, she loosens her grip around him. Leon sniffles and clears his throat, trying to pull himself together as Danae looks up at her big brother's face. His lower lip quivers as she rolls up on to her toes to kiss his cheek.

"I'll do everything in my power to find us peace," she says.

He nods. She loops her arm through his. They slowly climb the spiral stone staircase out of the present cavern.

"We need to rest before going on this fool's errand," Danae says, stepping up the last step into the rear landing.

"Teuta mentioned different living quarters," Leon says. Danae nods but doesn't look up from the floor.

"The mural on this floor has changed," Danae says. She kneels to inspect the mosaic tiles more closely. "This one had five archways and red flames yesterday. What do you make of this?"

She stands back up, pointing out one archway that is connected to a ring.

"Odd," Leon says, silently counting. "There are twelve points inside the ring. A clock?"

"Maybe?" Danae says. "All the riddles end with time. Illyria ember of mine, uncover the maze you will embrace all treasures in time." Danae looks away from the floor and up the stairs behind them. She takes the steps two at a time.

Leon follows nearly on her heels. "What has your pants on fire?"

She stands at the window on the landing, looking out over the inner courtyard. The hedge maze is still intact, and the stone figurine of a fairy-like girl in the middle has not changed.

"When Itra and I were about to come out to you, Ember transported us there," she says, nodding towards the maze. "I saw a woman, I believe, was Medusa standing here at this window." She shivers. "Then the statue, animated to life and twirled away, revealing an opening to a set of stairs. That is the only entry I know of that goes to the vault."

"Ok, but why did you sprint up here?"

"It's still here, with so much change elsewhere—" she starts but sighs. She turns to rest her back against the window.

The moonlight streaming in creates an odd shadow on the next flight of stairs.

"Leon, what is that?"

He turns to follow her gaze. A large, dark figure stands motionless in the threshold between the second-floor landing and the adjoining balcony.

Danae pushes away from the window and starts up the steps. When she clears the second to last step, she jumps back. Leon catches her before she stumbles down the entire flight of stairs.

"Sorry!" she says, releasing his forearm. "It's Junior."

Junior is frozen to stone with his arms raised and hands clinching a large dagger.

16

"Medusa got to him before you and Itra encountered her in the present cavern below?"

Danae nods.

Leon takes a few steps up to inspect the statue. He whistles. "I understand your alarm. He looks terrifying in that position."

"Just a bit," Danae huffs.

"Was Junior, the oldest living descendant of Mui?" Leon asks.

"Yep, Mui Junior." Danae turns away. "If that seven-foot giant man failed to protect and serve Ember and this castle, what chance do we have?"

He points to the stone walls on either side of the landing. "Why are there walls here now?"

Danae turns back and takes a step up. The archway openings leading to the suites are gone. She shakes her head. "Guessing the old suites are off limits?" She leans against the wall and slides down.

"Teuta mentioned some changes, maybe we can ask her?" Leon squats to her level. "And we're both exhausted, sleep, then we can figure out the rest."

Danae nods and blinks away a tear. Leon offers her a hand, and they stand together. They slowly walk back down to the rear landing and through the conservatory. The plants sway at their entrance, and the shadowy movement makes Danae jump. Leon laughs and plucks a tomato as they pass.

"Teuta," Danae calls as they enter the red and purple war room.

Teuta appears and twirls towards another door on the far side of the room. "Follow me, I'll show you to your suites."

Leon hesitates, looking over at the wardrobe with the feathered cloaks.

"Later, brother," Danae says, "we need to sleep."

"Fine," Leon says, following Danae and Teuta up a flight of stairs.

"That's odd. I don't remember another section of the castle large enough for a wing of suites," Danae says, stopping at the next floor's landing. A large archway opens to a long stone corridor with several wood and iron doors lining each side.

"Each line that has served the goddess Ember has a unique wing of suites." Teuta opens a door midway down the corridor. "When the sun rises, you'll no longer find Mui's suites by the stairs near the maze. The castle has a full reset in progress."

Danae nods. "Noted. The entrance is already gone. What about the portraits in the suites and other keepsakes?"

Teuta waves her hand. "They still exist but are hidden from the current descendants." She gestures to the open door. "Leon, this is your suite and Danae's is directly across the hall."

Danae stands at the threshold to her suite, examining the lavish interior. The ruby red linens with dark purple accents contrast with the large ornate furniture. A swirl pattern is carved on the bedposts and wardrobe.

A tingle between her shoulder blades pushes her further in the room. She pushes open another door on the far side to find a large living room. She's instantly drawn to the windows. The moonlight shimmers down on waters of the lake below. She follows the water to the dark outline of the Montenegro mountains. The land at the lake's edge looks desolate. No traffic, homes, or any light minus the moon. She and Itra stood on a balcony in the castle only a few weeks ago and were puzzled at the vacant appearance of modern life.

And if the shield is down, wouldn't I see an active border crossing, roads, lights, people, or boats? Another question to add to the ever-growing list.

Danae turns towards the bedroom to find a new door leading to a large bathroom. A large copper tub sits centered like an artist's masterpiece on display. She opens the drawers next to the sink to find toiletries and bath salts. She takes advantage of the tub to soothe her nerves and unwind.

The water never cools, but the warmth doesn't soothe her wave of emotions. Her tears fall while she soaks, replaying the loss of Iana and Kaly. The discovery that she is carrying not one but two babies. The water ripples as her chest heaves in sobs. She longs for the comfort of Itra and his embrace.

The ember amulet around her neck glows and floats to the surface. She stills her movements and feels a wave of relief from her scalp to her toes. She closes her eyes and only twitches when she hears the door open to her suite.

"Danae?" Leon calls.

"In the tub," she whispers. She doesn't hear him respond. She repeats herself louder. "In the tub!" She then hears him just outside the door. There is a soft sound of his shirt scraping the wall as he slides down the wall to sit on the floor near the bathroom door.

"I can't sleep," Leon says.

"I can't stop—thinking," Danae responds.

Leon bangs his head against the wall and curses under his breath. "I haven't even tried to call Kaly's mom."

Danae submerges under the water in response. An image of a red book fills her mind. She emerges with a gasp of clarity. "Leon, the archives!"

Leon leans forward. "What about the archives?" They spent the first few hours of the battle sequestered in the archives, a large hall with a collection of paintings, books, and a three-bedroom suite hidden far below the castle.

Danae stands as the tub drains automatically, and she grabs a warm towel hanging on a rack near her head.

"There was a book about Medusa in the archives. Maybe there is a remedy to the snake charm."

She steps out and dries off. She envisions an outfit ready for action and feels the familiar sensation of clothes draping around and covering her curves. She steps in front of the large mirror as her dark pixie hair dries and styles. The magic of a thought provoked wardrobe never gets old.

19

Danae opens the door and Leon stands, his posture hunched and broken. When his eyes meet hers, the red rims and puffiness mirror her own.

"Teuta, can get us to the archives," Danae says with a small smile. "It's portal access only, remember?"

"Ugh!" Leon groans, rubbing his stomach in anticipation. Danae pats his shoulder in reassurance.

"Teuta!"

A few seconds later, Teuta appears with her eyebrows lifted. "Ember will knock you out if you two don't sleep soon."

"While we were in the archives, I found a book—"

Teuta snaps, interrupting Danae. A large stack of books lands in the middle of the bed with a muffled thump.

"Now sleep or else. We need to be ready at first light." Teuta twirls and vanishes.

"That will never be normal!" Leon hisses. Danae shrugs, moves to the side of the bed, and picks up a few volumes.

"She's an odd little fairy queen," Danae chuckles. She holds up a familiar red book with Medusa on the cover. "Take this one." She hands Leon the book.

He turns the book over and opens it to thumb through the text. "It's blank. What was the phrase to unlock the books?"

"Hapur," Danae states. She picks a book on ancient charms. On contact, her ember amulet lifts away from her chest. She places a hand over the amulet. It is pulsing.

"Hapur," Danae whispers over the book. She clears her mind and thinks only of the snake charm Leon showed her after Kaly was turned to stone. The book lifts from her hands and snaps closed. Another book flies towards her face. The book tilts and opens to a drawing of the snake charm with ancient text and symbols. She attempts to grab the book, but it flies just out of reach.

"What the—" Danae sighs and tries a second time to reach for the book, and it flies higher. "Leon, a little help please!"

He calls his ember staff and snares the book, lowering it back down to the bed. The book shakes under the weight of his staff and then snaps shut with a force that knocks Danae back to the wall.

"Ugh!" Danae gasps after air returns to her lungs.

"Are you ok?"

"No," Danae grunts. "I saw a page with the snake charm and then it wouldn't let me near it!"

"What did it say?" He rummages through the pile. "Which one was it?"

"Gold spine, black cover." Danae remains near the wall.

"I don't see it!" Leon tosses each book off the bed without care.

"Careful!"

They each vanish before they hit the floor.

"Danae, what did it say about the charm?" Leon holds the only remaining book, and its red.

"I tried to bring it closer to read, but you saw what happened." She steps towards the book, but the amulet propels her back. She frowns.

"What is it?"

"It's pushing me back." She attempts to move against the force. She's stuck. "What book is left?"

"The one you gave me about Medusa, but it's written in a different language." He shows her the cover.

"The amulet is for protection." She tries to calm her racing heart. "If the text could bring me or my family harm, it will instinctively protect us. Maybe the text is the curse. Either way, we'll need someone else to translate it."

Leon snaps and points at her. "Wasn't Itra's Uncle Vincent, gifted with the ability to read, write, speak, and translate any language by the goddess Ember? Do you think he still has his gift?"

"Teuta!" Danae calls. The last book vanishes from Leon's hand. He steps back in surprise as Teuta appears between the two of them.

"Yes, the former descendants keep their gifts," Teuta answers before they can even ask.

"Were you listening to our conversation?" Danae asks, realizing she can move freely again. She steps closer to Leon.

"Doesn't matter," Teuta says, rapidly tapping her foot. "You have one minute to lie down in your respective beds or be placed there by Ember. We have a mission to complete at dawn! I need you both well and rested!"

They stare at her.

"Thirty seconds," Teuta chirps.

Leon mumbles a curse. He walks across the hall to his suite and slams the door.

Danae moves to her bed and sits on the edge. "We aren't twelve, you know."

"Ha!" Teuta vanishes.

Danae feels a weight on her chest, lowering her towards the bed. She doesn't fight the feeling and pulls in a pillow to hug as darkness overwhelms her.

5

Leon's watch beeps. He jumps from the bed, calling his staff and crouching in defense. He scans the room. A large window creates just enough light to make out the large ornate furniture. *Castle.* He exhales and straightens.

He leans over to the other side of the bed to check that he didn't wake Kaly, but his bed is empty. He recoils as he recalls the previous day. He shudders and taps the staff once. A warm ember light fills the space. He checks his watch. *It's only five in the morning.*

He peers out the window. Heavy clouds hang low overhead, masking any star in the night sky. A small trace of dawn is just beyond the eastern peaks of the Albanian Alps lining the far side of the valley of Bajze. He moves closer to the window, noticing movement below.

"Headlights?" He shakes his head. "If I can see lights, they can see the castle!"

"Danae!" Leon barrels out of his door across the hall to her suite. He doesn't bother knocking and throws open her door. "Danae!"

Danae sits up and launches a pillow towards the noise. Leon ducks the fluffy assault. "Leon?" She squints to make out her brother's form. She scans the room, trying to recall her surroundings.

"Who else?" He chuckles. "We have a problem!"

"What time is it?" She clears the remnants of sleep from her voice.

"Five am. Danae, I can see movement in the valley below. The remaining barrier is—"

"Gone!" She leaps from her bed and races to the window in the adjoining room. Leon slides to a stop beside her. She points to a border patrol boat in the lake below. "We're doomed!" She leans forward, placing her forehead on the cool glass and squeezing her eyes shut.

"So dramatic," Teuta sings from a chair across the room. Danae and Leon jump.

"Seriously!" Leon shouts. "I'm putting a bell on you!"

Teuta smiles. "We need to get moving, much to do. Meet me in the war room in ten minutes. And Leon, you smell!" She wrinkles her nose before vanishing.

Leon gives a middle finger salute to the vacant chair.

"She's not wrong, brother," Danae says after sniffing the air. "Go shower, and when you are done, just imagine your wardrobe." He raises an eyebrow. "It's thought provoked." He rolls his eyes before returning to his room.

Danae's gaze lingers on the lake. A second boat pauses near the border patrol vessel and a wave of movement happens on board. She squints, trying to make out the figures. *They're pointing up!*

Leon finds the vanity has deodorant along with a much-needed toothbrush. He considers the razor and shaving cream in the drawer, scratching the two-day scruff on his chin, but closes the drawer. The shower is well stocked with a bar of soap that smells like pine and a shampoo. He takes a military style three-minute

24

shower: soak, lather, and rinse. While drying off, he imagines the dress blues he used to wear for ceremonies. He drops the towel when he feels the tingle of clothing drape around him. He leaps back from the mirror. Every medal, including his purple heart, is fastened to his pristine uniform. Leon reaches up and touches his white waistband.

"Leon, are you ready?" Danae calls from the bedroom door.

"Um…"

Leon cracks open the door.

Danae's jaw falls open.

"It still fits?" she asks.

Leon chuckles. "Apparently, or it was magically adjusted."

"Ah, well, you might want something less formal for this task." Danae gestures to her quick-dry hiking pants and boots, along with a fleece. Leon nods and shuts the bathroom door.

"Does it tingle?" Leon calls out when the wardrobe changes in to combat boots, pants and a layer of shirts topped with a jacket.

"Yes!" she responds.

Danae nods when Leon exits the bathroom. "Much better."

They go downstairs to the war room. Danae freezes in the doorway. Leon bounds into the room.

"Good," Teuta calls as she turns and reveals a man. Leon jumps back in alarm. "This is Noel. Noel, this is Leon and Danae."

"Oh dear," Danae whispers. "They're almost identical."

Noel and Leon stand a foot apart, inspecting each other. They laugh in unison with the same low, throaty tone.

Danae steps beside Leon. She nudges him with her hip and extends her hand towards Noel. Noel looks down at her, shakes his head, and gives her an enormous hug.

"Well, hello to you too!" she says in surprise.

Noel releases her and chokes back a sob. "Hi, sorry, I'm a hugger. Plus, you look like my sister. She's been gone for nearly a decade."

"Gone?" Leon asks, stepping closer to Danae.

"Ovarian cancer."

Danae shudders, cradling her abdomen.

"So sorry," Leon says, lowering his gaze to Danae. She looks up and a single tear falls down her cheek.

"Well, it's a pleasure to meet you, Noel," she says, discretely wiping her cheek. "Revolutionary or Ottoman dimension?"

"Sorry, what?" Noel turns to Teuta in question.

"The five ember archways, an extension of the goddess Ember's hand, provide a portal to five dimensions. Over the last century, the portals have earned the nicknames revolutionary, communist, Ottoman, past, and future."

He shakes his head. "Dimensions?"

Teuta turns to Danae and Leon. "I found Noel in the Ottoman dimension. You two will need reinforcements, considering the veil is completely gone. The locals can plainly see the Castle of Teskom in all dimensions."

"You're a descendant of Zeus as well?" Leon asks.

"This is all news to me," Noel says. "Teuta appeared with a gold box and some story about my family needing my assistance. I can't explain what on Earth possessed me to believe her, but I took her hand and landed here." He runs a hand over his head. Danae laughs. He glances at her with an eyebrow raised.

"Sorry, the gesture is so similar to Leon's," Danae says, smiling. "Has Teuta explained where you are now?"

He nods. "Not sure I believe any of this or if I'm still dreaming in my bed."

"Oh, it's very real," Leon says, scuffing his boot.

"Now that introductions are out of the way, I need to give you each a task," Teuta says, twirling in circles around them. "But Danae and Noel will require a few gifts from Ember. Noel, catch!"

A staff falls from above, and Noel catches it with ease. Leon calls his staff and shows him the tap sequences. Noel curses at the new forearm ink that now holds his ember staff.

Danae feels the amulet vibrate against her chest. She scans the room in alarm.

"No threat," Teuta says. Her voice is a whisper behind her.

Danae whirls around, but Teuta is nowhere to be seen. Even so, Danae can sense her presence about a foot away to the right. She reaches out and pats Teuta on the head.

"Good," says Teuta. She reappears. Noel shuffles back.

"See!" Leon points to Noel's frightened expression. "You really do need a bell!"

Teuta's wide smile doesn't soothe Noel's nerves.

"Danae, the gift of perception heightens your ability to sense any object, animal, person, living or dead," Teuta says. Then she turns and opens the wardrobe with a flick of her wrist. "Next!" The red and purple cloaks fly out of the wardrobe towards them.

They all duck and stumble back. The cloaks hover in the air above their heads. Teuta giggles.

"They didn't fly out last night," Leon says, attempting to gain control of his nerves. He glares at Teuta. She gives a slight bow. Leon rolls his eyes.

"Danae, you and Noel will locate and retrieve the shield."

"Hard pass!" Leon thrusts an arm in front of Danae.

"Leon, you'll stand guard in the clearing. We have several locals climbing the hillside, likely more once the sun rises. We need to move now."

A single cloak lowers and hovers near Danae's back. The other cloaks drift back to the wardrobe. Noel inspects the garment with the same eagerness Leon had done the night before. Danae smirks.

"Hold out your arms," Teuta instructs Danae. She follows her command and the cloak drapes like the other pieces of her wardrobe. Then it disappears into her clothes.

"It's invisible?" Noel asks.

"It conforms to the user," Teuta says, heading towards the door leading to the dining hall.

Danae twists her neck to inspect her back. "Wait! How does it work?"

Teuta doesn't pause her little stride. "Thought provoked, of course."

They fall in line behind Teuta and sprint to keep up.

"She may be tiny, but she is quick," Noel mutters.

Leon snorts. "Sneaky as well!"

"And I can hear everything," Teuta calls from the door leading to the conservatory.

Danae's eyes fall to the floor of the dining hall. She slows her pace. Before the castle reset, the mosaic tiles showed the castle and vacant valley the night before the battle—an image of the rogue descendants surrounding and attacking the castle. Now it displays the castle but with a valley that alternates between historic, modern, and futuristic structures but all in a state of flux. People are running towards the hill, towards the castle. *Itra is out there.*

"Danae!" Leon calls from the doorway.

She looks up at Leon and nods. She catches up with Noel and Leon waiting in the conservatory.

The plants wave, as if breathing, when they rush towards the main entry. They look down at floor tiles, which transform as they head for the open door. Noel is added to the scene and a set of wings is faintly visible behind Danae's figure.

Teuta waves the gold cube to get their attention. They look up in unison. She presses a corner, and the cube sides collapse.

"We believe the shield is here." Teuta points to the now third line down in the string of text. "Once you cross under the ember archway, select this line only. After you retrieve the shield, select the second line to return."

"Where does the first line return us to?" Danae asks.

"At the bend near the archways," Teuta says, nodding towards Noel. "Same place we dropped in earlier."

"And if the attempt fails?" Noel asks.

Teuta ignores his question. "Don't get caught. This is Ember's magic, and if in the wrong hands we could have another disaster like the battle we just fought."

"And if the shield isn't there?" Danae asks.

"Ember will interrogate Medusa," Teuta states. Leon flinches.

"Excuse me?" Leon says, rolling up on his toes. "Medusa is alive?"

Teuta nods.

"Son of a—"

Danae pushes Leon away from Teuta and points a finger inches from Teuta's face. "What do you mean, alive? We saw her stone figure in the present cavern!" Danae freezes, sensing movement in the clearing. "I think we have company!"

6

A woman in white stands at the base of the four enormous castle steps with her hands raised and her chest heaving. Leon nearly trips down the first step to get a closer look, but Teuta floats down to inspect the lady, blocking their view.

"My name is," the lady says, but gasps for a breath, "Avi."

Noel looks from Leon to Danae for an answer. Danae shrugs, but Leon leaps down the steps.

"You're one of them," Leon says. Leaning closer, he inspects every inch of her face. She resembles Kaly, but she couldn't pass for her.

"One of who?" Noel asks, joining Leon and Teuta. Danae remains a few paces behind.

"A grey sister," Teuta says.

Avi frowns. She holds up a card.

Leon snatches the familiar stationary, calling his staff. He taps once and lowers the ember glow to the card. The text changes from Time to Time to Serve.

"Where did you get this?" Leon asks, clenching his jaw and flaring his nostrils.

Teuta and Danae exchange a worried glance.

Avi takes a step back when Leon double taps his staff. The scythe glows ominously in the remaining darkness.

"It arrived two days ago," Avi says, her voice quiet and shaking.

"What's the significance of the card?" Noel asks.

"My wife, Kaly, had this card with her before she—" Leon turns his glare towards Teuta. "You're the only messenger for this castle and Ember, correct?"

Teuta nods.

"Did you deliver this card?"

"No!" Teuta places her hands on her hips and sticks her chin in the air. "We don't have time for this. Noel and Danae need to leave now the sun is rising." She hands the cube to Danae and points towards the archways. "Go!"

"Wait," Danae calls as a force beyond her control propels her forward off the last step and towards the clearing. "Leon, please don't do anything you might regret!"

"Come back in one piece!" Leon returns his focus to Avi. "Who delivered this card?"

"I wish I knew. It was on my nightstand with this." Avi hands Leon a gold cube.

Teuta plucks the cube out of Leon's palm and turns it over. "Is this how you got here?" she asks.

Avi nods.

"How did you know how to use it?" Teuta asks.

"I didn't." She shrugs. "It was an accident. My cat, Jinx, knocked it off the nightstand this morning. I got out of bed to inspect the damage. When I picked it up with the card, I heard a click and then I was standing at an archway." Avi points towards the revolutionary archway.

"Where are you from?" Leon asks.

"Greece, but I live in London. Where am I now?"

Teuta twirls and suddenly disappears.

Avi yelps in surprise. "What is she?"

"My worst nightmare," Leon mumbles. "Teuta can appear and disappear at any moment."

Avi shivers. Leon studies her closely. She's dressed only in a fluffy bathrobe and no shoes. "I don't trust you," he says, "but I can't leave you out here dressed like that!" He extends his hand to help her up the first giant step.

She narrows her eyes at Leon. "Who are you?"

Teuta reappears between Leon and Avi.

"Geez!" Avi stumbles back and falls hard.

"To answer your question," Teuta states, pointing at Leon. "Leon, a descendant of Zeus and I'm Teuta, the messenger and mark maker for the Castle of Teskom."

"And this castle is where in the world?" Avi asks, looking up from the damp ground.

"Albania," Teuta states, holding up a piece of parchment. "And you are Avi, daughter of Gage and Pam?"

Avi gets to her feet. "And how do you know my parents' names?"

"A family tree." Teuta hands Avi the parchment. "Come inside, let me show you who and what you are."

Avi goes pale. "What I am is lost, confused, and cold."

"You are also a descendant of Deino, a grey sister, and of Phorcys!" Teuta sings.

Leon flinches.

"Come along," Teuta sings, "no time to wait." She twirls and bounds up the large stone steps towards the main archway to the castle. Leon and Avi watch as her figure disappears through the open door.

"Seriously, is any of this real?" asks Avi.

Leon turns to glare down at her. "Unfortunately, yes." He extends his hand again, but she ignores the gesture and climbs up the first step herself. He shrugs and bounds up the thigh high steps with ease.

32

Avi slowly follows, but hesitates at the open doorway. She glances back out at the clearing. She watches someone land and the two figures disappear under an ember archway.

"You can fly?" Noel asks.

Danae silently lands with a grin. "I tripped and then, lift off!"

Noel gapes at her response. He takes Danae's hand on instinct as they walk under the ember archway. She doesn't resist, but she releases his hand the second they pass safely under.

Danae pulls out the cube and taps the corner. The cube flattens. She uses her finger to select the third line down.

Noel scans the path, but Danae looks up, sensing another person. The barrel of a rifle rounds the boulder at the bend in the path. She grabs Noel's hand, squeezing it tight, and grasps the cube. *Three, two*, the stranger cocks his rifle, *one*.

7

"Are you just going to stand there?" Leon asks, pacing impatiently in the entry.

Avi tears her eyes away from the clearing. She watches colors swirl under Leon's pacing feet. The colors stop and she is looking at herself standing next to Leon and the two others she saw a moment ago. "What is this?"

"A reflection of events," Teuta calls from the conservatory. "Please follow Leon to the war room."

"War room?" Avi exhales in a whisper. The air from the conservatory warms her chilled skin. She touches the leaves on a few plants as she follows Leon around the curved path. Leon holds open the door. She halts just inside. "Sensory overload," she whispers.

The purple walls and high ceiling leave her breathless.

Leon closes the door and strides across the room. "Follow me," he says.

Her eyes wander from the large glass dome, warm with the colors of dawn, to the dining table centered below and the large mural on the mosaic tiled floor. She slows, trying to understand the chaotic scene changing under her bare feet.

"You can look at this later," Leon says, noticing her hesitation.

Avi hustles behind Leon.

"Good," Teuta says as they enter the war room. "Avi, step behind here and change." She gestures to a tall dressing screen of red silk and dark wood in the corner of the room.

Avi peeks her head around the screen. "No clothes?"

"Think of something warm to wear," Teuta says and raises a finger, "preferably something you can fight in."

Leon looks up from the parchment with Avi's family tree. "Imagine the wardrobe," he explains.

Avi's brows furrow.

"It's thought provoked." Leon thinks of a red hat and it appears on his head. Her eyes widen. "Your turn."

Avi vanishes behind the screen. Leon leans over the parchment and traces Avi's lineage back to Phorcys. *Like Kaly.*

Behind the screen, Avi closes her eyes and pictures standing at her mirror just before leaving the house yesterday. A tingle starts at her toes, travels up her spine, and she feels her hair lift from her scalp.

"What the—"

Avi glances down, startled by her clothing. She is fully dressed in riding boots, dark fitted jeans, and a long cardigan over a fitted tee. She peeks under the shirt at a soft bra. "How?"

"Ember," Leon says from beyond the screen.

Avi clasps a hand over her mouth to smother a squeak of surprise. She steps out from behind the screen.

Leon glances up. "Are you wearing make-up?"

She glances down at her hand. A touch of her signature berry red lip gloss is painted on her palm. "My lip gloss, but how?"

"Your thoughts included hair and make-up?" Leon points from her glossy lips to her long, straightened, dark hair.

Avi blushes. "I'm usually very tidy with my appearance."

"Eat and read quickly," says Teuta. She flicks her wrist and a chair near Avi scoots back. A tray of pastries, sandwiches, and fruit

35

appears on the table, and the aroma of coffee fills the air. Leon sits and pours a cup of coffee, offering her the first mug.

Avi stares at the table, then up at Leon. "This is real?"

He nods.

"Sit and read," Teuta says before vanishing.

Avi slaps her cheeks and frowns at the pain before slumping into the chair. "Not a dream."

Leon sets a steaming mug of coffee within her reach. She glances up as he pops a whole pastry in his mouth. She lifts the mug and sips the warm, rich blend of her favorite morning coffee. "Is this a special blend?"

"It is if that's how you like your coffee."

"How?"

"The thought provoked wardrobe and food are the luxurious benefits of life here at the Castle of Teskom."

"Life?"

He shakes his head. "Maybe if we can't find the shield."

"We?" Avi asks, gripping her mug tighter. "And what shield?"

Leon shrugs. "A shield was stolen from the castle vault and the veil hiding the castle was disabled, exposing it to this world and the others."

Avi gapes at him. "Others?"

Leon points to the books. "You might want to read first, then ask questions later."

Avi doesn't break eye contact with Leon for several seconds but feels drawn to look down at a book with the title 'OPEN' written on the cover. She pulls the book closer, moving her coffee aside.

"Wait," Leon says, crumbs spitting out from his very full mouth. "My sister was expelled from the castle the first time she opened that book because she was not a descendant of the current bloodline." Leon picks up the parchment. "Who was your grandmother on your father's side?"

"Eliza."

36

"And Eliza's father?"

Avi tilts her head, lost in thought, before answering. "My father always referred to him as Chop, but I believe his name was Garon or George."

Leon nods. "Garon. It's probably safe, go ahead."

Avi blows out a long breath and opens the book. She reads quickly, turning page after page. She glances up at Leon and down several times until she finishes the book. "An infinite promise to protect and serve the goddess Ember and the Castle of Teskom?"

Teuta appears, standing next to Leon. He jumps. "Bell, freaking bell!"

Teuta jingles a small wooden handled brass bell.

Ding, ding

Leon shakes his head. "It's before you appear, not after!"

Teuta shrugs. "It's time."

Avi feels a weight wrap around her throat. She panics, touching her bare neck.

"Ember provides a gift to each descendant," Teuta says. "Avi, your gift is persuasive communication." Leon and Avi exchange a confused glance. "You can now persuade any living or past being to do what you command. Choose your words wisely."

A whoosh of wind barrels through the war room, slamming a door. Leon stands in alarm.

"Intruders have entered the clearing," says Teuta. "Go!" Leon bounds out the door. Avi remains glued to her chair. Her hands linger on her throat. Teuta taps her shoulder. "You need to go, too. Tell the intruders there is nothing to see. They'll listen to you."

"What do you mean?"

"Speak and they will listen," Teuta says, nudging her out of the chair. Avi stands and feels an urgent desire to help. She rushes out the door, through the dining hall, and the conservatory, and out the entry overlooking the clearing. Leon is running across the clearing with his ember staff as three figures stride toward him.

"Turn around," Avi whispers. The three advancing figures hesitate and glance around. *It works?* She bites her lip and exhales. "Horror will harm your family. Return at once to save them!"

Leon is within a few steps of the first intruder when the man turns and runs away. Another hastily follows. The third intruder is still approaching and gaining speed.

"Leon is the grim reaper."

Leon understands her threat and double taps his staff. The shimmering scythe glows brighter as the sun crests the hill, shining directly behind him. The last intruder skids to a stop and immediately retreats, stumbling several times before turning to sprint across the clearing.

Avi joins Leon at the base of the steps.

"Only three?"

"For now," Leon says. "Do you think you can do that again?"

"Um, scare people?"

Leon nods with a grin.

Avi shrugs with a slight nod.

"Great, follow me!" He bounds up the castle steps.

Avi follows him inside. Leon jogs up a flight of stairs in the entry foyer.

"Where are you going?" Avi asks, trying to keep pace with him, but she pauses to stare at the hedge maze from the landing window. She presses against the glass, drawn to the stone figure in the middle.

"Tower!" Leon calls down to her from a few flights up. "Come on!"

She pulls her attention away from the maze and back to climbing the stairs. She reaches a spiral staircase with a narrow opening. "Leon?"

"Up here!" Leon says, poking his head down. "Hurry! Two groups are near the clearing."

She scrambles up the stairs into a square glass box. "What is this, a lighthouse?"

"Not quite. The castle's concealment veil was anchored by the two towers." He points to an identical tower across from theirs. "It creates a concealment bubble over the castle, clearing and archways."

"But now?"

"When the Medusa Shield was stolen from the vault, and the bubble popped leaving it exposed."

"As in DaVinci's Medusa Shield?" Avi asks, turning to look at Leon.

"Can we discuss that after we get rid of them?" Leon points to a group running towards the castle. "Do your thing! I'll stand guard at the door for those that don't heed your warning."

"Wait!"

He doesn't wait but yells. "You got this!"

She counts five people, two women and three men.

"Stop! You are running towards certain death," she whispers in a low, menacing tone. Four out of five, stop running and look around. "Turn around and never return!"

They duck in response, and four of them slowly turn and run away. The last one sprinting towards the castle is a man. He hesitates and glances at the fleeing group.

"Go now!" Avi shouts.

He jumps and takes off towards the group, nearly out of the clearing.

"Keep it up!" Leon says.

Avi jumps and spins around, looking for him. She's alone. *"How can I hear you?"*

"Ember's magic," Leon states. *"The descendants are blessed—or cursed, if you ask me—with thought-provoked communication. The last family nicknamed it eDrum."*

"Every thought?" She paces the tower, trying to manage a rational explanation for the last three hours of her life—asleep in her London flat to now warding off intruders with her words from an ancient castle in Albania.

"Only those thoughts you intentionally communicate."

Avi slaps her palm to her forehead. "Wake up!" The scenery doesn't change. She sighs.

"Heads up!" Leon shouts.

Avi looks up automatically, then laughs at her response.

"One more has entered," Leon says. *"They're attempting to remain in the shadows."*

Avi scans the shadows before spotting the figure lurking in the shadows. She whispers, "Boo!"

The figure in the shadow leaps back in alarm.

She smirks and tries another tactic her roommate in college would do when trying to get her attention. "A, B, C, D," she says in a monotone voice.

The figure spins around, scanning the clearing and shadows.

"The alphabet?" Leon asks.

"It always got my attention."

"I'll get you, my pretty," Avi sings in her best wicked witch voice. The figure bolts out of the shadows and the clearing.

"And your little dog too!" Leon sings, finishing the famous line.

Avi laughs. *"Fan of the Kingdom of Lost?"*

"Kingdom of Lost?" Leon repeats.

"A musical about a girl named Larissa and her dog, Monty."

Leon laughs before responding. *"Danae watched, the Wizard of Oz, at least once a year our entire childhood. Remind me later to compare notes on movies with your dimension."*

Teuta appears in the tower beside Avi.

Ding, ding

"Geez!" Avi shouts, pressing her hand against her racing heart. "Leon's right, you need to ring it before you enter."

Teuta tilts her head to the side and smiles. She holds up a book with three haggard women on the cover.

Avi squints to read the loopy text below. "The Grey Sisters?" Teuta nods and hands her the book. She barely grasps the book before Teuta vanishes again. She gasps and shakes her head.

Avi scans the clearing. *Clear.* She carefully opens the book. A mist immediately fills the tower. She snaps the book closed in alarm. She is not alone. Two figures hover next to her. She drops the book and steps back, raising her arms in defense. The mist clears, and it's two women nearly identical to herself.

They look her up and down before advancing towards her. Avi bolts for the stairs, but they split and cut her off.

"What do you want?" Avi asks, her voice shaking.

"A legacy," one answers.

"Without betrayal," the other answers.

"Join us," they say in unison, each moving in closer to Avi.

"Join who?" Avi asks in a whisper.

"Your sisters," they say in unison before fading and merging into Avi.

Avi sucks in a ragged breath before collapsing.

8

Danae feels the ground under her feet.

Noel is bent at the waist, coughing when they land in a lightless space. The air feels damp and cool. Danae sighs. They're in or near a bunker or cave.

"A little light would be nice," says Danae.

Noel straightens and strains his eyes. "Yeah, I can't see a thing."

"Dude, really? You have a light embedded in your arm!"

Noel calls his staff. His mouth is twisted, and he stares at her blankly as the light fills the space.

"Your 'not funny' face is just like Leon's," Danae says with a smirk.

He tries to hold the expression but cracks a small smile.

Danae laughs and looks around the space. She finds a pile of chains in the corner and grimaces. She scans the rest of the space, swearing under her breath. "It's empty, no shield."

Noel creeps to the door and listens. Satisfied, he tries to move the door, but it doesn't budge. Danae helps him push, but a screech of metal on metal makes them cringe and step away.

Noel kicks the door.

"It's like this door hasn't been moved in centuries," he says.

Danae faces him. "Say that again."

His eyes go wide. "Centuries?"

Danae takes his staff. She kneels to inspect the chains in the corner. She picks up a link, and it falls apart in her hand. She stands quickly. "We need to go back."

"In time?"

"No, to the castle." She takes the cube from her pocket. She activates it, scrolls past the first four and selects the fifth line.

"Wait!" Noel objects. "Teuta mentioned that line to return." He points up to the first line.

"And face the barrel of a rifle?" Danae says, shaking her head. "No thanks."

"Are you sure you don't want to check the other bunkers—just in case?" Noel gestures to the door.

Danae glances from the broken chains to the heavy door. "Did she say three bunkers?" Noel nods. "Fine, but quickly. And no splitting up, deal?" He nods again.

They push harder on the door, barely budging it open. Danae squeezes out, but Noel struggles with his broad chest. He finally shimmies through. The only sound is a faint dripping further down the corridor.

Danae closes her eyes and reaches out with her gift. She feels at least three breathing bodies, human or animal. She holds up three fingers. Noel takes the lead with his staff.

The first corridor ends at a small faucet with a slow drip. Noel catches a drop. "It's fresh and cold."

"The lake is spring fed," she whispers.

He nods and continues. He chooses the wider of the two corridors to check first. She follows. Her footsteps seem to echo, but his are silent. He pauses about every ten steps to listen.

"There is something ahead," he whispers, double tapping his staff, creating a clatter of noise. The scythe is too long for the narrow space. He mutters a curse.

Danae reaches for her amulet. It is still.

"No threat ahead," she whispers.

Noel looks back at her; she shrugs and passes him, taking the lead.

The glow from his staff lightens the opening ahead, and a stone figure stands near the center. She moves past the frozen guard and notices another stone statue.

"They were definitely here." She closes her eyes again. She feels a pull to her right.

Noel finds a small passage leading to another bunker. The door is wide open, but there is nothing inside.

They step back out and look at the two other corridors.

"Divide and conquer?"

"No, sir!" Danae glares at Noel. She tilts her head to the right. "This way!"

They walk for several minutes, pausing every few steps. A small chirp makes Noel freeze mid step. He makes eye contact with Danae for five long seconds before crouching low and moving quickly towards the noise. He skids to a stop as they clear the opening. Two guards are frozen in stone up to their shoulders, but they're alive. A yellow canary is chirping from a basket overhead.

"İşletmenizi belirtin," one guard commands.

Noel turns to Danae. She shrugs.

The second guard struggles to move his jaw. "State your business."

"Who did this to you?" Danae moves closer to inspect the stone.

"The white witch," the second guard answers with a heavy accent.

Noel approaches the door behind the guards.

The second guard frowns.

"State your business!"

Noel smiles but doesn't respond as he moves past the guards. He steps inside the entry. "Danae, it's here."

44

Danae feels a presence and turns. A giant object launches out of the shadows. Her amulet yanks her to the floor, barely missing the impact.

"Noel!"

He whirls, but it's too late. The object shoves him hard in the chest. He crashes against the wall, dropping his staff. Then the object retreats with the same speed. Noel regains his balance and calls his staff again, but the door slams shut. "Danae!"

The ember amulet pulses against her chest as she pulls on the heavy bunker door. "Noel!" She balls her fists and pounds on the door. "Can you hear me?"

"I'm here! What was that thing?"

"I think you tripped an alarm." Danae sighs. "A giant log on a pendulum?"

He tries the door, pulling and then pushing. He finally gives up and kicks the door. "It's not budging."

"Can you stand far away from the door?"

"Sure, why?"

"I'm going to try to bust you out of there." Danae holds up the ember amulet. The guard watches her unamused. She tilts her head and grins.

"Ready?" she calls.

"For what?" Noel asks through the door.

"Just stand far back."

"Ok," Noel says, moving away from the door.

"Open!" Nothing happens. One of the guard's smirks. She frowns, but feels the amulet vibrate. "Open says me!" The door rattles and then bursts open. Dust fills the space. "Noel?" she asks, coughing.

"Alive." Noel coughs. "What did you use, dynaflight?"

"Dyna what?" Danae chokes on her laugh. She wipes the dust away from her eyes and mouth with the inside of her jacket.

"You know, the red sticks with the wicks at the end," he says.

"Dynamite?"

He lifts an eyebrow and shakes his head. She taps her ember amulet to explain. He looks from her face to her chest. His brows furrow, and he wipes his face down. "I don't get it?"

"The ember amulet—blew the door." She frowns at his expression. He is still staring blankly at her chest.

"Danae, I don't see an amulet." He meets her eyes, and she looks down at the amulet in alarm.

"What do you mean?" She holds it up for him to inspect. "You can't see this hanging from the chain?"

"Your hand is empty." He shrugs and looks through the rubble from the door.

"How is that possible?" Danae mumbles. She moves beside him and helps lift a large piece of rock out of the way. "Shit!"

"What?" Noel asks.

"That's Kaly's pack," Danae exclaims, picking up the pack, brushing off the dust, and unzips the main pocket. Two books and three journals are inside. She thumbs through the journals. All appear to be Kaly's handwriting, but one phrase makes her pause. She hands the others to Noel. She reads the passage.

Time to Serve?

If Leon and I are tasked as the protectors of time, including the vessel, what does that mean for Danae? Are we infinitely bound to serve? How does this impact the alliance?

"What did Kaly do for a living?" Noel asks as he thumbs through the other books and journals.

She turns to him with glassy eyes. "A college professor," she says, her voice shaking. "Her research focus included anthropology and mythology of the Balkans." She lets a single tear escape and reads the passage a second time.

"Hey, you good?" Noel asks.

Danae shakes off the emotions and nods. She holds the pack for him. He slides the items in before zipping it back up. He shrugs on the pack and clips it in place after adjusting the waist strap.

"What did you find before the door incident?" Danae asks, looking around the space.

"Just the pack, no shield."

A wave of frigid air makes her shiver. She feels her skin rise into a thick layer of goosebumps. "What is standing behind me?"

"Not what, who," he whispers, watching a scene unfold. The color drains from his face in an instant.

She slowly turns to a faint glow of three figures. One is a man crouching against the wall in chains. She recognizes him immediately as Unis Beard. The other two, a woman in white and a man—likely Medusa and Poseidon—facing away from them. They're standing over a covered object shaped like a shield.

Danae searches the bunker, expecting to find Kaly, but the second set of chains lies open.

"Who are they?" Noel whispers.

Danae explains. Poseidon vanishes with the covered object. The woman releases Unis, and he vanishes. She slowly turns while lifting a veil.

"Run!" Danae turns towards the opening and sprints between the two guards, making a hard left down the passage. She can hear Noel on her heels. She doesn't slow her pace or pause until they reach the next opening. She pants, trying to breathe normally.

Then she reaches in her pocket for the cube. It's empty. She pats down all of her pockets before looking up at Noel.

"The cube is gone!"

Noel frantically checks his pockets, Kaly's pack, and then he pats her down. He stands back. "But how?"

9

"Avi, another group is heading our way," Leon calls. He paces the front foyer, waiting for her response. Silence. *"Avi?"*

"Avi!" He sprints up to the tower. *Why isn't she responding?*

He climbs up the final spiral staircase and finds Avi on her side. "Avi, wake up!" He kneels down, checking her pulse. She's alive but out cold. "How did this happen?"

"Her sisters are here," Teuta calls from the landing below.

"Her what?" he asks, standing to look down at Teuta dancing from foot to foot. Movement outside catches his attention. He looks out from the tower. An approaching group is too close.

He maneuvers down the spiral stairs. "Take care of her!" He doesn't wait for Teuta's response before sprinting back down to the front entry.

He jumps down the last four steps, activates his staff, and blocking the entry to the castle, startling the leader of the group. The man stumbles back.

"Leave now!" Leon shouts and double taps his staff and swings the scythe in an arc mere inches from the man's chest. "Now!"

The man swallows a loud gulp and glances down at his pants. Leon follows his gaze. A large wet spot expands down his leg.

Leon curses and looks the man up and down. He's a teen, may be still in high school. The group scattering behind him looks even younger. *Great, I just scared the pee out of a teen.*

"Go!" Leon shouts.

The boy jumps. "Ok!" He chases after his group.

Leon scans the clearing. The sun is higher, lightening the shadows of the morning. He identifies no further threats and sags against the archway.

"What is Avi's status?" Leon asks.

"Resting," Teuta responds. *"I moved her to her suite."*

"Explain what you meant by her sisters are here."

"Ember instructed me to give her a book. I sensed two additional beings with Avi. I believe they're here."

"Where are they now?"

"In her—part of her?"

"Is that a question or a statement?"

"I'll know for sure once she is awake."

Teuta tucks a blanket around Avi. She's too anxious to sit with her and opens the suite's adjoining door. The room is clean and ready like the other suites, but a picture hanging over the fireplace is pulsing. She crosses the room in a blink. It is a portrait with two women painted in profile on either side of a third woman centered on the canvas. Their long oval faces, olive complexion, and dark wavy hair are painted as if their hair joins them as one. Teuta floats up to exam the painting at eye level. An ember pendant hangs around the middle woman's neck in the shape of an hourglass.

Leon shakes his head and jumps up and down, trying to soothe the adrenaline still surging through his veins. He glances towards the archway where Kaly's stone figure stands. His eyes drift over to the Ottoman archway. *Where's Danae? Is she safe?*

10

A knock at the office door wakes Itra. He sits up and rubs his eyes.

"Uncle Itra?" The door cracks open, and the wild curls of Elis's hair pop around the door.

Itra kneels on the floor and opens his arms. "Hey buddy."

Elis launches himself into Itra. Itra rocks back and squeezes him tight.

"What time is it?" Itra asks into Elis's hair.

"Time for you to buy a watch," Elis laughs.

"Ha, ha!" Itra releases one final tear as a small smile tugs the corner of his mouth. "Did you eat?"

"Twice!" Elis says, smiling. "Nada brought over two pizzas and cookies after Grandma made pancakes."

"Did you leave any for me?" Itra scoffs with a grin.

"Nah," Elis says, patting his belly. "It's all right here."

Itra tickles Elis's sides. He squeals in response and bolts from the room.

"Easy!" Anton side steps Elis's retreat. Itra meets Anton in the hall. His hair is standing on end, clothes disheveled.

"Did you sleep at all?"

"About an hour," Anton says. "I kept waking up hoping this was all a nightmare. This is the worst reality ever."

"Uncle Vincent called the family," Itra says. "He is on a flight over. The rest of the family will be here by morning. Do we need to do anything else, or does that cover it?"

"We still need to pick out the casket and the flowers," says Anton. "I have no idea what she would've wanted. Did you two discuss this at any point?"

"I remember her saying keep it simple—with mom and again with dad. She's never been one for flashy anything."

"Simple it is," Anton sighs. Elis laughs from the kitchen. Anton smiles. "He woke up calm and happy. I'm thankful but confused at his ability to bounce back."

"Did he ask for Iana?"

Anton shakes his head. "He said something about an ember healing his broken heart."

"What is an ember?" Itra feels his scalp tingle.

"No idea," Anton says and shrugs.

Itra pulls down the gravel road towards his house. He dials Danae. The phone rings only once before going to the message that her voicemail is full. He tries Leon and Kaly again with no success.

Itra jumps out to open the gate. Then he hops back in and drives the borrowed car down the drive, anchored on both sides by blooming vines. His truck, along with Anton's SUV, is still parked in the drive. The new roses tickle his nose as he exits the car and jogs back down the drive to close the gate.

When he turns back for the house, his gaze is drawn to the rising hills of Mokset. A new structure is visible at the highest point.

Odd. He can only recall the ruins of a few old forts and the old Mokset Castle, but not any sizeable buildings.

He raises his phone to take a photo of the hills. The structure is blurred. He tries a second time but gets the same result. He pockets his phone and paces back and forth a few times before heading inside.

"Danae? Are you home?"

He checks the bedrooms and the kitchen which are empty. He opens the office door last and goes to shut it, but the camera bag catches his eye. He pulls out the digital camera, attaching its longest lens.

He walks back out and lifts the camera to his eye to focus. The outline of a structure clears in the viewfinder, but it is too close. He twists the lens counterclockwise, but a blur of movement just before the image focuses again makes him pause. He scans the area. *There are no birds or limbs in the way...* Leveling the camera back to his eye, he finds the features of a man staring down the lens of his camera.

He stumbles back in alarm. He quickly draws the camera back up and finds only the outline of giant steps leading up to a dark opening.

He checks the display screen on the camera. He finds he was in video mode while focusing. He watches the jumpy coverage on the tiny display and catches the movement. He rolls it back and pauses the image. *Is that a scythe?* He lets it play a few seconds forward a man's face fills the screen.

Itra rushes inside, taking the memory card out of the camera and firing up Danae's laptop. He steadies his trembling hand and slides in the card. His foot taps while the video loads. He presses play and slides the video forward, freezing the frame at the first movement. *That's definitely a scythe.* He rolls it forward and pauses at the man's face. *Leon!*

Itra rushes back outside just as a car pulls up to his gate. Ermal jumps out and waves to Itra. The comfort of seeing his childhood friend, a local police officer, makes the last five minutes less surreal. Itra waves back. Ermal slides the gate open and pulls down the drive.

52

Itra walks towards the car to greet him. He stops at sight of the tight frown etched on Ermal's face.

"What's happened?" Itra asks.

Ermal's frowns deepens. "I'm here to pay respects for Iana. I wasn't sure you would be here, but my sister just left Anton's and said you had returned home to get some items for the funeral."

Itra chokes back a sob. "I can't locate Danae. I thought—maybe you had news."

"What do you mean, locate?" Ermal walks beside Itra down the drive to close the gate.

"I've called her phone several times. There's no answer, and her voicemail is full."

"When is the last time you saw Danae?"

Itra stops walking and drags a hand over his face before releasing a long sigh. "Two or three days ago when we hiked with you, Iana, Anton, Leon, Kaly, and Vincent to the old Mokset Castle ruins. Do you remember the hike down?"

Ermal raises both eyebrows, and his jaw falls open. He shakes his head once before responding. "Danae was with you inside the Castle of Teskom. She didn't return with you?"

Itra grabs Ermal by the shoulders and shakes him. "Castle of Teskom?"

Ermal glances towards the hills.

"Start talking, Ermal," Itra grunts, his hearing nearly muted by the pulse drumming inside. Ermal takes a step back.

"You recall nothing from the last few days?" Ermal asks.

"I remember arriving at Anton's apartment in the city. I don't know how I got there. And before that our hike on the hills."

Ermal walks past Itra and closes the gate. He returns and playfully loops an arm around Itra's neck. "Did we drink all the whiskey?" Itra breaks loose with a glare. "We drank a fair amount before the second hike."

"What second hike?" Itra asks.

"You're going to need raki or whiskey and a solid chair under your rump before I talk." Ermal turns for the house and glances over to see Itra standing helpless and confused in the middle of the drive.

"Come on, you want to know where Danae is, right?"

This question reanimates Itra's face, and he follows Ermal inside.

"Sit," Itra instructs, taking two low ball glasses from the cabinet and picking up the nearly empty bottle of whiskey. He exchanges the bottle for the raki and takes the glasses to the kitchen table. He pours a finger-width into each glass before he hands one to Ermal.

Ermal raises his glass. "Glory to Jesus, may God give you strength, may Christ have her in paradise, may he watch over you."

Itra raises his glass in return. "May Christ help you and guard you too."

They each sip and wince as the raki slowly burns.

Itra pulls out a chair and sits. "Start from the hike."

Ermal nods. "We hiked to the ember archway right after we left the castle ruins." Ermal pauses, but Itra's expression remains blank. "We followed Vincent and the rest of the family under the ember archway. You held on to my arm as we went under."

"Why would I hold on to you and not Danae?"

"I'm not of Mui's lineage," says Ermal. "It was just in case— it rejected me."

"Wait, Mui? Are you talking about the giant from the old folk tales?"

"Itra, you're the one who told me all of this after you and Danae went missing a few weeks ago. You seriously can't remember anything?"

Itra raises the glass and takes a large gulp. "I feel tingles of recollection. I know something very important happened. But I can't recall anything after we made it to the castle ruins." His eyes glass over and the color drains from his face. "Is Danae in danger? Do you know where she is?"

Ermal reaches into his pocket and withdraws a card. The parchment is gold with blue cursive writing. He hands the card facedown to Itra. Then he gestures for Itra to turn it over.

Itra flips the card over and reads. *Do you remember?* He freezes. All movements and breathing cease.

Ermal waves a hand in front of Itra's face, but he doesn't blink. "Itra?" Ermal touches Itra's wrist to take his pulse after a full minute with no response.

Suddenly, Itra inhales and blinks a few times before he can focus on Ermal. "Danae is with Leon. The blast killed Iana. And we failed."

"Failed?" Ermal repeats, shifting in his chair. "I arranged transport for Elis, Anton, and Iana off the hills and back to the city. When I left, Leon was with Kaly's stone figure in the clearing. What happened?"

"Unis Beard showed up."

"Hold up! We found Beard's body near the lake this morning."

"He was given a snake charm or curse, like Kaly's. His was a live snake wrapped around his ankle. If any harm fell on Medusa, the snake would strike and well the snake did its thing." Itra takes another sip of raki and feels his cheeks flush. "Leon and Danae's bloodline is now assigned to protect and serve. We failed to protect the castle and lost the shield that secures the veil, masking the castle's existence from all dimensions. That's why you can see it up on the hillside."

Ermal nods and drains his glass. He refills both glasses.

"How did you end up with this card?" Itra asks.

"When Teuta brought Elis to Anton in the clearing just before the chopper arrived, she handed me the card," Ermal says. "Her instruction was to only show you once until Danae returned."

Itra laughs. "Teuta, you clever fairy. Do you remember the present cavern?"

55

Ermal nods. "A window to communicate with those that have been blessed by Ember?"

Itra nods. "Danae reached out last night. I asked for Ember or Teuta to help with Anton and Elis. Their memories from their time at the castle were starting to fade." Itra shakes his head. "Ember helped. I have two memories now. One is of Iana falling down a flight of stairs while holding and protecting Elis. The other is of her standing in the ember archway with Elis and Anton moments before the blast." Itra chokes back a sob. "Both seem so real."

Itra and Ermal take a long swig from their glass.

Ermal winces and coughs, pounding a fist into his chest. "That burns."

Itra wipes a tear and nods.

Ermal clears his throat. "We have had reports of people fleeing down the hill in fear. One officer tried to question a few individuals, but they refused to say what had them running."

Itra stands and motions Ermal to follow him into the office. He taps the keyboard and Leon's face fills the screen. He moves the footage back to the scythe.

"Ember's gift to Leon before I was booted off the hill was a glowing staff that turns into a scythe." Ermal looks from Itra and back to the screen.

"Cool," Ermal says, grinning.

"Pretty sure this is the reason the people are scared."

Ermal laughs and places a firm hand on Itra's shoulder. "How can I help?"

Itra smiles, releasing a long sigh. "I came back to get Anton's SUV, Danae, and a few changes of clothes." He paces the office. "Can you keep an officer near the hills? Just in case Danae or Leon need help."

"I'll take the first shift. Do they know where the shield was taken?"

"Beard claimed Medusa had a shield-shaped object before he was sent to the clearing near the ember archway. But who knows if we can trust that information."

"Was Beard working with them or for them?"

"If you ask me, both. He was being paid to harass Danae, Kaly, and I. He even confessed to the tapping of our phones." Itra's frown deepens, recalling the invasion of privacy. "His real name was Earl Eunice McCoy."

"As in Hatfield and McCoy?" Ermal snarks. Itra raises an eyebrow. "What, you don't think I know American history?"

"Just surprised," Itra chuckles.

"I discovered the History Channel while visiting my cousin in Michigan a few years back. There was a whole series about the family rivalry."

"No idea of his connection to the family, but that is his legal name. Did you identify his next of kin?"

"No, the American Embassy was notified of his arrest and subsequent escape. We made the call this morning to update them of his death. They're sending an agent to assist with contact information for next of kin."

Itra checks the wall clock. "I need to get back. Can you keep me posted on any action near or on the hill?"

"I'll call you if anything comes up, I promise."

11

Noel and Danae quietly back track, inspecting the ground for the cube. Danae jerks her head up and looks around.

"Do you hear that?" she whispers.

Noel strains to hear beyond their breathing. Heavy footfall is heading in their direction. He switches positions with her. "Danae run!"

"I'm not leaving you!"

"I'm right behind you." He urges her away from the mess they made.

She jogs down the corridor ahead of him. "Left or straight at the next opening?"

"Left! We need to find an exit."

"Hey!" a shout echoes down the corridor. "I see a light ahead. Stop!"

Noel immediately releases his staff, blinding them in darkness. "Son of a—"

Danae slows her pace a few steps, allowing her eyes to adjust. The ember amulet is vibrating. She feels it shift to the left just as they clear the opening. She makes a hard left, sprinting down another corridor. It's wider than the last, but still dark. She can feel Noel directly behind her. The corridor breaks again in three directions. She feels the amulet move, tapping to her right. She goes right without hesitating. He follows without comment.

A small crack of light grows as they sprint down a narrow corridor. An opening with stairs is straight ahead. Noel takes the lead, calling his staff as they quickly climb up.

A shout from below makes Danae hesitate and trip. She mumbles a curse.

Noel scans the area. They're level with the lake and staring at the mountains of Montenegro across the water.

Danae turns to look up. She recognizes the boulders on the rise. "This way!" She tugs on his arm. He doesn't move.

Danae meets Noel's eyes. He glances left and flares his nostrils but doesn't make a move.

A shout from below spurs Danae into action. She shifts the amulet out from under her top and turns to Noel's left.

A single guard stands with a gun leveled in their direction. The amulet lifts from her chest and the guard's knees buckle. His face plants into the muddy shore.

Danae takes Noel's hand as they to run towards the boulders. The first step launches them into the air. Noel panics, nearly letting go, but Danae tightens her grip. They clear the first boulder in a single leap and land as guards pour out of the bunker.

"Wings?" Noel whispers.

Danae smiles. "I just thought it would be nice to fly away and then boom airborne."

They watch the group divide into three search parties. Two groups head away from their hiding spot, but a third group of four men are headed straight for them.

Noel grabs her hand. They move in tandem, away from the approaching men. He leads her up the hill, keeping low, weaving around boulders and bushes, attempting to keep out of sight.

Danae feels the amulet shift to the right. She taps his shoulder and points. The afternoon sun creates a shadow from a tall boulder near a few thick bushes. They squat low behind the largest bush and wait. The first guard passes, only glancing towards them. He doesn't slow his pace. They continue to wait. The next two guards scan the area but do not give a second glance in their direction. The last guard passes, keeping his eyes focused on the rocks above.

After a few minutes, Danae sucks in a big breath. "Too close." She brushes a leaf from her hair. "We need to return and find the cube."

Noel's eyes go wide. "Are you nuts!" Danae flinches. "That place is probably swarming with an entire army of men. You set off what looks like an explosion down there."

"Teuta said—we can't leave without the cube." Danae sighs with notable frustration. "The other coordinates could lead to the shield."

"Pretty sure Teuta documented the coordinates. It's too risky."

"You want to talk about risks? One sister-in-law is dead, and the other is stone. If the cube falls into the wrong hands, more lives will be in danger." She lowers her tone. "We can't leave it behind."

"I hear you." Noel stands and scans the area. He creeps forward and peeks around the boulder. He motions for her to follow. They slowly creep back down. She glances back every few steps. He signals for her to pause and squat as they reach a spot where they can clearly see the entrance to the bunker. Two men are guarding the entrance and a third is pacing nearby.

Danae bites her lip as the amulet jumps from her chest like it is charging forward. The pacing guard doesn't have a weapon drawn, but the other two are resting with their fingers on the triggers of their large guns.

"Can you draw the two guards away from the entrance?" Danae asks Noel.

"And leave you alone with that guy?" Noel lifts his chin towards the pacing guard. "Hard pass."

60

Danae narrows her gaze at the pacing figure. It's the guard she disabled earlier. "Ha! He won't be expecting us to return."

Noel smirks and shakes his head. "I'll see what I can do—but if this goes sideways..."

"It won't." Danae stares at Noel.

He nods. "Take the same path down and stay low."

She nods.

Noel picks up a handful of sizeable rocks and heads to the far side of the bunker. He does not quiet his progress, drawing the attention of the pacing guard.

Danae inches further down, keeping a line of sight with the bunker. She steps and snaps a branch.

The pacing guard turns in her direction. Noel nails the guard with a rock square in the back. The guard whirls away from Danae, searching the hillside while pulling a gun from his side holster.

"Incoming," the guard yells to the two by the entrance. They split, abandoning the entrance and maneuver around the bunker, keeping their eyes high.

Danae exhales. The amulet is still pulling her forward. She doesn't slow but stays low.

"Bro, did you see the size of his gun?" Noel shouts before laughing. He lowers his tone before answering himself. "Like they stand a chance against this!" He cups his mouth and whistles. "Pew, pew, pew!" The sound is a dead ringer for an automatic rifle.

The guards duck and look around for any damage. They make a few hand signals and split up.

Danae bites her fist to keep a bark of laughter contained. Leon used the same distraction tactic when they were kids. Noel's weapon impressions are just as impressive. The amulet stops pulling her forward. She squats low and waits.

The pacing guard approaches her. She can just see his boots when Noel shouts again.

"Take the one on the right!"

The guard near her turns and bolts towards the other men. She stands and scans the area before leaving the cover of the boulders. She catches a figure running on the ridge and freezes.

"Clear!" Noel shouts in the lower tone he used to answer himself. Danae sprints to the entrance and ducks just inside the door, out of the guards' line of sight. Noel lets out a long, high-pitched whistle that sounds like a firecracker.

"Take cover!" a guard yells in response.

Noel throws down a handful of rocks. The guards curse, dodging the rocks, and continue their climb. The first guard to reach his hiding spot falls hard when Noel trips him with his scythe. He cries out in pain, holding his shin. Noel disarms the man before hiding behind a bush. A second guard approaches slowly from below.

"Which direction did he go?" the guard asks in a hushed tone. The injured guard just groans in pain. The guard kneels to check his partner's injuries, coming eye level with Noel.

Noel just smiles before punching him squarely in the jaw. The guard crumples unconsciously on top of the other guard. Noel disarms the guard, pocketing the side pistol and extra ammo. He dismantles the large gun with ease. Taking the cuffs from their belts, he secures them to each other, wrist to ankle, and pockets the keys.

"Here, kitty, kitty!" Noel says, taunting the third guard.

The third guard moves low. He remains close to the boulder, keeping his footsteps silent.

Noel lets out another long whistle. He chucks pieces of the dismantled gun in various directions and fires the guard's pistol in the air.

Danae covers her mouth, squashing a scream. She listens for Noel.

The third guard cowers, raising his weapon and scanning the ridge.

"We can do this all day," Noel answers himself. "Right bro?" Danae sighs in relief.

62

The last guard fires toward Noel's voice.

"Wrong move, bro!" Noel locates the guard and fires the pistol. He nicks the guy in the arm, forcing him to drop his gun. "Make a move and I will shoot to kill. Kick the gun away and lie face down on the ground."

The guard sneers up at him but complies.

Noel fires a round to the ground. "Last one down!" Noel calls in the lower tone. The guard flinches but doesn't move or protest when cuffed wrist to ankle.

Danae sneaks a peek around the bunker just as Noel comes into the clearing, now fully loaded with the weapons from the three guards. He hands her a loaded pistol. "I assume your brother made sure you knew how to handle a weapon." Danae nods, releasing the magazine—five bullets left. They scan the area once before entering the bunker.

12

Avi stirs and opens a single eye. *A pillow? It was a dream, or rather, a nightmare.* "Jinx." She pats the blankets down behind her back and feet, expecting to find fur, but the room is quiet. No purring. She opens both eyes and slowly sits up. *Not home, not my bed.* Her pulse races. *The message, cube, archway, castle, tiny woman, and the ghostly figures...all real?*

She stands and scans the room. The sparse, dark, ornate furniture is large, filling the space. She tiptoes to an open door and peeks through—a large furnished living room with a mosaic tile floor.

She creeps in slowly. A portrait on the far side of the room pulses with a faint light. She walks over and to inspect it. Her mirror image looks back at her.

Unexpectedly, a cool object falls in between her breasts. *What?*

She swats her neck and chest. Then she pulls back her shirt and pulls out a long, slim chain with a pendant shaped like an hourglass. She turns the chain, looking for a clasp. No beginning or end. She tries to pull the chain over her head, but it shrinks and gets caught under her chin. "Come on!"

"Avi?"

She freezes and whirls around, expecting to find someone standing in the room. A conversation with that brute of a guy from the morning replays and she recalls the connection to talk using thought. *What was his name?*

"Yes?" she replies.

"Are you well enough to help me out down here?"

"Who is me?"

"Leon."

The name sounds right. *"How did I get from the tower to here?"*

"I found you unconscious. Teuta transported you to your suite. Is she not with you right now?"

"My suite? And how could that tiny woman transport me?"

"Like this!" Teuta laughs, appearing next to Avi.

Avi jumps back and feels a small punch to her gut. The floor falls from under her. Her feet make contact a second later. She sucks in a long, ragged breath. She looks up and finds Leon standing just outside the open door of the front foyer.

"What was that?" Avi looks from Leon to Teuta.

"A portal." Teuta reaches up to Avi's neck. Avi steps out of her reach. Teuta shrugs and disappears.

Avi glares at Leon. "Explain."

He smirks. "I know the feeling all too well. She doesn't ask permission."

She fingers the new chain under her collar.

He narrows his eyes. "Is that new?"

She nods. She pulls the chain out. She palms the pendant to show him. "I didn't put it on and now I can't take it off."

Leon steps back. "Who did?"

"Not an actual person—I think. There is a portrait of me with two other women hanging above a fireplace in one of the rooms in my... suite? The woman in the portrait had this painted around her neck." She places it back under her top. "I felt it around my neck the second I stood in front of the painting."

"I would be mindful of its presence," Leon says, pacing the foyer. "The last chain that was unwillingly put around a descendant's neck—turned her to stone when it was accidentally removed."

Avi feels a tremor of dread wrap around her neck. "You think this is cursed?"

"No idea." He stops pacing. "Who was in the tower with you?"

"Teuta gave me a book with three haggard women on the cover—a mist filled the room and two figures cornered me. Then I was in darkness until I woke up in a bed."

"Seriously, it only gets weirder the longer I'm here." Leon turns towards the archways.

A person is standing near the past archway. Leon swiftly moves in front of Avi as the person draws a weapon from their back and starts to cross the clearing.

"Who is that?"

"Could be any of the past or a rogue descendant—maybe?"

Teuta appears next to them. Leon doesn't react to her appearance, never taking his eyes off the approaching figure.

"Ember identifies the approaching woman as Enyo."

"As in another grey sister?" Leon stiffens.

"Yes, but an original," Teuta sings. "The message on Avi's card is documented in the archives as a calling card for their services."

"You think she received the same message I did?" Avi says.

Teuta nods and taps the pendant under Avi's top. "The pendant is noted in the archives and a painting. The one in your suite is documented as the Protectors of Time."

Leon double taps his staff as the woman approaches the bottom step. "State your name and your intentions."

She is holding a large bronze sword in one hand and a small dagger in the other. Her flowing red coat hides her frame and possibly other weapons. Her dark hair is platted into three thick braids.

66

"My name is Enyo." She bows just slightly but keeps her eyes level with Leon. "I was summoned here."

"By whom?" Leon growls.

"Ember."

Leon flinches in response.

Avi steps out from behind Leon.

Enyo's eyes go wide. "Deino?"

"Do I know you?" The pendant shifts under her top. She presses her palm against her chest. The pendant vibrations seem to pulse in time with her racing heart.

Enyo studies her face before answering. "Yes." She sheaths her blades. "May I enter?"

Leon stiffens.

"You may," Teuta responds. Leon and Avi look down at Teuta, their mouths agape.

"She's armed!" Leon protests. "Leave your weapons. I'll gladly give them back once I've seen some proof of your lineage."

Enyo lifts her hands. "May I retrieve an item from my inner pocket?" Leon nods. She releases the hook, holding her coat closed and reaches in slowly, keeping her eyes on Leon and his glowing scythe. She pulls out a single card.

Teuta moves down the steps to examine the card. "It's the same message."

Leon sighs and releases his staff. "I'll keep watch from the tower."

Avi grabs his arm as he turns to run up the stairs. "It's pulsing." She meets his eyes and glances at her palm on her chest. "Is that normal?"

"Is any of this?"

She opens her mouth to respond, but zero words form. Teuta and Enyo join her in the foyer.

Enyo extends her hand towards Avi, but she steps back out of her reach.

Teuta shakes her head. "Avi has had a rough morning," Teuta explains. She twirls towards the conservatory.

Avi glares at her tiny figure skipping ahead. She can feel Enyo's gaze but keeps her eyes pinned on Teuta.

"Come along." Teuta dances through the curved rows of plants. She stops and opens a door.

Avi waits for Enyo to fall in line behind Teuta. She examines the hilt of the dagger visible from the sheath strapped to her back. *Renaissance or bronze age?*

Enyo glances over her shoulder. Avi immediately looks down and away. The pulsing pendant is only increasing her anxiety. They follow Teuta through the dining hall. Enyo doesn't slow to look around.

"Odd," Avi mutters. *Has she been here before?*

13

Avi and Enyo enter the war room. Teuta gestures to the chairs. Avi shakes her head and remains standing near the door. Enyo removes her sword and dagger, lying them on the table before sitting.

"The Castle of Teskom and Ember appreciate the answer to her call," Teuta begins. "Yesterday, the former bloodline assigned to protect and serve failed when the Medusa Shield was stolen from the vault. Also Medusa trespassed and killed at least three people."

Avi walks closer to the table, legs visibly shaking.

"A blood oath signed by Zeus and Phorcys to protect and serve has been reinstated. Leon, the man you met upon arrival, his sister, Danae, and another man, Noel, are from Zeus's line." Avi sits, too unsteady to remain standing. "Ember expects the sisters to work in tandem and restore the shield, fulfilling their duties as the blood oath commands."

Enyo holds up a hand. "Medusa was here?"

"Is here."

"Alive?" Enyo stands, grasping the hilt of her sword.

"Frozen in stone," Teuta says, smiling. "But yes, alive." She vanishes.

Enyo stares at the vacant space where Teuta had been standing and slowly turns to look at Avi. "What is she?"

"Annoying," Avi answers with a shrug.

Teuta reappears with three books. She places each book down carefully. "Avi, start with the Medusa book." She points to a red book with an illustration of Medusa. "Enyo, please read the OPEN book. It is required reading for all new arrivals. An orientation to the castle, magic, and knowledge held here at the Castle of Teskom. Any questions?"

Enyo points to the last book with red lettering on the cover. "And the last?"

"Your legacy, should you choose to accept."

"Legacy?" Avi whispers, standing to read the cover. "Protectors of Time."

Teuta nods. They stare at her for an additional explanation. Teuta smiles. "Sit and read. Leon will need your help soon." She twirls and vanishes.

"That is not normal." Enyo turns to Avi.

Avi nods.

"Shall we?" Enyo asks, gesturing to the books.

Avi stands to pick up the Medusa book, and the pendant vibrates. She releases the book. The pendant goes still.

"What's wrong?" Enyo asks.

Avi pulls out the pendant. Enyo's eyes go wide. "Do you know what this is?" Avi asks.

"Yes, may I ask who gave it to you?"

"Not who, but what."

Enyo shakes her head.

"I was standing in front of a painting when I felt something on my chest. I've tried to remove it, but there is no clasp. It shrinks when I attempt to pull it up over my chin." She lifts the chain to demonstrate, but Enyo reaches over and slaps her hand away. Avi lurches back. "What the hell?"

70

"Sorry!" Enyo holds up her hands. "You must never attempt to harm or remove the necklace."

"Why?"

Enyo shakes her head. "Can you tell me about the painting?"

"Three women, two painted in profile, standing on either side of a woman who looks just like me. This necklace was painted around her neck."

"Was painted around her neck?" Enyo asks, leaning forward. "It's missing from the painting now?"

Avi nods. "Can you explain why I'm stuck with this?"

"It's an infinity loop."

Avi picks up the pendant and holds it level with her eyes. She sucks in a breath. "And that means what?"

"Our legacy."

Avi exhales a long sigh and sits. Her foot starts a rhythmic tapping under the table.

"The grey sisters are infamously portrayed as those that gave up the location of Medusa." Avi nods. "But the truth is that— Perseus, the son of Zeus and Danae, was Ember's messenger and mark maker."

"Like Teuta?" Avi asks, leaning forward.

Enyo nods. "Zeus and his bloodline were the first to protect and serve the Castle of Teskom. Athena was the daughter of Zeus. She cursed Medusa using Ember's magic. This action betrayed the family's oath to protect and serve."

"So, this is cursed?" Avi holds up the pendant.

"Not exactly. Ember instructed Perseus to give the ember infinity loop as a peace offering to Phorcys." The book with the Medusa illustration opens on its own, startling Enyo. She picks up the dagger and scans the room. She looks down at the page and gasps.

"Enyo, have you been here before?" Avi stares at the page. There is a painting of a woman in a flowing red coat, holding a sword and dagger. It's Enyo, even the hair braids are identical.

"Yes."

"When?"

Enyo blows out a long breath. "Three months ago. What year is it now?"

"Twenty twenty," Avi answers, swallowing hard. "What year is it for you?"

"First century, eighty-sixth year."

"And you are how old?"

"Thirty-six. You?"

"Thirty-three," Avi responds but raises a hand. "Hold up! We are three years apart in age, but two thousand years apart in reality?"

Enyo nods. "A little more, but yes."

"How?"

"Ember."

"That explains nothing. Remember, I'm new here!"

"The ember archways are an extension of the goddess Ember. Three go to parallel dimensions and two go to time, the future and the past."

Avi squeezes her eyes shut and taps the table. "You came through the archway to the castle from your time three months ago?" Enyo nods. "This painting is of you standing like you did today at the bottom of the steps." Avi points to the open book. Enyo nods. "How did you gain access to the castle if Zeus's bloodline was—or is—still in power?"

"Perseus's never made it to my father. My sisters and I saw him coming in a vision and waited for his arrival. He offered the pendant as a token of peace initially, but we had already seen his future."

"I don't understand."

"He had other orders to find and behead Medusa, but this would sever Zeus's line to the Castle of Teskom and Ember. He was torn. We proposed a new deal allowing Perseus to complete his orders but for the lineage to still have ties to the castle."

72

"The blood oath?"

Enyo nods. "It isn't Zeus and Phorcys thumb prints, but mine and Perseus." Her eyes glass over. "We buried the oath along with an eye, a tooth, and a tiny shard of ember from the pendant. That is why there is a scratch on the back."

Avi inspects the pendant and finds tiny dip in the back where it looks like it was scraped off. "What made you come to the castle?"

Enyo wipes away a single tear before hardening her expression. "I was sent to the Castle of Teskom by my father, Phorcys, to petition for our bloodline to take over for Zeus after Perseus beheaded Medusa." She bites her lip before continuing. "Ember listened to my petition and asked me to return only after I received a summons."

"She knew of the oath and Perseus's betrayal?" Avi leans back.

"I assume Ember knows all."

"So, the pendant?"

"A merger of my sisters. Our essences."

"Translation, please."

"You can summons our souls."

Avi flinches. "That's a little dark and witchy. Why would I do that?"

"You would do it for counsel. You may need guidance of one or all three of us from time to time. The soul bond was forged into the metals of the chain. A blend of Ember's magic and the power of three."

Avi looks down at the pendant and back up to Enyo. "I have this for life?"

"You were chosen."

"And what happens if the necklace breaks?" Avi asks.

Enyo opens her mouth to answer, but Avi holds up her hand to stop her.

"I could use a little help!" Avi hears Leon huffing, descending the stairs at a full sprint.

"On my way," Avi answers. "Stay here. Read the book, Teuta suggested. I'll return shortly." Avi stands and heads for the door.

"Wait!" Enyo exclaims, standing and picking up her dagger. "I'm coming with you?"

Avi gives her a fierce glare. "No, sit and read."

Enyo backs up as if punched. "What was that?" She rubs her chest.

"My instructions." Avi swings open the door and sprints to the front entrance. *"How many?"*

"A dozen or more, but fair warning several are kids."

"Are you still in the tower?" Avi asks. The plants sway as she bolts past them to the main foyer.

"Here!" Leon pokes his head out of the front entrance.

"You said a dozen. That looks like fifty or more." Avi stands on her toes watching a continuous stream of people filling the clearing heading towards the castle.

Leon shrugs and double taps his staff.

Avi steps away and focuses on the lead group. "Today will be your last if you continue."

A few members of the group yelp and turn away. The others stop and look around. Only six continue unphased by the warning. Leon leaps down the steps to the path and runs in their direction.

"Your death is now certain." She renews her focus to the next group. "Death is certain!" She can hear cries of alarm. "Go back and never return!" Several sprint away, but a few people fall to the ground crumpled in fear and cover their heads. "Five, four, three, two, one!"

Leon enters the clearing as she calls one. A shrill scream comes from the first group.

"You were warned."

Leon starts his assault in a full sprint towards the group. They flee, screaming for mercy. Avi covers her mouth to smother a bark of laughter.

Only two trespassers remain on their knees in the clearing. Leon nudges the first remaining trespasser, a teenage girl. She looks up and screams, seeing him for the first time. He reaches down to help her up. She springs back, scrambles to her feet and runs away. Her scream draws the attention of another kneeling figure, an older woman in a red dress. She stands and boldly walks towards Leon. He raises his staff but then stops. She is smiling.

"Nice to see you too, Leon," the woman states with calm confidence. He narrows his eyes, trying to place her face with someone he should know. Her accent is familiar. "You have no idea who I am?" He doesn't answer or move an inch as a shiver races down his spine.

"My name is Xena. I'm Kaly's aunt."

He sucks in a breath and steps back, releasing his staff.

"Who is that?" Avi asks.

"Family."

14

Danae follows Noel, trying to keep her steps light. The amulet lifts from her chest as they reach the first opening. He looks back, and she motions straight. They move silently, not alarming any additional guards.

At the next right, they're facing the two guards from earlier and the crumpled opening to the bunker. Noel spins slowly, checking each entry and shadowed corner.

Danae enters the bunker. She picks through the rubble until the amulet pulls hard, yanking her level with the floor. An object flies just over her head, crashing against the wall. A scuffle of noise escalates just outside the opening.

"Noel?" She scrambles out of sight against the bunker wall. A shot echoes in the small space. She flinches and covers her ears. "Noel!" She risks a look out of the opening. Noel is panting, standing over the two guards. "What the hell happened?"

He gestures to where the guards stood in stone only seconds before.

"How did they break free?"

"I heard a small crack before the first one swung a rock towards my head," he says, fighting to catch his breath. "No idea how or who busted them out."

"Are they dead?" Danae steps out of the bunker to inspect the guards.

"No, but one will probably need a hospital. Did you find the cube?" One guard groans. Noel bends to secure their hands using the guard's belts.

"Not yet."

Danae steps back inside to continue her search. She kneels down and moves a few larger rocks to uncover the lost cube next to one of the shackles still chained to the wall. She shudders, picking it up to inspect it for damage. Turning it carefully over, it appears intact. "Got it!"

Noel steps inside with a finger raised in front of his mouth. She listens and can hear approaching footsteps and chatter. She quickly steps beside him and taps the cube. It flattens. She grabs his hand before selecting the coordinates near the archway and presses in the sides.

Their feet fall and connect with land a few seconds later. Noel exhales, raising his borrowed gun and scanning the area.

Danae palms the amulet. It remains still. "Clear," she says, marching towards the ember archway with confidence. He follows but keeps his back to hers as they approach and cross under.

As Noel and Danae approach the castle, they see that Leon is standing in the middle of the clearing with a woman. He waves them over. "Any luck?"

"Yes and no," Danae answers. She gives Leon a hug. Then she turns to greet the newcomer. "Hi, I'm Danae, Leon's sister."

Xena smiles. "Kaly always said you were warm and friendly."

Danae tilts her head to study the woman.

"I'm Xena, Kaly's aunt from Greece."

Danae's mouth falls open. Leon nudges her in the side. "Sorry, my manners, it's nice to meet you." She extends her hand and Xena shakes it.

"You're expecting?" Xena asks.

She nods in surprise. "How did you know?" She smooths down her top.

"Call it a woman's intuition." Xena turns to Noel. Her glance goes from Leon to Noel several times. "Kaly never mentioned you were a twin."

"We're not," Noel and Leon answer in unison.

Danae chuckles until her stomach groans loud enough to draw their attention. "Sorry, I'm starving. Can we go in?" She looks at Leon. He nods.

Noel and Leon pace ahead, discussing the events at the bunker and finding Kaly's pack.

Danae falls into step beside Xena. "How did you end up here?"

"Kaly called me four days ago on her layover. She mentioned a recent discovery that linked to the death of her father, my brother. She was very cryptic, but also excited. When she didn't call after a few days, I got in the car and headed north. I arrived in town this morning and there was a buzz of chatter in every cafe about a new structure on this hill. I heard a group of kids planning to climb up and investigate. My gut said to follow, and here I am."

"Did Leon fill you in on what has happened?"

"Yes. His pain surrounds his energy. I knew something was wrong the second I saw him. And for you, to lose two sisters in one day, the pain must be unimaginable."

"It's not real, not yet," Danae whispers.

"Who are they?" Noel asks.

Danae hears his question and looks up. Two women are standing at the entrance to the castle. Danae recognizes the one from this morning, but the other is new.

"Avi and Enyo," Leon answers.

78

Xena places a hand to her chest. She moves forward and wordlessly climbs up the four giant steps.

Danae searches Avi and Enyo for a similar reaction, but both have their brows lifted with a question. Leon and Noel extend their hands to help Danae up the first step, and they follow Xena to the top.

"Are you a descendant of the sister Pemphredo?" Enyo asks Xena.

"Our family tree has links back to Phorcys and Ceto," Xena responds.

Enyo grabs Xena and Avi by their wrists. "We are three, hear our plea," Enyo recites, lifting her chin up. Avi and Xena freeze with their eyes locked on Enyo. "To protect the ember in time, Illyria of mine." A whirl of air gathers around their ankles and blows straight up, lifting the loose hair of Avi and Xena. "Unravel the weave and hear us breathe." Enyo continues as her braids release and her hair lifts and connects with Avi and Xena. "Bind our line to protect time, our legacy thine." A final push of air lifts their hair, twirling and intertwining their thick brown locks as one.

Danae steps back as air pushes away from the women and ruffles their clothes. Leon steps in front of Danae and calls his staff. Noel watches with wide eyes as the women's hair falls back down and untangles.

"What did you just do?" Avi asks, her voice trembling. She pats her hair.

Enyo lowers her chin and smirks. Her hair, free from the braids, is wild around her face, making her expression more menacing than happy. She releases the women and takes a giant step back. "I fulfilled my promise and duty."

"Promise and duty to whom?" Leon asks, deepening his tone to a growl.

"Ember," Enyo says and turns, nearly skipping back inside.

The five of them watch her move through the conservatory before speaking.

"Was that a curse or blessing?" Xena asks.

"To be determined?" Avi strokes her hair and straightens her top. She shakes hands with Xena. "It's nice to meet you."

"What did this look like before we left?" Noel asks, staring at the mural on the foyer floor. "Three, right? Now six." He points to the figures painted on the floor.

"Bizarre," Danae mumbles.

"Teuta," Leon calls. She appears with a slight curtsy. "Can you keep watch while we eat?" She nods and vanishes.

Xena points to where Teuta appeared and vanished. She then laughs, her chuckle nearly identical to Kaly's. Leon and Danae make eye contact and his eyes glass over.

Noel leads them through the conservatory to the dining hall.

The table is formally set for seven with fine china and purple plate covers. Enyo is pacing under the dome with her head tilted up, watching the colored glass shift with the changing sunlight. She looks over at the group as they enter and motions towards the table.

Leon pulls out a chair for Xena. He sits down next to her, and Danae sits to his right. Noel and Avi sit across from them with Enyo, leaving the head chair vacant. Once they settle, a hush falls over the group.

"Shall we eat?" Danae asks. She smiles at Noel and Xena. "Imagine the meal you desire, a house chef to inspire."

Noel raises an eyebrow.

Leon wastes no time and removes the formal cover. The aroma of freshly grilled steak and roasted vegetables fills the air.

Noel licks his lips and uncovers his plate. "So good!" he mumbles around a mouthful of shrimp.

Avi wrinkles her nose at the smell and at his manners.

Avi, Xena, and Enyo lift their covers in unison, revealing identical meals—pasta with grilled chicken with white sauce, along with a side salad, feta, and olives. They laugh and shake their heads.

Danae uncovers her perfectly cooked banana pancakes and a side of bacon and eggs. She grins widely, picking up her fork.

Just as she lifts the first bite to her lips, the middle door opens on the far side of the hall. Noel stands with his fork and knife in hand, ready for a fight. No one enters.

"It's just the door to the library," Danae says before taking a large bite.

Danae recalls her first step inside that door when she was briefly locked in with Itra. Her desire to return home becomes urgent. She focuses her thoughts on the Medusa Shield.

A book floats into the room and lands on the table next to her. The group exchange looks before turning to her. She shrugs and swallows. "It's thought provoked, think of a subject and it delivers."

The book opens. Pages flip and stop at a portrait of a bronze shield. The caption is not legible. She attempts to turn the page, but the book resists.

"What am I missing?" Another book lands and opens to a page with an illustration of Medusa's head on a podium and a person's back sitting with a paintbrush in front of a bronze shield.

Leon leans over to look at the two open books. "Well, that isn't exactly helpful."

The group looks over from their plates. Danae sighs and holds up the first book. "A bronze shield." She holds up the second book. "The painting of said shield."

Enyo leans closer. "The shields are different."

Leon and Danae scan the details of the illustration with the artist and the portrait.

"She's right," Leon murmurs.

"Does that mean we're looking for two shields?" Noel asks.

Danae and Leon look up from the books and at each other. "No clue," they say in unison.

"Can anyone make out the caption below the bronze shield?"

Xena shakes her head as Leon passes her the book for a closer look. Noel and Avi take a closer look but frown.

Enyo takes a sip of wine before speaking. "Wield the shield or mirror the field. Time will bend until Kelmend."

"Kelmend? The area north of here is called Kelmend. I wish Itra was here."

"Who is Itra?" Enyo asks between bites.

"My husband and a descendant of Mui, the previous protectors of Ember and the castle." Enyo frowns. "Mui's line was the fourth line to serve. We intend to take up Zeus on his alliance once I pop."

Enyo nearly chokes on an olive.

"What alliance?" Enyo asks.

A book narrowly misses Enyo's head. She pulls her dagger in alarm. The book lands on the table and opens to the page, discussing the merger of Zeus and Mui's lineage. Enyo reads the page. "If this is true, what will happen to the blood oath of Phorcys and Zeus?"

Avi's eyes dart between Enyo and Danae.

The door from the conservatory opens with a loud howl of air. The group stands in haste. A breath later, a tall narrow figure fills the doorway.

"You made your plea," says a deep voice that fills the hall. "Your legacy is secure, but the blood oath is null and void."

Enyo bolts away from the table, knocking over her chair and draws her sword.

A man smiles before making a small bow and stepping into the room. "My name is Pax." The resemblance to Teuta is shocking. He has the same piercing green eyes, dark wavy hair, and full lips outlining a wide smile.

Leon and Noel quickly move between the door and the table.

"Friend or foe?" Leon asks.

"Family," Pax replies.

"Whose line?" Noel asks.

"The second line. The Illyrian Queen Teuta is my sister. We are the second line to serve and protect Ember."

82

Teuta appears next to Pax, at her full height and curves, dressed as the queen—blue gown and crown.

"Teuta—the pirate Queen Teuta?" Xena asks.

"One and the same," Danae answers. "Teuta, I need to ask you about—"

"Tani!" Teuta responds. Danae vanishes. Leon just rolls his eyes while the others curse in surprise.

15

Danae curses as her feet connect with the floor of her bedroom at home. *How in the hell did Teuta know I was going to ask to leave?*

"Itra, are you home?"

Danae searches the house. There is a note on the fridge in Itra's handwriting.

Left the truck, see you at Anton's tonight. I hope. Love you!

She checks the time. It's ten till four. She has just enough time to shower and drive south to the city. She packs a change of clothes for the funeral and throws in a few extras for Itra.

After a quick shower, she stands at the mirror, waiting. *A thought provoked wardrobe would be nice right now!* She now finds the action of physically dressing cumbersome.

She steps out onto the front porch and drops the bag to lock the door. Her gaze instantly goes to the hills.

"Danae?"

She searches for the voice. A person is standing at the end of the drive. The backlighting of the evening sun makes it hard to distinguish who is walking towards her. She instinctively reaches for the amulet. It is still. She raises her hand to shade her eyes, straining to make out the approaching figure. It's just the neighbor. She sighs.

"Hi Franc."

"We noticed lights and movement in the house. Mira thought you were in the city with Itra."

"Um, I had to come back and get a few items." She picks up the bag and locks the door. "Thanks for checking on the house."

"I know it's not the best time to ask," Franc says and lets his eyes float up to the large castle on the hills, now clearly outlined by the setting sun. "Any chance you know what that is?"

Lie or truth? She keeps her face calm and lies. "I heard it's a temporary set for an indie movie."

"Well, that explains its sudden appearance. I won't keep you." He takes a step back towards the drive but turns. "And Danae, my condolences. Iana was a wonderful woman and a great mother and sister. She will be missed." Danae nods and sucks in a quivering breath.

"Thank you," she whispers, trying to choke back the grief tightening her chest.

He tips his hat and jogs down the drive and slides open her gate. She pulls through and waves. She pauses to check the rearview mirror to ensure he had no trouble closing the gate. Then she releases the brake and rolls down the road.

"Why!" Her emotional flood gates rip open. She beats the steering wheel and weeps as she steers down the road and out of town with blurry eyes.

Danae parks the truck and checks the mirror. She lets out one final exhausted scream. She steps out, straightens her clothes, and grabs her bag.

She can hear the whispers of a crowd two floors up as she slowly climbs the stairs to Anton and Iana's apartment. Her feet feel like three hundred pounds of weighted dread. She pauses, sucking in a deep breath before facing the family and friends here to pay their respects.

The people lingering near the door nod and acknowledge her as she climbs the final steps.

"Danae!" Elis shouts, climbing off Anton's lap and running towards her. She drops the bag and lifts him into her arms. She squeezes him in a tight hug. Itra joins Elis.

"Hi buddy," she whispers into his hair. She kisses his curls and leans into Itra as he wraps his arms around them.

"You made it," Itra whispers. "Are you ok?"

Tears are streaming down her cheeks. She nods, unable to speak as she takes in the mournful state of the room. Vincent and Anton join them. She hugs each of them, with Elis still wrapped tightly around her. She shifts his position and sits down next to Itra.

"Are you going to leave me like mama?"

She squeezes him tighter. "Itra and I will always be here for you."

He sniffles and places a hand on her ember amulet. "And Ana? When can I see Ana?"

She swivels to look at Itra.

Itra's eyes are equally large. *How does he remember his mother's doppelganger from the revolutionary dimension?*

"You remember Ana?" Itra asks.

"I'm the compass to time and time is growing." He wiggles and turns to face Itra. "Mama didn't fall down the steps." He stares at Itra, waiting for a response. Anton shifts in his chair to look at the three of them.

"What is he talking about?" Anton whispers.

Danae and Itra make eye contact but can't respond before the next round of mourners comes through.

The visitors for the next three hours are continuous. Around eight, Anton's mother collects Elis and puts him to bed. Hours and countless faces later, they sit for the traditional midnight meal.

86

Anton corners Itra and Danae. "What was Elis talking about? Who is Ana? What compass?"

Itra bristles, and Danae's ember amulet shifts under her top. She pulls it out. Anton's eyes narrow, waiting for a response.

"Anton, do you trust Itra and me?" She holds the amulet within reach to Anton. He nods. "Hold this for a moment."

"Hold what? I see nothing!" She guides his hand to the amulet. He barely touches it and his knees buckle. Itra catches him before he falls.

"What's happening?" Itra asks.

"I remember everything," says Anton. He shakes his head. "A spinning image of Iana up till the part she stopped breathing." He clears his throat and straightens his posture. His vision clears and he can make out the ember amulet. "Elis touched this?"

She nods.

"So much for the cover story," Itra grumbles. "How long will the memories last for Anton and Elis this time?"

She shrugs.

"You knew?" Anton asks Itra.

"Teuta gave Ermal a card. He showed me when I was home."

"And Danae, where were you?"

"Honestly, getting shot at while trying to track down the Medusa Shield in the Ottoman dimension with a man named Noel, Leon's doppelganger." Anton flinches. Itra immediately pats her down. She bats his hands away. "I'm fine." She taps the ember amulet. "The grey sisters have united at the castle, including Kaly's aunt, Xena." All color drains from Anton's face at the mention of Kaly's name. "Anton, it is not your fault Kaly is stone. This is one hundred percent Medusa's fault." Anton frowns.

"Who are the other sisters?" Itra asks.

"Avi arrived as Noel and I were leaving, and Enyo arrived while we were gone. Enyo did some kind of chant when they were united with Xena." Danae taps her chin. "We are three, hear our plea. Protect the ember in time, Illyria of mine. Unravel the weave and hear us breathe." She pauses, trying to recall the last line.

"Bind our line to protect time, our legacy thine?" Vincent asks, joining the three of them.

"More riddles?" Itra mutters.

Anton mumbles a string of curses.

Danae nods. "That sounds right. How do you know the phrase?"

"I think I read it in an old book." Vincent yawns. "But no idea where I was when I read it." The ember amulet lifts from Danae's chest, nearly hitting Vincent in the face. He feels a tickle of something nearby and swats it away. Upon making contact, his eyes go wide. "Ember!"

Danae nods. "Sorry, it has a mind of its own." She places the amulet back under her top. "Was this book at the castle?"

"Yes. It was an ancient book called Protectors of Time."

"Is this a good or bad thing?" She reaches for Itra's hand. He laces his fingers around hers as they wait for Vincent to respond.

"If you're carrying time," Vincent says, glancing down at her waist, "then it's a good thing." He smiles and pats her shoulder. "Coffee?" He scans their faces. They shake their heads.

"Have you heard of a man named Pax?" Vincent freezes, and his jaw falls open.

"Who is Pax?" Anton asks.

"A man claiming to be Teuta's brother. He arrived just before I was booted out."

"He is Teuta's brother, but he's also bad news if the stories are true." Vincent paces back and forth. "Is the castle visible from your house?" The anxiety of his tone sends a cold shiver down Danae's spine.

"Yes," Itra and Danae answer in unison.

"We failed," Vincent says, his eyes glassing over.

16

Teuta and Pax glide into the dining hall with postures straight and chins lifted. Noel stammers about Danae's disappearance. Enyo sheaths her sword and bows. Avi and Xena make eye contact with each other, but neither move.

Pax pulls out the end chair for Teuta. She stands in front of the chair and gestures for the rest of them to find their seats at the table.

"Where did you send Danae?" Leon snaps.

"I sent her home," Teuta says.

"Why?" Leon asks.

"Iana's wake is tonight, funeral tomorrow."

"And who is watching the clearing if you're in here?" Leon asks.

"The sun is setting. I closed and locked the front door. You may go to the tower to keep watch if you like." Teuta sits and the others follow.

Leon turns but spins back. "Why is he here?" he says, pointing to Pax.

"Ember."

He looks from Pax to Teuta, furrowing his brows. "Xena is my family by marriage. She is not to be harmed."

Pax and Teuta nod in response.

He meets Avi's eyes. *"I'll be listening."* She nods. His exit leaves the room silent for a full minute.

"Danae and Leon are the descendants of Zeus." Teuta's voice startles the others. Her sing-song tone is now smooth and elegant. "Danae is pregnant with an heir foretold for centuries, aligning the lineage of Mui, the former bloodline to protect and serve, with that of Zeus."

Enyo shifts in her chair, but the group remains silent.

"And upon Danae's delivery, the descendants of Mui will join the descendants of Zeus and the Protectors of Time."

Avi raises a hand. "Who are the Protectors of Time?"

"We are," Enyo says, pointing to herself, Avi, and Xena.

"According to our records, the gift of time has never been extended to anyone. But Danae's child is time, according to Ember. Once her heir crosses under the ember archway, time will freeze in every dimension."

"Her child will essentially hold the start and stop to all things?" Avi furrows her brows and looks to Enyo, who is staring at the table. Then she turns her attention to Xena. "How are we supposed to protect a child?"

Xena meets her eyes with a small smile. "Children."

"What?" Enyo asks, whipping her head up, searching the others for answers.

"She is carrying twins," Xena answers with a smile.

"Leon!" Avi panics. *"Is Danae pregnant with twins?"*

Leon chokes back a curse of surprise. *"Maybe. She hasn't been back to the doctor to confirm."* He stares out of the tower. No movement in the clearing, but the valley is busy below. The number of headlights streaming towards the hillside is increasing by the minute. *"We may have a mob at sunrise."*

"Why do you say that?" Avi responds.

"A stream of headlights heading this way, and it seems to be endless."

90

Avi states. "Danae hasn't confirmed that she is carrying twins and Leon says there is an endless stream of cars heading for the hillside."

Xena lifts a brow. "How did you speak to Leon?" She looks around the room.

Before Avi can respond, Enyo raises her hand.

"What are cars?"

Noel and Xena gape at Enyo.

"Where are you from?" Noel asks.

"Illyria," Enyo responds.

He sputters a few incoherent words before asking. "What year is it there?"

Enyo looks from Avi to Teuta before answering. "According to Avi, the year here is twenty twenty, but I am from the eighty-sixth year."

"First century—BC," Avi adds.

"I'm sorry, what?" Noel asks.

"How are you a few thousand years in the future?" Xena asks.

"Ember," Enyo states.

Teuta raises her chin and claps twice. The lights dim and a three-dimensional image of a throne hovers above the table. Teuta stands. "The Castle of Teskom and the grounds here date back to 1 BC. The knowledge, power, and technology held within these walls are bestowed to a bloodline by the goddess Ember, in order to protect and serve." The picture wavers to a woman inserting her hand into the ground and releasing a warm ember glow. "The five ember archways are an extension of her hand and power. The archways provide a portal to five dimensions. Over the last century, the portals have earned the nicknames revolutionary, communist, Ottoman, past, and future."

A series of images appear: the caverns, the castle's construction in various phases, and the finished castle.

Noel, Avi, Enyo and Xena watch in rapt attention. Pax drums his fingers on the table and yawns.

"The knowledge stored here will rival any historical collection the world over. We hold the keys to every past and current monarchy, ruler, dictator, government, and empire. The documentation here could easily rewrite history, as some of you know it—and Enyo, the future."

The color drains from Enyo's face.

Avi and Xena shift in their chairs and glance from Enyo to Teuta.

"What is the blood oath you were speaking of?" Xena asks Enyo.

Pax stands from Danae's spot at the table. Teuta graciously nods, giving him the floor to speak as she sits. "When Athena cursed Medusa using Ember's magic, Ember sent a peace offering to Phorcys via her messenger, Perseus. He was intercepted by the grey sisters."

Enyo doesn't look up but sinks lower in her chair.

Pax paces the room. "The grey sisters knew he was also tasked to assassinate Medusa. If he didn't complete this task, harm would come to his mother, Danae."

"Leon! Are you listening to this?" Avi tries to keep from squirming in her chair.

"Yes!" Leon leans his forehead against the cool glass of the tower.

"The sisters and Perseus struck a deal." Pax pauses mid stride in front of Enyo. "Shall I finish, or would you like to explain?"

Enyo raises her eyes to meet Pax's coy smile. Her face hardens. She remains silent.

"Very well," Pax says, continues pacing. "The sisters and Perseus forged the blood oath using their father's names to pledge an oath to protect and serve Ember and the Castle of Teskom for eternity. It was buried with an eye, a tooth, and small sliver of ember from the peace offering Perseus was supposed to deliver to Phorcys." He stops again in front of Enyo. "Did I miss anything?"

She doesn't answer. Her lips set in a straight line and her focus remains on the chair in front of her.

"Son of a—you've got to be kidding me!" Leon yells.

Avi winces. "If this is all forgery and Phorcys's line was never meant to serve, why were we summoned here?"

Pax looks from Avi to Enyo. "Interesting. She hasn't told you everything?"

"It's been a very busy day," Avi states, glaring at Pax.

"The sisters were summoned to Ember after the interception and forgery," Pax says. Enyo shifts, straightening her posture. "Enyo answered the summons and made a deal to keep herself and her sisters alive."

Noel glances around, feeling a little out of place.

"Ember assigned the sisters to be the protectors of time as penance for their actions, but the essence of their legacy is tied to the life of time. If time dies, so does their line."

Xena and Avi blow out a long breath in unison. Xena reaches for Avi and Enyo's hand. Enyo ignores the gesture. Avi takes her hand and shifts to face Enyo.

"Is this true?" Avi asks.

Enyo faces Avi. "I did it to save my sisters." Her face remains hard.

Xena leaves her hand open to Enyo. "I understand the decision."

Avi tightens her grip on Xena's hand and extends her other hand to Enyo.

"What's happening?" Leon asks, pacing the tower.

"Waiting," Avi responds. She focuses on Enyo's face as her eyes dart between her and Xena.

Enyo shifts in her chair and hesitantly places her palms to theirs. A punch slams into her gut and the room falls away, leaving the three of them standing in blackness. The cool dampness of the space feels vacant of any air movement. They each spin around looking for the others, but the ladies are alone.

"Leon!" Avi yells. *"Can you hear me?"*

Leon doesn't respond but moves towards the stairs. Teuta appears on the top step back in her fairy form. He jumps back.

"BELL!" Leon shouts in Teuta's face.

Ding

Teuta let the bell drop to her side. He attempts to move around her, but she blocks his path.

"They're fine!" Teuta twirls. "The future cavern has a message for them. Keep watch while I show them." She doesn't wait for his nod before vanishing.

"Teuta is coming to explain," Leon answers. Avi doesn't respond. He checks the clearing once more. No movement. He bounds down the steps towards the conservatory, nearly running in to Noel.

"Any sign of the ladies?" Noel frowns. "They vanished except for Pax and I."

Enyo inspects the space with a dagger and sword in each hand. Xena and Avi remain back-to-back, slowly turning, straining to see anything in the pitch black.

"Coming!" Teuta calls. Her voice echoes in the space. Enyo lashes out with her sword, barely missing her as she appears a foot away.

A light is hovering over her tiny figure. Xena stammers in surprise and points to the light. Teuta opens her palm to catch the stone, and the light falls. They blink, trying to readjust their eyes.

"This is the future cavern. It has been dormant since the fall of Mui's bloodline. But it has a message for you three."

Enyo joins Xena and Avi.

Teuta sings, "We are here. We are open. We are present."

The wall flickers with a fuzzy image, then clears to three women standing over a crib. The image fades to three women chasing two figures in a dark forest. The image goes dark before the three are able to catch up.

94

"Was that us?" Avi asks.

"Did you see the red coat?" Xena asks.

"What's happening?" Enyo asks in a menacing tone.

"A future clip of events." Teuta taps her light stone, and it hovers back above her head. "Come along." A door that wasn't there a minute ago opens to a stairwell. Teuta skips towards it. The three women stare at her, unmoving. "Did you really think Ember would summon you three here and then lock you up?"

Xena closes her mouth and swallows hard. "I wasn't summoned here."

"Kaly's call was a summons. Was it not?"

"No," Xena says, wringing her hands. "It was never an invitation. I came on my own free will, I was not compelled or summoned."

Teuta smiles. "Did you not dream of the sisters? Did you not feel drawn to the hills once you arrived?"

Xena's face falls. She hadn't told a soul about the dreams that had been haunting her since the death of her daughter over a decade ago. She drops her hands and straightens her spine. "How long will we be forced to stay here?"

"Who is forcing you to stay?" Teuta tilts her head with a frown. She turns and bounds up the stairs.

Avi is the first to follow. Enyo nudges Xena and nods with a small smile. Xena takes a small step and then another. Enyo falls in behind Avi but checks Xena's progress as they climb the countless stairs.

At the last step, Avi hesitates. She spots two figures standing in the shadows near the conservatory doorway. "Leon?"

"And Noel." Leon taps his light stone. "What did you see?"

"Two scenes," Avi says. "Three women standing over a crib and a second where three women were chasing two figures in a dark forest."

"Not chasing, hunting," Enyo corrects. Xena and Avi turn to stare at her. "Call it hunch."

"We still have business to discuss regarding the missing shield," Teuta says. "Plus, Xena and Noel need to read the manual."

"What manual?" Noel asks Leon.

"It's a book about the castle, the knowledge and magic held within."

Teuta lifts an eyebrow at Xena. She nods and follows the group back to the dining hall.

Noel places Kaly's pack on the table—the meal and dishes vanish. "Where do you want me to start?"

17

The room is quiet, minus a few snores from Vincent propped up in the corner. Anton shifts in his chair for the twentieth time. He gives up, standing and stretching before pacing the room. The extended family left the apartment an hour ago. The absence of quiet conversation to distract his thoughts making reality nearly intolerable.

Danae watches Anton pace. She leans against Itra. Her eyelids droop. He kisses her temple.

"I need two minutes," she whispers, falling asleep before hearing his response.

"You should try to sleep for a few hours," Itra whispers to Anton.

He stops mid stride and slumps in the nearest chair.

"It's called a wake, not torture," Itra says kindly.

Anton looks up with puffy red eyes and a deep frown, and shakes his head. "Iana's last words replay the second I close my eyes."

Itra nods towards the liquor cabinet. "Let the raki burn it away. Elis will need us in a few hours. Nada gave me a double espresso before leaving, so I'm wired. Just rest for a few hours."

Anton stands and pours two fingers of raki. "Wake me up in two hours." Itra nods as Anton swallows the raki in two big gulps. He grimaces as the liquid burns all the way down, and then he coughs. "What did you make this with?"

"Mulberries." Itra smirks. "Sleep now, two hours, go!" Anton nods and trudges down the hall.

Itra adjusts his shoulder and Danae stirs. He gently strokes her cheek. She relaxes. He feels a gentle vibration. He pats her down looking for a phone but realizes it is the ember amulet. He gently pulls the chain and lifts it out from under her top. It's almost pulsing in his palm.

"Itra?"

He twists around, looking for anyone else awake in the room. Vincent is still softly snoring in the corner.

"It's me, Leon," Leon says, standing in the present cavern.

"I can hear you," Itra whispers. "Are you ok?"

"Yes. We found a lead to the shield and are going after it at first light." Leon watches the color drain from Itra's face. "We need to be sure Danae doesn't come back until we return. There are too many people wandering the hillside. They could be rogue descendants or innocent civilians. Either way, we need her to remain with you for now. Do you understand?"

"What do you mean, 'for now'?"

"She is carrying time, remember."

Itra cocks his head to the side. "Also known as our child, or children."

"Ember will call her back, eventually."

Itra narrows his eyes. "Danae will do what is best for our family, and that includes you, so don't do anything stupid!"

"Yes, sir."

"And Leon, who's 'we' in this hunt for the shield?"

"Noel, Xena, and Enyo."

"Who will be left to defend the castle?"

98

"Avi and I, plus Teuta. Pax disappeared after exposing the blood oath was forgery. Teuta hopes to have additional help by dawn."

"It's a forgery? By whom?"

"Perseus and the grey sisters."

"Wow." Itra searches the room for a clock. It's just past two in the morning. "Anything we can do from here?"

"We need a text translated. After the service tomorrow, any chance we can borrow Vincent?"

"You could ask me yourself," Vincent says, clearing his throat.

"Sorry, didn't know you were listening." Leon watches the view shift to show the whole room, including Vincent.

"I'll head north after the service and meal tomorrow—ah, later today—with Itra and Danae."

"Don't let Danae convince you it's safe for her to return. I'll send Teuta to collect Vincent."

"Deal! Don't break anything!"

"Yes, sir."

Itra releases the ember amulet. "Are you sure you want to go back?"

"I'm surprised I can," Vincent answers, "to be honest." He rolls his neck side to side and sighs. "The lines before us never entered the castle except Teuta and now Pax. I never knew it was possible until the attacks."

"The first line was Zeus, the second was Teuta's family, right?"

"Yes, but it was her line, not King Agron."

"Her line?" Itra raises an eyebrow.

"Ardiaei tribe." Vincent nods with a grin. "They once ruled from the Lezhë Castle."

Itra's mouth drops open. He took Danae to this castle during her first year in Albania. It sits high on a mount overlooking the city of Lezhë, with views all the way to the Adriatic Sea.

"Zeus to Ardiaei and Mui was the fourth, but who was third?"

Vincent stares at him, unresponsive.

"Vincent?" He waves his free hand up and down. No response. He slides his arm out from under Danae and gently lays her on his chair.

He kneels on the floor in front of Vincent. He gently shakes him. "Hey Vin, come on!"

Vincent opens his mouth, but no words come.

"Vincent, you're scaring me. I'm calling for a medic." He jumps up to look for his phone.

"Wait," Vincent whispers.

He pauses after tossing a couch cushion aside. "Vincent, what's wrong?"

"The third line before Mui was Kelmend."

"Like the Kelmend area in northern Albania?"

Vincent nods.

Itra shakes his head. "Wait, wasn't Mui technically of Kelmend?"

"No Kastrat. Although some historians argue his father was of Kelmend. Ember selected the Kelmend line to protect and serve, after the Adriaei line got greedy with the knowledge stored inside the Castle of Teskom."

"What happened to the Kelmend line?"

Vincent frowns. "I only found one line documenting Kelmend in the castle library—Kelmend end, Mui begin." Vincent shrugs. "Ivan and Teuta were very mute about this line. I dug deeper on my third visit to the library. It was like the history of the Kelmend line didn't exist. There was nothing, no other mentions, just that one line."

"But why did you go all rigid?"

"The Kelmend line still thrives in the highlands. If they were part of the rogue descendants that attacked the castle, and they know the defenses are down… with the shield gone, the threat up north is very real and possibly catastrophic."

100

"The families left in the highlands aren't warriors, they're farmers."

Vincent holds up his hands. "Have you heard of Fort Kelmend near Nikç?"

"Other than a sign on the road near Tamare, no. Why?"

"Ancient folktales allege conquering Fort Kelmend will unlock Chronos."

"As in Zeus's father, Cronus?"

Vincent shakes his head. "C-H-R-O-N-O-S," he spells out. "Father Time."

Itra sits. "Time." He mulls this over, trying to recall any history of the Kelmend tribe. He can only recall their resistance against the Ottoman's and the stories of fairies in the Accursed Mountains. "Who defends the fort?"

"Fairies?" Vincent says, biting his lip.

"Ha!" Itra stands and searches the bookshelf next the dining table. "Iana had an art history book of Albanian tribes." He quickly scans the titles. "Got it!" He pulls the heavy volume from the shelf and flips to the back, searching the index for Kelmend. "Page thirty-two." He flips to the page and holds it up for Vincent. It shows a seventeenth century painting of Chronos with wings wielding a harvesting scythe holding a child by the leg.

18

The image fades to darkness. Leon turns to glare at the stone figure still standing in the corner. "You will pay for all that you've done."

Noel clears his throat from the door. "Who are you threatening?"

"Medusa."

Noel enters the present cavern and walks near the open edge, drawn to the moon's reflection on the lake below. He follows the lake to the shore and his eyes meet the ground. He immediately steps back. "Whoa! Why is this just open?"

"It's thousands of years old, maybe it wasn't at the beginning of time." Leon remains in the middle of the cavern. "Why did you follow me down here?"

"Couldn't sleep and heard your door open," Noel says, turning to look at him. "You moved too fast for me to call out after you. I didn't want to wake the ladies."

Leon stares at him. "Your poker face is worse than mine."

Noel scrunches his nose and frowns. "What is poker?"

Leon laughs. It echoes in the cavern. "A card game where you often bluff to win the bets on the table."

"You think I'm bluffing?" Noel narrows the gap between him and Leon.

"I know you are." Leon shifts his posture and staggers his stance. "Tell me, why did you really follow me?"

Noel looks down at the floor. "Curiosity and grief." He scuffs the floor with his boot. "My sister, towards the end, would sometimes talk in her sleep. She repeated one phrase several times the day before she died. Ember of mine, Illyria of time."

Leon blows out a long breath.

"I thought it was a song or a poem."

Leon nods. "You said when we first met that your sister died nearly a decade ago."

"Yes."

"Xena's daughter, Pemphredo, died in a car accident a decade ago. Remind me to ask Avi about her timeline and events around the same time as your sister's passing." He tilts his head and twists his mouth. "It could be nothing."

"Noted." Noel inspects the rest of the cavern. "How does this work?" He nods his chin towards the dark interior wall.

"I don't know the science or magic behind it, but it acts as a window to the present. If the person on the other end has crossed through the ember archways or has held an ember stone, they can sense someone is watching. However, when Itra and Danae first used it, they could communicate with Itra's sister Iana and even his nephew Elis heard them speak." Leon laughs. "I didn't believe Iana or Danae when they shared this story. Teuta and Itra's ancestor Ivan had never heard anyone answer until that day."

Noel fights a yawn. "If this is the present, and the ladies were in the future cavern earlier, is there a past cavern?"

"Not that I've seen, but Teuta could probably confirm."

"Confirm what?" Teuta asks, appearing between Leon and Noel. They jump back. She holds up a brass bell and jingles it softly.

Ding, ding

Noel's laugh consumes the cavern, bouncing back and gaining volume. Her smile broadens as Leon fights to keep his grim face from cracking a smile.

"A warning bell is for before you appear, not after." Leon glowers and then laughs as Noel snorts, trying to control his laughter.

"Is there a past cavern?" Noel asks, still snickering. Teuta tilts her head and frowns. Her reaction makes him fall silent.

"No, only a past portal." She twirls to face Leon. "Who did you contact?"

"I spoke to Itra and Vincent," Leon says. She raises an eyebrow. "Vincent agreed to help with some translations we need. He'll ride up with Itra and Danae after the funeral." She frowns. "I also said you could give him a lift here?"

"I'm Ember's messenger, not yours!" she mocks and vanishes.

"That will never be normal," Leon says, shaking his head.

"Says the man with a floating light stone hovering above his head in a magic cave."

"Ha! Point! Noel one, Leon zero." He walks toward the door. "I'm done down here. Are you going to creep about or are you heading back to the suites?"

"Suites." They climb the stairs in silence before Noel asks, "Do you think Itra believed you?"

Leon trips up the next step. "I think he'll keep Danae safe."

"Why did you feel it necessary to lie to him?"

"What did I lie about?"

"We don't have a lead on the shield or a plan to go at first light."

He looks over his shoulder and smirks at Noel. "The scene you described in the bunkers with Danae left us a major clue." He continues up the stairs.

"What clue?"

"We know from the half stone soldiers, Kaly's pack, and the illusion of the woman in white hovering over a chained man that this was the holding location Kaly, and the blogger described."

He looks back, observing Noel's frown. He skips up the last three steps and waits for Noel to join him.

Noel breathlessly follows him to the foyer. He waits for him to continue.

"If we return to the same bunker in the past by only two days, we can intercept Poseidon and take the shield."

"Can we control how far back in the past we travel?"

Leon shrugs. "Hoping we can confirm this in the morning with Enyo," he holds his hands in air quotes, "and 'her'."

Noel laughs. "Is she like Bumblejuice? Say her name three times and she appears?"

Leon cups a hand over his mouth to stop a laugh from spilling out.

"What?" Noel shrugs.

"The movie was Beetlejuice."

"Not where I'm from," Noel scoffs.

"Avi quoted a line from the Wizard of Oz, but she said it's called Kingdom of Lost. Have you heard of that one?" Leon asks, walking into the conservatory.

Noel doesn't respond.

Leon turns to find Noel staring at the mosaic tiles. "What's glued you to the floor?"

"The shield."

Leon jogs back to Noel's side.

"Bloody hell." Leon calls his staff and lowers the warm ember glow, slowly moving over each tile. He takes a step back beside Noel. "Do you see a dark cave opening with a pulsing light in the middle shaped like a shield across from a large stone fort built in the side of a mountain?"

"Yep!"

"Does this valley in between the cave and the fort look familiar?" Leon gestures toward the center.

"No, afraid not."

"If the Ottoman soldiers intercepted Poseidon, would they have hidden it?"

Noel shrugs. "Maybe, anything is possible."

"Maybe one of the sisters has seen this valley before." He takes off at a jog after releasing his staff.

"Do you think we should wait till morning?" Noel calls a few paces behind.

Leon ignores the question. He doesn't slow his pace until he barges through the door to the dining hall. He halts at the presence of three figures standing in the dark under the glass dome. He double taps his staff. Noel skids to a stop behind him. One figure activates a light stone, illuminating the ladies.

"Why are you standing in the dark?" Leon scowls.

"Why are you prowling about in the middle of the night?" Avi asks in return.

"We found a lead to the shield." Leon turns back towards the conservatory, swinging his arm for them to follow. Noel steps out of his way and shrugs an apology to the women. They follow his lead to the rear foyer. He taps his staff, waving it over the tiles.

"Do you recognize this landscape?" He looks at each of them carefully.

Enyo moves around the perimeter and stops near Leon. "Fort Kelmend."

Avi stands beside her. "Are you sure?"

"American here, care to fill me in?" Leon raises his free hand.

"An ancient fort, embedded in the side of the Accursed Mountains deep in the Cemit Canyon," Xena answers. "Old folklore describes it as the timeless fort, never conquered or occupied."

"Never occupied—then why is it called a fort?" Noel asks.

Xena points to the tiles. "What else would you call this?"

106

He examines the image again. The solid stone perimeter is set with small notches for lookout posts.

Leon faces Enyo. "What was the caption you translated about the shield?"

"Wield the shield or mirror the field. Time will bend until Kelmend."

"How far is this fort?" Leon asks.

"It's just north of here." Xena taps her chin. "Maybe twenty miles, but two hours by car. The road up there is not great."

"Any clues if it's conquered in other dimensions?" Leon paces the small foyer.

"I've never heard of it till today," Noel says.

"Not in our timeline," Xena answers.

Avi nudges Enyo. "What about yours?"

"You mean ours," Enyo answers, "and no, not thousands of years ago." Avi rubs her arms as her hair rises.

"Do you think there are any answers in the library?" Noel asks Leon.

"Maybe not the library, but definitely in the archives."

"Archives?" Avi asks.

"It's portal access only," Leon explains. "Teuta will need to either retrieve the text or send one of us down there." Noel and Avi shake their heads in unison.

Xena raises her hand. "I'll go and get what we need. Kaly got her love of research from my side of the family." The others nod. "Kelmend and the Ottoman bunkers, plus any history related to the shield or Medusa?"

"The research we did after Noel's recount of the bunkers came up with theories but no real answers." Enyo yawns. "Will this be a waste of time?"

"My only other plan was trying the past portal to the bunkers where they found Kaly's pack and try to catch Medusa or Poseidon with the shield." Leon faces Enyo. "Can you control how far back or ahead you can travel through the portals?"

"How would I know?"

"You're the only one to travel here using one of those portals."

"No, sir. I only came using the cube to this time. My first trip was directly under the revolutionary archway."

"Hold up," Leon says with a frown. "The cube can cross time as well as space and dimension?"

"Apparently."

Leon shakes his head and marches towards the dining hall. "Who wants coffee and breakfast?"

"It's three in the morning," Xena says.

"And?" He holds open the door to the dining hall. "The three of you are up and were standing in the dark." He cocks his head at Xena. "Why was that?"

Xena doesn't meet his eyes as she shuffles past. The others follow her in silence.

"Secret sister sorcery?" He mocks, closing the door. Noel laughs at his comment, but his laugh cuts short.

"They're gone."

Leon spins around, looking for any sign of the ladies.

19

Danae sits up and rubs her eyes. Her movement startles Itra and Vincent. They had been wordlessly looking at the painting for several minutes.

"What did I miss?" Danae asks.

Itra opens his mouth to explain. She goes rigid, searching his face for an answer.

"What's happened?" She stands looking from Itra to Vincent.

"Nothing." Itra stands and strokes the ridge of her scrunched nose. He kisses her forehead before embracing her in a tight hug.

"Can't breathe!" She pushes away from Itra. "You're worried," she says, looking over his shoulder at Vincent. "You both are. Why?"

"Leon reached out." She opens her mouth to interrupt, but he holds a finger up. She nods. "He was checking on you. And they need Vincent to assist with some translations."

"It's the middle of the night. Why would Leon reach out now?"

"He probably couldn't sleep." Itra frowns. "And we're at a wake."

"And the shield, did he mention any leads?"

"Yes, they're going at first light to check out a lead." Itra motions for her to sit. "He wants you to stay away from the castle until they get an all clear. The hill is crawling with people and we don't know if they are innocent civilians or rogue descendants."

"You think the people we just fought have returned?"

"We don't know, and neither do they. We were discussing Vincent's return and—" Itra fails to finish his thought.

Vincent stands. "Danae, when you were in the archives, did you happen to research the previous bloodline?"

"No." She searches his face for an explanation. "Why is that important?"

"Proximity, mostly. Have you heard of Kelmend?"

Her eyes open wider. "Wield the shield or mirror the field. Time will bend until Kelmend."

"What?" Vincent and Itra ask in unison.

"It's a caption underneath an illustration of a bronze shield."

Vincent nods. "The last line to protect and serve Ember before ours was Kelmend."

"Why is this a bad thing?"

"If they were part of the rogue descendants that attacked the castle…"

She runs a hand through her hair. "They're close enough to see the shield is down."

Vincent and Itra nod.

"Did you warn Leon?"

"We only put the pieces together after we talked with him." Itra reaches for her hand. She grips it hard.

"What do you know about their line?" she asks Vincent.

"Next to nothing, except for the folktales. But Itra found this." Vincent hands her the book, open to a painting. She looks down and back up with her brows knitted together.

"Chronos," Itra says. "Otherwise known as Father Time."

"Allegedly conquering Fort Kelmend will unlock Chronos," Vincent adds.

She glances down at the scythe-wielding man in the painting. "Is Leon supposed to be Chronos?"

Itra sits down hard and breathes out a string of curses.

110

"Language!" She scolds him and frowns.

"He can't be Chronos, right?" Itra faces Vincent.

Vincent remains silent.

"Vincent?" Danae faces him too.

"I'm thinking." Vincent pulls his white hair, leaving it standing on end. "Kelmend end, Mui begins." Vincent shakes his head.

"What does that mean?" she asks.

"It's the only line of text I found related to Kelmend from the castle library."

Danae chews on her bottom lip, trying to recall any useful information from the manual. "If the castle did a full reset like it has now, it could be stored in the archives and not in the library." She focuses on Vincent. "I need to go back with you this afternoon."

Itra jumps up. "Were you listening? Leon says you need to stay put and I second his opinion. Vincent can relay this concern and assist with the research."

Danae sits back in her chair and glares at him. "Did you really just pull the mansplaining card?" She raises an eyebrow.

"Whoa!" Itra holds up his hands. "I did, but not on purpose. Can you tell me why you need to go with him?" He holds a hand to his heart. "I'm listening."

Vincent chuckles at the exchange but stops when Danae cuts a glare in his direction. "Sorry." He motions for her to continue.

"I'm bound to protect and serve. If there is a known threat to the castle and I idly standby regardless of my physical state, we may lose more than just the shield." Itra raises a hand. She shakes her head. "I didn't leave an army behind, just five souls plus Teuta and now Pax, if he counts."

"Speaking of Pax," Itra says with a grimace. "Leon said he disappeared after dropping a bombshell of news." She leans forward. "The blood oath was a forgery."

"By who?"

"Perseus and the grey sisters."

"Itra," Elis says. They turn in surprise. He is tugging on his pajamas, standing just behind the couch.

"Hey buddy," Itra kneels next to him.

"Ember called." He rolls up on his toes and hops side to side. "She wants our help."

"Our help?" Itra looks over at Danae and Vincent. They shrug in response. "What did Ember say?"

"The shield is near, check the rear, face old Kelmend to start again."

Itra blinks several times before responding. "Anything else?"

He nods and his brown curls bounce around. "Illyria, ember of mine, recover the shield or yield the line to end all time. Illyria, ember of mine, the new stone will shatter at night and breathe with light when all is right, Illyria, ember of time." He smiles. "That's all." He turns and skips back to his room.

Itra stands and follows him. Elis climbs back in bed and tucks himself in, patting the blankets around his chest. Itra watches him relax, and he falls asleep immediately.

Itra returns to the living room and finds Vincent and Danae in a heated whispering match.

"Hey?" Itra interrupts. "What's going on?"

Danae ignores Vincent. "Is Elis ok?"

"He's fine, already back asleep."

Vincent nods. "I'm going to start a pot of coffee."

"What were you two arguing about?" Itra asks her once Vincent is out of earshot.

"Nothing."

"Didn't look like nothing." He pulls her in for a hug. "Don't keep me in the dark."

"He thinks the cave Elis referenced means that Medusa wasn't the only enemy we missed during the battle." Itra steps back to look her in the eyes. "I saw Poseidon take a shield from Medusa while Noel and I were in the bunker. The timing doesn't add up with the blast that killed Iana."

He paces the space before throwing open the door to the balcony and letting out a strangled scream of exhaustion.

She closes the door to the balcony behind her, giving them some privacy. "Just breathe."

He releases another ragged breath. "It's all a damn riddle! We've lost so much already." Tears are streaming down his cheeks as he faces her. She tugs his chin, pulling him closer and softly kissing each damp cheek before hugging him tightly.

20

"Enyo."

Enyo wakes, rolls over, and searches the room. "Who's there?"

"Ember."

Enyo throws back the blankets and gets out of bed. "I've followed our agreement."

"Yes, but I have a task only you can perform."

"I'm listening." Enyo's wrists twitch. The instinct to draw a weapon heightens with each breath.

"Go the present cavern. Speak to Medusa. Recover or yield the line."

Enyo shifts nervously from side to side at the entrance to the present cavern. She draws her small dagger and taps the pommel against her hip.

"I'm here, now what?"

She feels a push on her back. She tries to fight the propelling movement, but can't until she is standing directly in front of the statue of Medusa. She keeps her eyes lowered towards the ground. Sweat dampens her spine and her palms, making her grip slippery, she tightens the dagger. She pulls and vigorously shakes her shirt away from her spine. The cool night air from the cavern opening soothes her nerves.

"Show me Medusa."

She hears the words exit her mouth but doesn't recall saying them. The head of the statue moves. The veil covering the face ruffles. *It's breathing.* Enyo tightens her grip around the dagger.

"Gorgon to Grey, it's good to see a familiar face."

Enyo doesn't flinch. "Medusa."

"Enyo."

"Where is the shield?"

"Gone."

"Where did you hide it?"

Silence.

Enyo sheaths her dagger and draws her long sword. She takes a swing towards the head.

"Stop!" Medusa screams.

Enyo halts just before the blade makes contact.

"So hostile!"

"Speak and tread carefully," Enyo states, moving the sword back to swing again. "My patience is running thin."

"I'm the victim here," Medusa whines, "don't you see. It's our right to be here!"

"Ha!" Enyo smiles and bites her knuckle to stop a loud laugh. "You think you're so clever! You fool. The blood oath was forged."

"Forged by whom?"

"My sisters and I struck a deal with Perseus."

"You didn't, you wouldn't."

"Get over it! Start talking. Where is the shield?"

"Why would you betray me?"

"Old news, talk!" Enyo swings and strikes the statue, slicing a sliver of stone with ease. "Now!"

"You'll pay for your betrayal!"

"Talk or my next swing will be your head!"

"Threats to an unarmed woman. Where's your honor?"

Enyo raises her sword and swings directly through an elbow. The severed stone drops with a loud thud. Enyo raises her sword and aims for the other arm.

"Wait!" Medusa shouts. "I don't know where the shield is!"

"Ha!" Enyo rolls her shoulders back to strike again.

"Poseidon moved it last!"

"Moved it to where?" Enyo taps her sword on the bend of the elbow, leaving a mark.

Silence.

Enyo twirls and strikes the statue just below the knee. She pulls back in time before completely severing the leg.

"You know I can't feel that, right?" Medusa taunts.

"Doesn't matter, you've always been stone cold and heartless. Where did you hide the shield?"

"Kelmend."

Enyo smirks and sheaths her sword. "And the snake charm you gave Kaly? Permanent or temporary?"

"Does it matter?"

"Ha! Rot in hell." Enyo takes two steps back. "Hide Medusa." The ruffle of the veil stills. She inspects the entire statue for any defects minus the marks she left and tosses the severed arm over the edge of the cavern opening.

She skips up the stairs and nearly collides with Teuta when she enters the rear foyer.

"Do you know where the shield is?" Teuta sings.

"Yes."

"And?"

"I need to wake the others."

"It's almost dawn, they'll rise soon enough." She tilts her head. "You don't trust me, do you?"

Enyo tucks her chin to stare directly into her eyes. "Not even a little."

Teuta grins and blows dust in Enyo's face. "Tani!"

The ground falls out and Enyo free falls, landing on a soft bed. The room spins as she tries to sit up. She falls back to the covers and darkness closes in.

21

Anton staggers into the living room just as the sun rises, soaking the room in new light. Vincent stands, pouring a new cup of coffee, extending it to Anton.

He nods, accepting the warm mug. He sips before making eye contact with anyone. "Is Elis up?"

"He was only up for a few minutes around three," Itra says from behind him.

Anton glances up through the rising steam. "A few minutes?"

"He had a message from Ember," Danae says, joining Itra. Anton lifts an eyebrow. She steps closer and takes one of his hands. He doesn't resist as she places the ember amulet in his palm.

His grip tightens around his coffee. "What does she want now?"

"More riddles," Itra says. "The shield is near, check the rear, face old Kelmend to start again. Illyria, ember of mine, recover the shield or yield the line to end all time. Illyria, ember of mine, the new stone will shatter at night and breathe with light when all is right, Illyria, ember of time."

The color drains from Anton's face.

Danae ushers him to a chair. "We think the ending of the riddle may mean that we can save Kaly."

Anton blinks rapidly.

"Anton?" Danae kneels to his eye level. "This is a good thing."

"I can't," he whispers. "Elis and I just can't."

"We understand," Vincent says, sitting next to him. "We're not asking Elis or you to join us."

"Us?" He cuts Itra a glance. "You're going back? When?"

"After supper this evening."

Anton nods and focuses on his coffee.

Danae and Itra exchange a worried glance. He nods for her to follow him. They step inside the hall bathroom and close the door before speaking.

"That was unpleasant," Itra says.

She scrunches her nose. "You use the word unpleasant now?"

He frowns. "You know what I mean. Do you think we should've—I don't know—not told him anything?" He drags his hands over his face and sighs.

She wraps her arms around his waist. "We can't keep Anton in the dark with Ember whispering to Elis."

Itra wraps his arms around her shoulders and kisses her hair.

"Are you ready for the day?" Danae asks him.

"I'll never be ready to bury my sister."

She flinches and leans back. "I meant, did you need to shower and change?"

He leans down and kisses her nose. "Yes, to shower and change."

She releases him and steps towards the door.

He grabs her arm and pulls her back. "Where are you going?"

"To grab your clean clothes and I brought your shaving kit," she says, scratching his three-day-old bristly beard.

He faces the mirror, turning his chin from side to side. "Trim or shave?"

"Your face, your choice."

"Mustache it is." She frowns. He grins.

Elis whistles when Itra comes around the corner in a suit. Danae takes in a breath before facing him. He's holding a hand in front of his mouth.

She sucks in a breath. "You wouldn't?"

He moves his hand. He's clean shaven. She exhales and smiles.

He pats his cheeks. "Smooth like butter."

"Uncle Itra, do you think I should wear the blue or red tie?"

"Blue, duh!" Itra teases and kisses Danae's temple. He whispers, "You should've seen your face!"

She halfheartedly punches him in the arm. "I'll go freshen up. Anton is on the phone on the balcony confirming the timing of events with the catering company and the funeral home."

"Where's Vincent?" he asks, looking in the kitchen.

"He stepped out to take a call. Something about a cousin needing directions."

"It's just you and me, buddy." Itra ruffles Elis's curls.

Elis marches over to the hall mirror. He tries to clip on the tie three times, but it remains off center. "Can you help me?"

Itra stands behind him and adjusts the tie. Their eyes meet in the mirror once it is straightened.

"Perfection!" Elis states, bouncing his eyebrows with a half-cocked grin.

"Oh dear, where did you learn that?" Itra laughs.

"Learn what?" Elis shrugs and heads to the balcony door. Anton is still on the phone. Elis taps lightly on the glass to get his attention. When Anton turns, his frown grows into a smile and he gives Elis a thumbs up.

"It's after seven," Vincent says, walking in. "The front door should be open."

120

Itra glances at the clock. He squints to make out the minute hand. "It's only two minutes past, and Danae is still getting ready."

A burst of air stirs the room as Anton enters from the balcony. "Catering and the funeral home are coordinating." He stares directly at Itra and Elis. "Nada is bringing over some food to keep these savages from passing out before the meal this afternoon."

"Who are you calling savages?" Danae asks as she slips on her cardigan, entering the living room. Itra and Elis raise their hands and turn with the same guilty grin. Vincent and Anton burst into a state of hysterical laughter. Danae laughs just as an echo of footsteps fills the stairwell. She covers her mouth and steps into the kitchen to try to contain her laughter.

Vincent and Anton straighten their jackets and ties, trying to squash their hilarity.

Nada fills the doorframe, holding a fruit tray in one hand and a meat and cheese tray in the other. "A little help here, please!"

Itra and Elis race over to assist. Anton snorts, trying to contain another burst of laughter. Nada glares in his direction.

"Sorry, you just missed a moment." Anton holds up his hands in apology. He glances over at Vincent. He has tears streaming down his cheeks and his lips are pressed together, trying to contain another laugh.

"Well, pull it together," Nada says. "There is a group downstairs waiting to come up."

22

"No!" Enyo cries out. "Stop!"

Xena sits up, squinting as the morning light filters in through a window near a wardrobe.

"Castle, right," she mumbles. She scoots to the edge of the bed. A quick staccato of footsteps rushes by her suite door. She jumps up and swings open the door. Avi is racing down the corridor.

"What's wrong?" Xena calls.

"Enyo!" Avi shoulders open the door to a suite a few doors down.

Xena rushes after her. Enyo is standing in the middle of the room. Both weapons are pointed at Avi and now Xena.

"Hey, it's me, Avi!" She holds up her hands. "I heard you scream and came to check on you."

Enyo shakes her head and inches further away from her.

"Is she still asleep?" Xena whispers, moving to Avi's side.

"I can't tell," Avi mumbles, taking the infinite pendant out from under her top.

Enyo's eyes instantly widen, and she charges towards them. Xena moves in front Avi, pushing her out the open door.

"Stop!" Avi screams.

Enyo freezes mid stride. She looks down at her white knuckles and loosens her grip.

"I think you were having a nightmare," Xena says, taking a small step closer to Enyo.

Enyo steps back. "Drugged."

"Are you ok?" Avi asks, stepping back into the room next to Xena.

Enyo lays the sword and dagger on the bed. She jumps up and down, shaking out her arms, and rolls her neck side to side. She turns to face Xena and Avi. "Teuta used some kind of powder to knock me out."

"I'm sorry, what?" Avi asks.

"I was summoned to interrogate Medusa. And when I was returning to the suites, I ran into Teuta near the conservatory. She blew something in my face after I refused to give her any details."

"You spoke with Medusa alone?" Xena asks.

"Ember was present, I think." Enyo undoes one of her braids and shakes out her long waves. "I think I have a solid lead for the shield." She releases the second braid and the volume of her hair springs to life, nearly standing on end.

"Why would Teuta press you for information and then drug you?" Avi asks.

"Old habits?" Xena shrugs. "She was pirate."

Enyo releases her last braid. "I don't trust her." She lowers her chin, making her look like a wild lion ready to attack.

"We should wake the guys," Avi says.

Noel peeks his head around the doorframe. "I heard Avi yell." He steps in, holding his hands up. "I'm unarmed."

Enyo nods. "Where is the other one?"

"Leon? In his suite, I guess." Noel takes a step back into the corridor but hesitates, turning back towards the three women. "How did you three disappear from the dining hall last night?"

Xena and Enyo look at each other and frown.

"So that wasn't a dream?" Avi asks.

"I thought the conversations we had with you and Leon were a dream."

"We?" Xena's frown deepens. "I haven't left my room all night."

Noel and Avi stare at her.

"Tell me what happened last night," Enyo states.

Avi wrings her hands. "I woke up after you two called for me. I met you in the dining hall."

Xena and Enyo exchange a glance and shake their heads. "Like Xena, I never left my suite until Ember summoned me."

Avi furrows her brows and purses her lips.

"Leon and I found you three standing in the dark, under the dome in the dining hall around three this morning," says Noel. "You came with us to inspect the floor in the rear foyer."

"That wasn't me," Xena states.

"Nor I," Enyo states.

"So, we were hallucinating?" Noel asks, pointing to Avi and himself.

Enyo points to Avi. "You're one with three."

"What?" Xena and Avi ask in unison.

"You are a shared consciousness with the ability to manifest us when needed," Enyo explains, gesturing to Xena and herself. "It's a gift or a curse, but as long as you wear the infinity charm, we are bound to you."

"So, we were chatting with your souls?" Leon asks, making the group whirl around. He fills the doorway behind Noel.

"You believe her?" Noel asks.

"After the last few days, it's not the strangest thing I've heard or encountered."

"So now what?" Noel asks.

"We decide who will go to the cave." Leon says, waving a hand towards Avi. "But how did you disappear last night?"

"I heard a whisper behind me and then I woke up in bed to Enyo screaming," Avi says. "That's why I assumed it was all a dream."

"Everyone has read the manual by now, right?" Xena asks. The four of them turn in unison. "Chapter fourteen describes the health of the line while serving. A vitals check is completed every hour. If there is any sign of fatigue or heightened stress, Ember compels the person to rest and recharge."

A bell rings behind Leon. He whirls to face Teuta but finds only a vacant corridor.

Teuta appears in a chair in the far corner of Enyo's room. "I see you're all up," she sings with a half grin. "War room, ten minutes." She vanishes.

"Shit!" Enyo curses.

"Was she in here the whole time?" Xena asks.

"Pretty sure we'll find out soon enough." Enyo scoots the group to the corridor. "I'm going to shower. We need a plan, so please wait near the stairwell before entering the war room."

They nod and disperse to their respective suites.

Thirty minutes later, they stroll into the war room, plan made. Pax and Teuta are waiting. Teuta gestures for the five of them to sit. Enyo and Leon glance at each other before sitting. Silence fills the space. Teuta transforms from her fairy form back to her queen height, dressed in a black gown with a crown.

"You have concerns about my loyalty to Ember and your line, don't you?" Teuta asks, focusing her attention on Enyo.

"Is that really so hard to believe?" Enyo responds coldly.

Teuta smirks. "You believe the rumors?"

"You mean the ones describing you as a vengeful pirate queen with no moral compass?" Xena states. "If the crown fits."

"Ha!" She taps her crown. "It does indeed. You think Ember would let me remain here?"

Leon leans forward, propping his elbows on the table, placing his chin on his fists before cocking his head to the side. "Says the woman that drugged Enyo last night. And blocked my exit when my wife was missing."

"I'm just the messenger," Teuta says, batting her eyes with childlike innocence.

"Ha!" Enyo snorts. "So was Perseus."

Teuta doesn't acknowledge Enyo. "It's not that simple."

Enyo stands. Leon follows her lead.

"We're wasting time here when we should be going after the shield," Enyo states.

"You know where it is?" Teuta asks.

"We know where it could be," Leon answers.

"Please share with the group."

"We know and therefore so does Ember," Xena says, standing and stepping next to Enyo.

Pax and Teuta share a brief look. "We're here only by Ember's grace. If she trusts us, so should you."

Leon ignores Teuta's comment and marches past her to the wardrobe with the feathered cloaks. He removes two and nods his head towards the dining hall door. The others follow his lead.

"Wait!" Teuta calls. The group doesn't hesitate in their departure. She transforms from queen to fairy and vanishes. She appears in Leon's path. He walks around her towards the conservatory door. Teuta slams the door with a flick of her wrist.

"Nice try," Xena says, flicking her wrist, and the door swings open.

"How!" Teuta shouts as the group continues to the front foyer.

"I read chapter eleven," Xena chuckles as she passes a wide eyed Teuta.

"Most people just skim read the OPEN manual," Teuta says.

Xena smiles. "I'm not most people." A full chapter on thought provoked abilities and actions. Examples include the wardrobe,

126

food, book catalog, and communication, but also included counter measures when threatened.

They reach the open door in the front foyer without any further protests from Teuta.

"Hold out your arms," Leon tells Xena.

"Like this?" She extends both arms. He nods and drapes the cloak over her shoulders. It fades into her clothes. She twists back to look at the effect.

"It's invisible?"

He nods. "Enyo your turn." She turns her back to him and lifts her arms like Xena had. When he releases the cloak, a deep purple glow surrounds the edges before vanishing into her red coat.

Avi's mouth drops open.

Enyo catches her expression. She looks back at Leon. "Is there a problem?"

"A purple glow appeared just before it vanished," Leon explains.

"And?" Enyo motions for him to continue.

"I don't know what that means?" Leon says before shrugging and gesturing for them to exit.

Noel hops off the last giant step and scans the clearing. The group had formed the plan to recover the shield in less than two minutes as they walked down the stairs to the war room. A flutter in his stomach confirms his nerves. He glances up as Xena and Enyo float down, testing their cloaks. Xena's grin fills her oval face. Noel smiles back until he catches Enyo's flaring nostrils and grim frown. They land on either side of him.

Avi and Leon stand just outside the arched entrance, watching the three of them join hands and take flight. They land near the Ottoman archway.

"Be careful," Avi whispers.

Enyo turns and nods to her before they walk hand in hand under the Ottoman archway and disappear.

The sun clears the far eastern ridge of the Albanian Alps, lifting the veil of night and bringing a warm morning glow. Avi spots movement in the clearing as the shadows lift from the rocky ground.

"Is that a person or an animal?" Avi asks Leon, straining to make out the figure weaving towards them.

Leon jumps down the four large steps without a response to inspect the newcomer.

"It's Ermal." He tells Avi as he approaches the familiar face.

"Friend or foe?"

"Friend."

23

Noel looks down and his vision dims as the ground drops further away. He tightens his grip on Enyo and Xena.

Xena shakes his arm. "Noel, stay with us." She glances over his head at Enyo's pale face. "If either of you fools decides now is a good time to pass out, think again. Do you hear me?" Enyo barely nods.

"I think I may have a considerable fear of heights," he mutters.

"You think!" Enyo says.

They fly over the valley of Bajze and Xena loses count of the clusters of cars parked along every road heading west to Mokset. She turns back to see movement of dozens of people climbing the hill.

"Do you think we should turn back?" Xena asks.

Enyo looks back at the chaos.

Noel chances a look down. "Shit!"

"Avi can manifest us if she needs to," Enyo says, "but we should make this quick."

They clear the valley and continue north. The Albanian Alps rise with rugged lines along the horizon.

"Beautiful," Xena whispers.

They clear a small village of sheep farmers and gasp as the height of the mountains drops into a deep canyon with a large river. Noel wobbles, and Xena tightens her grip.

The topography is just like the map Leon summoned from the library. The river splits just before a small town. They follow the river due east into the Cemit Valley to the tiny village of Nikç. The river is clear. Small cascades of waterfalls appear as the river rises with the elevation.

"I see the fort." Enyo points to stone walls on a far rise overlooking the narrow valley.

Xena turns to look on the opposite side of the valley for a cave and spots a small waterfall cascading down the face of the mountain. She sees a dark opening just underneath the stream of water and pulls the others in that direction.

"There, do you see it?" Xena says, pointing straight ahead.

Noel risks a glance and spots the cave as they are quickly approaching. "How do we slow down?" He panics and nearly lets go of their hands as they fly through the waterfall into the mouth of the cave.

They land in a pile, spluttering and gasping for air. Enyo untangles herself from the pile first and stands. She helps Xena up, and they extend their assistance to Noel. He shakes his head, flinging water in every direction.

Xena holds up her hands and blinks away his water assault. "Easy there, boy!"

"Ha!" Noel laughs. He calls his staff and examines the space. The opening to the cave is wider than it looked initially, with most of it hidden under the waterfall facing Fort Kelmend.

"From this angle, it doesn't look like a fort at all," Enyo says, joining him near the opening. "More like the ridge of a mountain shaped like a fort."

"I can see why it was never conquered." Xena points out the shear drops on either side.

Noel steps back, away from the edge. He uses the warm ember glow of his staff to inspect the space. It narrows to a passage. He turns to the side when his broad shoulders can't fit through. Xena and Enyo follow a few steps behind him.

He stops at the opening to an expansive cavern with tiered levels descending to what looks like a stone stage in the center. A small opening in the stone above allows in a single beam of sunlight, spotlighting a round mirror set on a podium center stage.

Noel takes a step over the threshold and feels every hair on his body lift at once. He hesitates before walking further in, but Xena nudges him forward. He rubs his arms and feels a slight shock of static. Xena's damp hair actually lifts away from her head. Enyo rubs her arms after crossing the threshold.

Xena pulls a light stone from her pocket, activates it and throws it towards the center of the cavern, lighting the entire space.

There are small, narrow, evenly spaced openings in a full circle, creating a dozen entries to the cavern.

"Any idea what this place was or is?" Xena asks Enyo.

"My sister, Pemphredo, described a room like this once," Enyo says, walking slowly around the perimeter, checking the next narrow opening. "Entries to space, is what she called it. She only had this vision once. We were kids. I didn't know what she meant, but this is identical to her description, right down to the round mirror."

Xena and Enyo continue to check each opening.

Noel moves down each tier with care towards the center. He turns to look back up. "Ladies, can you tell me which opening we came through?"

Xena rushes back and looks down at each opening. "Um, maybe this one?" she says, stopping at one with a few footprints.

"Are you sure?" he asks. "I thought it was a few more that way." He points to the right from where she is standing.

She checks the next two. "There are footprints here as well. I don't know for sure. Enyo?"

Silence.

24

Avi shifts side to side, watching Leon chat with Ermal. He isn't sending any communication back, but she hears the whispers between Pax and Teuta as they approach the open doorway.

"Avi," Teuta says, twirling to face her, blocking Avi's view of Leon. "Can you please tell me why you are choosing to keep me in the dark?"

Avi ignores her and steps around Teuta to watch Leon.

"Rude," Teuta huffs.

Leon sends Ermal back with a message for Itra and jogs back towards the castle.

"On my way!" Leon says to Avi.

Avi continues to ignore Teuta.

"You can't just keep me out of the loop," Teuta whines.

"We can," Avi says, smiling.

Pax is casually leaning against the large arched opening to the castle. Leon steps beside Pax. He doesn't move or acknowledge Leon.

Leon leans over and whispers. "Tani!"

Pax's eyes go wide just before he vanishes.

Teuta's mouth falls open. "How did you…? How could you…?"

Leon grins and winks at Avi.

"Teuta, we thank you for your service and sacrifice for the last nine centuries, but you are no longer needed."

"You can't fire me!" she shouts shrilly, transforming from fairy to queen.

"He didn't," Avi says, winking. "Ember did."

Teuta turns to face her.

Avi smirks before waving bye. "Tani!"

Teuta's face drains of color just before she vanishes.

Avi and Leon blow out a long breath.

"Do you think she will try to come back?" Avi asks Leon.

"Probably, her treasure is hidden in the vault below."

"I can't believe Xena retained all of that information from the OPEN book and formulated a back-up plan so quickly."

"No surprise to me. Kaly, my wife, reading comprehension was genius level amazing. She could read text once and recall every line." His eyes glaze over. "I remember a game night with friends who were brave enough to try to beat Kaly at a new trivia game. It was five against one, and she still beat the group."

"Uh, Leon?"

"Yes?"

"We have a line of people starting across the clearing."

He snaps his attention to the clearing. "Are you ready to start your word games?"

She smirks. "Word games?"

Leon shrugs. "Not sure what else to call it."

She nods, focusing on one end of the line. "In three steps you'll trigger a row of land mines that will tear you limb from limb."

Her tone rattles Leon. He shivers.

The line recoils and several people back away carefully before turning to run. This causes a ripple of confusion, and several others break off and follow those fleeing.

"Good," Leon says. "Keep the tone just as menacing."

A single man walks forward, poking the ground with a long walking stick. The line files in behind him.

"Kind sir," Avi whispers, "you're only inches away from the next line of land mines."

The man holds up a fist. He looks up, searching for the voice.

"Turn away and we'll do no harm. If you continue, we will be forced to take immediate action. Return to your loved ones or go home in a body bag, your choice."

Several men break off, holding up their hands in surrender as they walk away. But over a dozen remain.

Leon watches a heated discussion taking place among the remaining few. He cups his mouth and lets out a loud whistle. He lets it fade away like a bottle rocket. The effect makes the arguing pause and several men fall to the ground, covering their heads.

"BOOM!" Avi shouts, as Leon loses air. The people cower and scream. The few huddled on the ground lift their heads and check the others.

"That was a warning shot," Avi states. "The next time I have to speak, it will be to introduce you to death itself. Go!"

After that stunt, only four men remain in the clearing. Two appear to be in shock, unable to move. The other two look to be creating a plan using tactical hand motions.

"Show time," Leon says, rubbing his hands together.

Leon steps out of the shadows of the entry, calling and double tapping his staff. His movement and arrival startle the two who had been frozen in shock. They turn and run away. One of the remaining two holds a hand over his eyes and points to Leon.

"You were warned!" Avi cackles. "Meet death!"

Leon takes a leap down one of four giant steps. The remaining two scatter and sprint in opposite directions.

Avi waits for the two men exit the clearing before speaking. "One group down," she says to Leon as he saunters back up the stone step. "Coffee?"

"Absolutely."

Two steaming mugs appear on a tray near Avi's feet. Leon bends to pick them up. He hands her one that has a sprinkle of cinnamon on top. "White chocolate latte with cinnamon?"

"Guilty." She takes a long sip and sighs. "So, with Teuta gone, are you the messenger and mark maker?"

Leon nods before taking a sip.

"How do you feel about the messenger responsibility?"

"Processing that as we speak. I'll be close to Danae," Leon says, staring at the communist ember archway, "and Kaly." He takes another long sip. "After my last deployment and retirement from the military, I started a security consulting business. It was good, just not always busy. I'm better when I'm busy." He smiles and wiggles his eyebrows. "Plus, never doing laundry, dishes, or cooking is an amazing bonus."

"Ha!" Avi looks down at her mug and clothes. "Not a bad setup." They sit on the top step, letting their feet dangle.

"Do you think we should wear the cloaks just in case we need to create a diversion?" Leon asks, looking out over the clearing.

"Don't you think a diversion would draw more attention to the hill and castle?"

He sighs. "Maybe, but it might be necessary. Ermal says they lost count of the number of cars parked on the side of the road leading to the hill."

"Can we agree to use the wings only as a back-up plan if things go south?"

Leon nods and vanishes.

Avi drops her mug. "No, no, no!"

"No, what?" he says, reappearing next her with two of the cloaks.

"So, you can move around and vanish like Teuta now?"

135

"Apparently. I just thought about the wardrobe and retrieving the cloaks and then poof."

"You can't just vanish without warning!" She slaps his shoulder. "Aren't you going to wear a bell?"

Leon laughs. "Maybe I should!" Three bells appear between them. One is a small round bell hanging from a chain. The second one is a medium handheld brass bell. And the last is a ring with a tiny bell. Leon picks up each one and shakes it, testing the volume. The tiny bell on the ring is surprisingly the loudest.

Leon smiles at Avi. "You pick."

She picks up the round bell and chain. "This will be loud enough."

He slides the chain over his head and takes the last sip of his coffee. "Did you already finish yours?"

"Not quite. I dropped it when you vanished." A smaller mug appears in place of the two discarded bells.

"Drink up." Leon tilts his chin up. "I think our next round is about to enter the clearing."

"Yes, sir."

Three hours later, Leon and Avi collapse in a heap of exhaustion at the bottom of the steps leading to the castle. The continuous wave of people attempting to breach the castle started around eight and hasn't stopped.

"How many are still out there?" Avi asks, her hoarse voice nearly gone.

Leon counts the remaining heads. "A dozen or less." He pats her shoulder. "Rest your voice, I can take this last group on alone." She nods, too tired to protest.

He leaps up and calls his staff with a quick double tap. He starts out in a slow jog and then a full sprint towards the remaining intruders.

A woman screams and another man shouts in a language Leon doesn't understand. He doesn't slow his pace as he swings the scythe out with ease. The group bails and runs away as he quickly approaches. He gives full chase until they clear the archways. He stops to catch his breath and feels movement to his right. He swings on instinct, barely missing Xena.

Xena releases Noel's hand and side steps Leon.

"Sorry!" Leon shouts. "When did you get here?" He looks over at Noel. He is kneeling on the ground next to a round object. "You found the shield?"

Xena holds up her hands. "We're not one hundred percent sure this is the correct shield, but we have other problems." Xena looks over at Noel. He nods. "We lost Enyo."

25

In the final hour of the funeral, the priest arrives to share a few last words. After he finishes his final prayer, the family follows him out of the apartment and downstairs to the lobby. They file out, entering the awaiting procession of cars. Anton, his parents, and Elis ride in the lead car behind the hearse. Itra, Danae, and Vincent follow with Nada and her husband. The remaining cars are mostly first cousins and Iana's friends.

Itra checks his phone after they are on the highway leaving the city. Ermal left three text messages, and he has missed two calls. Danae feels Itra go rigid.

The car exits the highway to a small gravel drive leading to the family crypt.

Danae glances down at the screen just as their car comes to a sudden stop. They whip forward. The seat belts cut into their shoulders.

"Whoa!" Vincent shouts. "Why did you slam on your brakes?"

Nada's husband is mumbling an apology. Nada turns from the front passenger seat with a red trickle dripping from her temple. She wipes her brow and recoils at the sight of blood.

Itra checks Danae over for injuries.

"I'm fine," Danae says. "Nada, are you ok?"

Vincent leans over her to the center console "Where did the other cars go?"

Itra and Vincent exit the car.

Itra reels around. The road is empty in both directions.

Danae steps out of the car. The ember amulet vibrates and lifts from her chest. She yanks on Itra's arm. "Get back in the car!" He tries to process her words, but roaring thunder fills his ears. "Itra!"

Itra falls as the ground shakes beneath them. He scrambles to his feet, stumbling back to the car.

"Earthquake?" Nada asks from the car.

"Worse!" Vincent says, pointing up. The sunny afternoon sky is vertically unzipping to darkness.

A blur of light shoots across the darkened section of sky before vanishing into the sunny blue sky.

"Are we under some kind of attack?" Nada asks, holding a hand to her head as she exits the car. Vincent and Danae exchange a look and shake their heads.

"What did Ermal's messages say?" Danae asks. She taps Itra's chin with her finger. He drags his focus from the sky to meet her eyes. He withdraws his phone and hands it to her.

She taps to open the first message. "Just spoke with Leon. Two of the grey sisters and a guy from Ottoman just flew away from here heading towards Kelmend."

"Flew?" Vincent asks. Nada's eyes dart back and forth between Danae and Vincent.

"There are cloaks with wings, but there's more," Danae says, holding up a finger as Nada attempts to speak. "Teuta and Pax are not to be trusted." Itra and Vincent frown with concern. "And last, the hillside is full of civilians trying to get to the castle."

Another rumble echoes overhead and rattles the ground. They jump and take cover inside the car.

Nada turns around to face Danae. "Spill it! And no sugar coating."

Danae glances at Itra. He nods. "The Castle of Teskom holds the knowledge, power, and magic of the goddess Ember. She assigns a bloodline to protect and serve said castle, and before Iana's death, that line was the descendants of Mui."

Nada's eyebrows reach her hairline. All color drains from her husband's face.

"Yes, 'the' Mui the giant defender in Albanian folk tales," Danae says, rushing to explain talks faster. "Vincent and Itra are descendants of Mui from their father's side. After a recent encounter with rogue descendants, an artifact was stolen from the castle vault, destroying the barrier that shielded the castle from the other dimensions." Danae takes a long breath and swallows.

Nada barks out an anxious laugh.

"I know this sounds nuts," Itra says, leaning forward. "But we need to find Anton and Elis and head north as soon as possible."

Nada shakes her head. "Nuts? This sounds like you three are tripping, and the only place we're going is to bury my best friend and cousin, who is also your sister. Need I remind you. Start the car." She nudges her husband and turns her back away from them.

Vincent pats Danae's hand and shakes his head. "It's a lot to take in."

The car sputters and ticks but doesn't turnover.

"We'll walk," Vincent states, exiting the car. Danae and Itra follow his lead. Nada and her husband slowly get out and follow.

Danae reaches up to still the vibrating amulet.

Itra catches her action. "Are we in danger?"

She closes her eyes and reaches out, using her gift. She senses people ahead. "I don't know for sure about danger, but there are five people ahead."

Nada glances at her, meeting her eyes with a narrow glare. "Why do you think that? Do you have some superpower sensing ability now?"

"Something like that," Danae whispers.

140

Nada grabs her husband's arm and marches past Danae and Itra without a word.

"Nada, wait," Danae pleads.

Vincent shakes his head. "Later."

The cemetery comes into sight after ten minutes. Elis, Anton and his parents are standing next to the driver. The driver has a phone pressed to his ear, but he's waving his arms around like the listener can see him.

Elis is the first one to spot them approaching. "Dad!" Elis tugs on Anton's arm. "Uncle Itra, did you get lost?"

Anton sighs with relief. "Where have you been?"

"The car died," Vincent says, speaking over Itra as he starts to explain. "Did the rest of the cars make it?" Vincent looks around.

"No, we've been here a while, and you're first to arrive. Did you feel an earthquake and a few aftershocks?"

Itra nods. Elis tugs on his arm. "It wasn't an earthquake. It was Father Time."

Anton kneels to his level. "What do you mean, buddy?"

He points up to the vertical line of darkness as two figures descend from the sky.

Anton's mother squeaks out a faint scream before collapsing. Anton and his father catch her and lower her to the ground. The driver drops his phone and runs away screaming.

"Leon!" Danae shouts, as he and Avi land near the group.

"Anton, my apologies for dropping in like this," Leon says. "We have a situation." Leon tilts his chin up as the sky falls darker. "We need to return to the castle immediately."

Nada stammers before speaking. "You just flew here?"

Leon smiles and nods before kneeling to Elis. "Are you ready to earn your wings?" Elis looks from Anton to Leon.

"No! No way, no how." Anton rises from his mother's side.

"I will not argue with you," Leon says, holding up his hands, "but please understand Elis may still hear from Ember."

Itra steps between them. "Hey, let's take a breath." He holds Anton back from lunging towards Leon. "What's happened?"

"The short version is I'm now the messenger," Leon explains. "We expelled Teuta and Pax. We recovered an object from a cave near Fort Kelmend, but it is not the Medusa Shield. And we lost Enyo during the recovery mission." Leon points up. "The grand finale is that the veil between the dimensions is splintering with each passing moment."

"But why would anyone need to talk to a six-year-old boy?" Nada asks, stepping into the fray.

"I don't have time to explain," Leon says with a frown. "Just keep him close."

Anton glares back. "I don't need parenting advice from you!"

"Anton!" Danae scolds. "He's not here to cause you or Elis harm."

Anton twists his frown to a sneer, baring his teeth, creasing every line on his forehead. He takes Elis's hand and leads him away from Leon and Itra. Nada and her husband step towards Elis and Anton.

"Do we have time to lay my sister to rest?" Itra asks.

Leon glances over Itra's shoulder to the mahogany coffin just outside the family crypt. "Yes, but unfortunately not a second more."

Avi steps up beside Danae. "Sorry we interrupted."

Danae takes and squeezes her hand. "It's been a long day and night. Everyone is tired and on edge."

Avi squeezes Danae's hand in response.

Vincent assists Anton's father with supporting Anton's mother. They silently walk towards Iana's coffin. The car procession arrives a few minutes later. The cousins and friends gather behind the family. They recite the rosary and one by one they pay their final respects Iana with a single rose on the coffin and then to Anton and Elis before returning toward their awaiting cars. Leon and Avi keep their distance, giving the family space.

142

Anton's driver returns, pale and sweaty. He collects his phone as the crowd thins. He keeps his eyes lowered and returns to the driver's seat without a word.

"Do you think the driver will be ok?" Avi whispers, leaning closer to Leon.

"What do you think?" Leon softly chuckles. "We just descended from the sky into a cemetery." She attempts to hold her frown but gives in with a grin. "Exactly." He nudges her in the side.

Elis's attention wanders up to the sky as the last group leaves. He mouths a few words, catching Itra's attention.

Itra leans down. "What do you see?"

"Twelve flashes in a circle," Elis says, drawing a circle in the air. "Do you see it?"

Itra kneels to his level and follows his finger towards the sky.

A flash of yellow light follows another counterclockwise in a circle.

"I see it," he says, and stands. "Do you know what it means?"

"I'm six. What do you think?" Elis holds up his hands and shrugs. "I need to tell mama bye." He looks over as Vincent and Anton position Iana's coffin to push it into the family crypt.

Itra takes his hand and walks him over to Anton. "Can we have a moment?" Anton raises a single brow and frowns. "Elis would like to say a few words."

Anton nods and steps back beside him. His son's bottom lip quivers. "It's ok son, we can come back and talk to her anytime."

He looks up and lets the tears stream down both cheeks. "I need her to know that I will take care of you."

"And I you," Anton says. He leans down and kisses his son's cheeks before scooping him up in a big hug.

"Bye mama, I love you to infinity times infinity." He sniffles. "And more than chocolate chip pancakes."

143

Vincent and Itra slide the coffin into the crypt after wiping away their tears. They set the temporary marker in front her tomb and stand back.

After a few minutes, the earth rattles underfoot and shakes them out of the finality of the moment. The dark slit in the sky drapes them in a cool darkness, sending a shiver through the group.

Anton hands Elis off to Nada and nods for Vincent, Itra, and Danae to follow him towards Leon and Avi. "Elis will remain with me. Tell Ember if she attempts to contact, threaten or harm my son, I will demolish her precious Castle of Teskom stone by stone if I have to."

Leon and Avi nod.

Anton's rigid posture stoops. He whispers, "Leon, I'm sorry about Kaly and—" his voice catches. "And I'm sorry it was my grief that turned her to stone."

Leon steps forward and hugs Anton.

"It wasn't your fault," Leon whispers. "I will do everything in my power to shield your family from any additional harm."

Anton nods and turns to Itra and Danae. "Elis needs both of you. I need both of you. Do you understand?"

"We'll return, soon," Itra states before hugging Anton.

"Do you still have Ermal's number?" Danae asks, taking her turn to hug Anton. He stiffens in her embrace.

"Yes." Anton leans back, looking down at her. "Our phones are always compromised near the castle, but we can keep in contact with Ermal."

"I spoke to Ermal this morning," Leon says. "We set up a time to meet again tomorrow."

Anton nods. "Don't do anything Iana would deem risky." Itra smirks. "Seriously, just come back in one piece."

Vincent mock salutes Anton. "By the way," Vincent says, "we shared some details about the castle with Nada and her husband. She may have questions."

144

"Oh geez," Anton says slowly. He looks back at Nada. She is glaring towards the group. "Noted."

They watch a heated whisper exchange between Nada and Anton before the six of them squeeze into the car and pull out of the cemetery.

Vincent walks over to Avi and extends his hand. "Sorry, we've been rude. I'm Vincent, and this is Itra, my nephew."

Avi shakes his hand. "Avi. No apologies necessary since we literally fell from the sky and disrupted a funeral." She pulls out a small bundle from her back and shakes out a feathered cloak. Vincent and Itra immediately reach out to caress the feathers.

"Danae," Avi says, "according to Xena, the cloaks are linked to the assigned line, including the Protectors of Time." She points to herself. "I believe you can fly with Itra. Vincent, Leon and I will each take an arm to ensure your safety."

Itra and Vincent look up simultaneously. "What?"

Danae holds out her arms. Avi drapes the cloak over her back and the cloak disappears on contact.

"Fascinating," Vincent whispers.

"How?" Itra asks, patting Danae's back.

"Ember," Leon and Danae say in unison.

26

Vincent lands near the ember archway with Leon and Avi. He reaches up and rubs his tired cheeks, his grin still wide when Danae and Itra land a few seconds later.

"And I thought your bedhead was rough," Itra teases Vincent. Danae elbows Itra in the side.

"At least I still have hair." Vincent reaches up and pats Itra's nearly bald head.

"Ha!" Leon laughs. Avi and Danae roll their eyes at their antics.

"Good news!" Vincent nods towards the ember archway. "It appears the object you recovered is working to shield the castle once again."

The five of them stand near the statue of Kaly and look past the ember archway to an empty rocky clearing.

"Bad news," Leon says, patting his shoulder. "The rip overhead started after they brought it back."

Vincent tilts his head back to inspect the sky. The setting sun illuminates the remaining natural sky with a warm orange and pink glow in deep contrast with the black vertical division widening with each passing hour.

"Well, at least it is one problem at a time," Itra states, grasping Danae's hand.

"Vincent," Leon says, "take Danae's hand as we go under the archway."

Danae takes Itra and Vincent under the archway. The familiar crunch of ember rocks under their feet fills her with relief.

Avi takes a step forward to follow but hesitates.

Leon hangs back.

"Are you coming?" Avi asks.

His gaze is on Kaly's face, sculpted in stone. "In a minute."

She nods and follows Danae.

"I don't know how," Leon whispers to the statue, "but I will bring you back." He strokes her cheek before following the others.

Once inside the castle, Itra and Vincent gawk at the recent changes to the murals and the colors and details of the dining hall. Their eyes grow even wider when they enter the war room. They start with a round of introductions. Itra and Vincent meet Xena and Noel, who recount the moment they found the shield and the details of the space.

"Enyo was with you when you found the shield?" Danae asks. "And then she vanished to where?"

"We don't know for sure," Xena states. "I intend to go back and investigate at first light. The cavern had twelve narrow openings on the top level. Enyo and I were investigating each opening when Noel headed down to check the mirror."

"The openings all looked identical," Noel explains, shaking his head. "I asked them to backtrack and find the one we came through."

"But that's when we lost Enyo," Xena says, wringing her hands. "I stepped back to confirm our entry point and found footprints in a few openings. And when I asked Enyo for her opinion, she was gone."

"Neither of you saw what happened to her?" Itra asks.

"No," Xena and Noel state in unison.

"Is there anything in the library about that cavern or about the vertical line of darkness in the sky?" Danae asks.

"We've been pulling every detail we can think of from the library and archive since we returned." Xena gestures to a sketch pad and two open books on the table. "Before Enyo disappeared, she told us about a vision her sister had when they were kids. She described this space almost exactly according to Enyo. Her sister called it 'entries to space'."

Vincent and Itra huddle over the drawing.

"Who drew this?" Itra asks. Noel raises his hand. "Nice."

Danae looks at the open books and a title catches her attention. "Itra, what did Elis call the shaking we felt earlier?"

"Father Time." He looks up from the drawing. Danae holds up the book, open to a page with dark red lettering scrolled on top. "Father Time. How does he know this stuff?"

Vincent sits down and reaches for his reading glasses, finding an empty pocket. He tries to use the thought provoked wardrobe to make his reading glasses, but nothing appears. He mumbles a curse.

"Can someone conjure up a pair of reading glasses, please?" Four pairs appear on the table in front of him. He tries the first pair and shakes his head. The second pair works. "Thanks!" He motions for Danae to pass him the book. "And coffee?" Four mugs appear in unison. He grins and takes one.

"Ember gave Elis a message last night," Danae says, sitting down next to Vincent. The others sit around the table to listen. "The shield is near, check the rear, face old Kelmend to start again. Illyria, ember of mine, recover the shield or yield the line to end all time. Illyria, ember of mine, the new stone will shatter at night and breathe with light when all is right, Illyria, ember of time."

Leon stands. "New stone will shatter at night and breathe with light?"

Danae smiles and nods. "We don't know any more details yet, but we are hoping the archives can provide something to

148

reference." Nine books appear and drop to the table. The group yelps in surprise.

"Books need bells, too," Noel states, holding his chest. Avi laughs and Leon pulls out his new accessory and jingles the bell. Noel's laugh fills the room.

"Got it!" Vincent exclaims.

Noel stops laughing.

"It's here. Father Time, otherwise known as Chronos. He built twelve lines of time, a labyrinth of space and time to a fourth dimension. Each section of time represents a past, present and future in each dimension."

"A fourth dimension?" Itra asks. "Why would Ember only build a crossroads to three if there are four?" A book opens on the table and pages turn, settling on an image filling both pages. It is a circle split in four sections and again in thirds.

"According to this, the castle itself is the fourth dimension," Vincent explains. "The formal names for each dimension are ëndrra, makthi, lufta, and dija. English translation: dream, nightmare, war, and knowledge." Vincent points to each section. "Over the last century, the dimension names evolved. The revolutionary dimension is considered dream, the communist is nightmare, ottoman is war, and the castle is knowledge."

"And the cavern holds passages to every dimension's past, present and future?" Xena asks.

"Maybe, but according to this," Vincent says, pointing to the book open in front of him, "it requires a catalyst. The mirror shield could have activated the passages."

"Oh dear," Xena whispers. "When we removed the mirror shield from the center, the static energy I felt when we entered immediately stopped. Did we possibly lock Enyo out of returning when we removed the shield?"

Xena locks eyes with Noel. He blows out a long breath.

Xena turns to Avi. "Have you tried to manifest Enyo since we returned?"

"I haven't ever attempted to manifest anyone, at least not on purpose. I did do it that one time while I was sleeping. I'll try?" A book flies into the room and opens in front of Avi. "It comes with instructions. How thoughtful." She reads the text for several minutes.

Leon paces the room. His stomach growls. Danae turns to him, an eyebrow raised. He shrugs. A few pizzas arrive on the table. The group groans in appreciation. Leon immediately sits and shoves a slice in his face.

"Easy, brother," says Danae. "When was the last time you ate?"

Avi answers, not looking up from the book. "Hours ago, it was a busy day defending the castle." A glass of wine appears next to her, along with a small salad. "I think I can try this manifest thing now."

Avi drains the glass of wine and stands.

Xena joins her. Avi holds the infinity charm in her palm and closes her eyes. The room falls quiet and the temperature drops.

A ripple of chills slides down Danae's back. She feels the presence of someone new in the room. Her ember amulet vibrates beneath her shirt. She grasps Itra's hand and waits for the person to reveal themselves.

Xena feels a hand on her shoulder. She turns and finds nothing. Avi releases a loud exhale and opens her eyes. Enyo appears, standing next to her.

"My word," Vincent whispers.

"Enyo, where are you?" Xena asks, moving to Enyo's side. "Are you ok?"

"Lost," Enyo whispers. "I heard you call my name, but it was too late. I had already stepped through the passage and I couldn't get back."

"What passage?" Noel asks, standing next to Xena.

"In the past?" she says, looking down at her feet. "The valley below is just grass and a river, no structures or roads are visible."

150

"Are you still in the cave?" Xena asks.

She nods. "I can't fly. I tried. I'm at the mouth of the cave under the waterfall. There is no way down."

"Is the narrow passage still there?" Noel asks.

"Yes, but it's a solid wall of rock at the end." Itra stands up. Enyo furrows her brow. "Who are you?"

"Itra, Danae's husband," he says. "At the end of the passage, can you kneel down and feel if there is a seam at the bottom?"

Enyo cocks her head to the side. "I already tried to find any mechanism for a door. It's not like I've been sitting around here waiting for a rescue."

Itra holds his hands up. "I apologize, just trying to help."

"You want to help? Open the passage and get me out of this damn cave."

"Vincent," Danae says, turning to face him. "If the bronze shield was the catalyst for the space, does that mean we need to return it to get her out?"

Vincent flips through pages of the book about the lines of time. "If the passage is blocked for Enyo, it may be blocked for us as well."

Noel paces back and forth. "The passages were open when we left. We inspected each one while looking for Enyo before we returned." He stops pacing.

"I didn't hear or see anyone enter the passage after I went through," Enyo states.

"We shouted your name and ran down each one," Xena responds, "but they were all dead ends except one." She points to Noel. "Maybe we can still enter the same way? It was open when we left. If not, it may at least get us close enough to try the cube to enter a different time."

"The cubes can be calibrated to a different time?" Danae asks.

"Yes, at least my cube can," Enyo says. "Because when I was summoned, that's how I got to the castle in your time."

Leon stands and wipes his hands down with a napkin. "It's at least a starting point. Who has a cube?"

"I left mine on the table when we returned from the Ottoman dimension," Danae states.

Enyo nods. "Teuta took mine."

"Same," Avi states.

Leon vanishes from the room and appears back in a few seconds with a slight jingle.

"How did you do that?" Vincent asks.

"I'm the new messenger," Leon says, holding all three cubes. "Teuta had a suite in a tower I didn't know existed."

Danae taps a cube. The cube flattens and the numbers hover above. "Only one line, this must be either Enyo or Avi's cube." Leon taps the other two and only one has a stream of coordinates.

"Here," Danae says, "this the last jump we made." She points out the last coordinate.

"If we take the shield back to the cave," Itra says. "We risk exposing the castle again. Is there any other catalyst that may open the passages?" Three books fly open. The group leans over the table to peer at the new pages.

A gold cube nearly identical to the one Leon holds is illustrated on one page. The next book shows an illustration of the Medusa shield, and the last shows a book with a bronze shield.

"Wait, no mirror?" Danae asks.

"It's a bronze shield with a mirror on the other side," Noel says.

"Itra," Vincent says, "either Teuta lied about the item taken from the vault or both were taken."

"Leon, can you check the vault?" Danae asks. He nods and vanishes. She turns to Noel. "Where is the shield you brought back?"

"In the tower," Noel answers.

"Wait, what tower?" Itra asks.

"The one straight up the stairs from the front foyer," Noel says.

Itra and Danae start for the door.

"Where are you going?" Xena asks.

"The shield wasn't in the tower before all of this happened," Danae calls back.

Itra makes it up to the glass box of the tower first. He turns in a slow circle. "I don't see it."

Danae clears the top step and reaches towards the center. Her hand lands on something hard. She feels the edges. "It's here."

She guides his hand to the edge she is gripping. "On three, one, two, three." They pull and lift the shield out. Her grip loosens and the shield wobbles. Itra manages to hold the weight, placing it on the floor at their feet.

Danae straightens. "Itra look." She points up.

The dark vertical ripple in the evening sky slowly vanishes. The ground shakes under them as the last remaining darkness disappears.

"One problem taken care of," he says. She nudges him in the side and points to the valley below. The valley and their home are now clearly visible. "But now the veil is gone." He bends to lift the shield.

"Wait," Danae says. "Maybe it just needs to go back into the vault. Remember, it was stolen from there."

"If this is even the shield that was stolen."

"True." She begins to pace back and forth. *"Leon, can you join us in the tower?"*

A bell jingles as Leon appears between them. He looks up. "You fixed the sky!"

"At the expense of exposing the castle again," Danae says, pointing towards a lone man walking towards the castle.

Itra looks down. "I think that's Ermal."

She nods and turns to Leon. "We know from our first visit to the castle that the towers are the conduit for the veil. But we think that the shield was held in the vault, not in the tower. Did you find the Medusa Shield in the vault?"

Leon picks up the shield with no effort or strain. "There are no shields that fit that description, but there is some pretty cool stuff down there. I'll take this down to the vault." Leon points to her. "Stay here and let me know if the veil returns around the castle or if the ripple in the sky returns." He points to Itra. "Go check in with Ermal." He vanishes before either can object.

"Go," Danae says to Itra. He hesitates. "Ermal will have questions and if the veil comes back up with him in the clearing, he could get ejected."

"Ok, but can you call someone else to come up? I don't want to leave you here alone."

"Just go, I'll be fine, it's only for a few minutes." She kisses him and swats him on the rear. He smirks and descends the steps.

"Danae, can you hear me?" Leon asks from the vault.

Danae turns, and she laughs at her mistake. She answers back with a thought. *"Loud and clear."*

"There are two circular glass cases without labels. One looks too small and the other too big. Thoughts?"

"Turn the mirror towards the cases." She inspects the clearing. Itra is leading Ermal back to the ember archways.

Leon turns the shield around and looks at the reflection. Nothing unusual. He walks down to the other case again. Nothing out of place. He turns in a slow circle. *"What am I looking for?"*

"Enyo says she felt the earthquake," Avi says. *"Vincent keeps talking about the hedge maze and an illustration of the labyrinth of passages."*

"Leon, come back here with the shield!" Danae exclaims. He appears a second later with a small jingle. "Take us to the center of the hedge maze." She looks out at Itra, jogging back to the castle alone. "Now."

"Ok." He offers her an elbow, his hands full with the shield. She takes his arm, and the floor falls out. They land in the center of the maze.

"Somebody tell Vincent and Itra we're in the maze," Danae says after regaining her breath.

"On it," Noel states.

Noel catches Itra just before he starts up the stairs to the tower. "Leon and Danae are in the maze."

"Why?"

"Some connection Vincent found between the labyrinth and the maze."

Itra jogs up the first flight of stairs. Noel follows him. Itra knocks on the window. Danae turns and waves. Vincent and the ladies join Itra and Noel at the window a few seconds later.

"Where's Enyo?" Noel asks, looking around.

Avi frowns. "I lost my connection with her. She was there a second ago and gone the next."

"I think it goes here." Danae presses down on the statue's arms. "It can hold the weight." Leon nods. They attempt to balance the shield in the fairy statue's arms. She steps back, and he lets go. It shifts to the side, but then it stays.

"Can someone head up to the tower?" Danae looks back at the window. "We need to know if the veil returns or there are any changes in the sky."

Noel salutes and bounds up the stairs to the tower. *I can see the valley, including the cars and roads. The sky looks normal."*

"Maybe the mirror side needs to face away from the statue," Xena suggests.

Danae steps closer. She freezes as she sees the reflection in the mirror. "Leon, what do you see?"

The color drains from his face. "Teuta."

The mirror shows the of the same green eyes and wide grin they know all too well. Leon rests his hand on the edge of the mirror and the image ripples. The reflection transforms back into a fairy statue.

They hesitantly turn the shield around. The ground starts shaking after they step back. Leon dives forward to save the shield, but it stays in place. A rush of air rustles the surrounding hedges. They cover their faces from the blowing dust and debris.

"Look, doors!" Vincent exclaims, pointing to the walls of the hedge maze. Evenly spaced openings are visible around the perimeter.

"There's someone coming out of that one!" Avi points to an opening behind Leon and Danae.

"It's Enyo!" Xena exclaims.

"Hey guys," Noel says, *"the sky is normal, but the valley looks ancient. All the roads, buildings, and cars are gone!"*

The air settles in the maze. Leon and Danae straighten when they hear Enyo's approaching footsteps.

"Where are we?" Enyo asks, coming out of the maze.

"In the castle." Leon points up to the windows. Avi and Xena are waving.

"Guys, can anyone hear me?" says Noel nervously. *"Is everything ok?"*

"Yes, come on down and meet us in the war room," Danae answers.

Leon extends his hand to Enyo. She looks at him, then at Danae. Danae takes his other hand. "It's portal only," Leon explains. Enyo takes his hand, and they land in the war room.

The others come barreling in and a loud murmur of conversations erupts in the room.

Noel is the last to enter. He slides to a stop. "Is that the real Enyo or the ghost version?"

"Real!" Avi and Xena state in unison.

156

27

Anton quietly closes Elis's bedroom door. He turns, coming face to face with Nada. Her scowl tells him the conversation they started outside the car in the cemetery is about to continue.

"It's been a really long day." Anton moves past her towards the liquor cabinet. "Whiskey or raki?"

"Neither!"

Her harsh tone halts his pour. "Why are you angry with me?"

"You lied, they lied."

"Our memories of the castle only last so long. It's a curse or a gift, but that is the truth."

"And Mui, you expect me to believe that Iana and Itra are descendants of Mui, a freaking fairytale?"

"I've met Mui Junior. He was at least seven feet tall. I'm not going to question the nature of genetics, but his size alone could fit the bill."

"How long, Anton? How many times have you lied to me about this, about Iana?"

He takes a long sip from his whiskey. "Can we at least sit?"

"By all means." Nada waves her hand to the empty sofa. She remains standing.

"You recall when we asked you watch Elis when Danae and Itra were missing?"

"Yes, almost a month ago."

"That is when all of this started." She attempts to object, but he holds up a hand. "Please let me finish, and then you can ask all the questions you want. Deal?"

She nods and sits on the adjacent sofa.

"First, we never meant to lie to anyone. It's only been a month since this world dragged us in. We are still trying to navigate what is reality."

She bites her lip to remain quiet.

"When Itra and Danae returned, they gave us a detailed account of their hike. When they were lost, they found a castle and survived an encounter with Poseidon, who we now know was doing Medusa's bidding."

Nada shakes her head. She marches over to the whiskey and grabs the bottle, but no glass. She unscrews the top and knocks back two long gulps before wincing. She motions for Anton to continue.

"Medusa believed her bloodline had a right to the castle after a blood oath was discovered signed by Zeus and Phorcys. She attempted a coordinated attack on the castle using rogue descendants. Mui's line was responsible to protect and serve and therefore defend the Castle of Teskom and the goddess Ember."

She takes another long drink from the bottle but remains silent.

"But Mui's line failed the morning Iana was killed. A blast of air shot her through an ember archway. They tried to get her back, but she died on that blasted hill." He drains his glass. "And I turned Leon's wife to stone when she tried to hold me back from lunging towards the woman who called Iana's time of death."

"Are you done?" says Nada.

Anton shakes his head. "Leon and Danae are descendants of Zeus and are now bound to protect and serve. This nightmare continues." He gestures for the bottle. She pours him at least two fingers. "There is an ancient alliance between Zeus and Mui's line.

158

Their heir will unite the lines, and their child will be gifted with the ability to start and stop time. According to Teuta, Danae is carrying this heir."

"The Illyrian Queen Teuta?"

Anton nods.

"And Medusa and Poseidon are alive?"

"Poseidon was killed just before Iana. And Medusa was turned to stone in the Castle of Teskom."

"Danae said something about dimensions?"

"From what I understand, there are five archways that lead to three different universes, as well as past and future timelines."

Nada laughs, but then covers her mouth to muffle the volume. She quiets and listens for Elis. "You actually believe all of this? And Vincent, he's in on it?"

"Vincent found the castle in his twenties. Every time he left, his memory would fade after a day or so."

Nada sighs loudly.

"You know how Iana would talk about his ability to have a conversation with anyone regardless of their language." She nods. "He was given the gift to read, speak, and translate any language by the goddess Ember."

"A gift works outside of the castle, but not someone's memory?"

"Yep," Anton says, fighting a yawn.

"And Elis, what does he know?" Nada sets the bottle down on the coffee table.

"Too much." Anton drains the rest of his glass, sitting it down next the bottle. "He is the compass to time." Nada sits forward. "Elis and Danae created a veil that dropped over groups of people trying to invade the castle. Time froze under that veil. If I didn't witness it, I wouldn't believe it was possible."

Nada stands, holding a finger in the air. "When Danae and Itra lost their memories of the hike a few weeks ago?"

"It was after their time in the castle." He fights another yawn.

159

She moves around the coffee table. "How did they remember? Why did you go back?"

"Teuta dropped off a message that ignited their memories. It worked with Vincent as well. He came to visit shortly after we received the message. He was convinced it was the calling card of a coming war. I fought our participation, but you know Iana."

She stops pacing. "The last time I saw Iana, she was sitting there." She points to the dining table. "She was in a state of shock. What happened?"

"Ember's gift to Iana was vision, but she didn't have time to train before we were booted out. She kept seeing stuff from the future and had a panic attack before you arrived."

Nada stares at the chair. She turns back to Anton with tears streaming down her cheeks. "We lost her, for what?"

"I don't have an explanation or a reason," he whispers. "The question, 'why her?' is on constant repeat. I know Elis needs me and I need to try to navigate this madness."

"I'm here," she says, sitting next to him. "How can I help?"

"Elis," he says, "I want him to remember Iana." She nods. "Iana talked about her parents almost daily with Elis, keeping their memory alive. Her name will never be off limits and it's ok to talk about her anytime."

"Deal." Nada hugs him. "Go shower, you smell. And please sleep, you look like hell." She stands and heads to the front door. "There is enough food in the freezer and fridge for a week or more."

"Thank you."

28

Leon drains his beer in one long gulp. Another appears before he sets down the empty glass.

"Slow down," Danae mocks. "We're still missing the Medusa Shield."

Noel holds up a hand. "Is it still necessary to locate the stolen shield?"

Vincent nods. "Ember's artifacts are more than just antique relics. Most hold a piece of her magic. And in the wrong hands, they can create the chaos we have experienced during the last few days."

An open book with the illustration of the Medusa Shield lifts and the lights dim.

"What's happening?" Avi asks.

"Ember," Leon whispers.

A holographic scene plays out in the center of the room. A man holding a bronze shield stands alone in a field with an army charging towards him.

"Is that Alexander the Great?" Xena whispers.

The next scene appears with the action in slow motion. The lead soldier on horseback draws his sword and swings to strike the lone man but is ejected from the horse after striking an invisible barrier. The other riders plow into the barrier before they can stop. A second unit of soldiers on foot encircle the man, using their swords to poke at the barrier.

The next scene rapidly flickers with a sun and moon behind the man until it slows to show the soldiers whittled to bones, attempting to keep their posts around the man. The man inside remains standing and unchanged, minus his face. His beard is now snow white, touching his waist.

"Chronos?" Vincent whispers.

The next scene shows the last standing soldier fall in exhaustion and starvation. The bearded man drops the shield, picks up a scythe, and steps carefully over a pile of bodies.

The scene fades to an art studio. The same shield is set up on an easel. Only the back of an artist can be seen with the tip of a brush to the shield. The next image shows the finished painting of Medusa on the bronze shield with an ember glow surrounding the edges. The room goes dark, and the book falls closed on the table with a loud thud.

"Eek!" Avi yelps.

The lights come back on to a few blinking faces and a few flying books. Noel ducks as one flies just over his head.

"Stop thinking for a minute!" Leon swats a book away. The books fall to the table and some vanish before hitting the floor.

"What was that?" Enyo asks.

"Ember's way of showing the importance of recovering the Medusa Shield," Itra says.

Danae stands, too anxious to sit any longer. "Enyo, do you think you can talk with Kaly? Like you did with Medusa?"

Leon stands. "You think she is alive under the stone?"

"I don't know, brother." Danae faces him. "But Kaly was the last person to speak to Poseidon. I don't want to think that she is trapped alive, but I don't want to think of the alternative either."

"I can try," Enyo says.

"Good, let's go." Leon marches towards the dining hall door.

"I'll need a cloak, it's not my dimension."

The wardrobe opens. A single cloak flies out and hovers behind Enyo. She scoots back her chair and stands, extending her arms. A purple glow surrounds her again as the cloak blends in with her red coat.

Leon is halfway across the clearing when Enyo exits the castle.

Enyo pauses at the bottom step. *Fly or walk?* She chooses to keep two feet firmly on the ground.

"You should stay on this side," Enyo says, approaching Leon.

"No way," Leon protests. "I'm coming with you!"

She places a hand on his shoulder. "If she's still in there, I promise I'll call for you."

"Fine, but I'll wait here, not inside the castle."

"I understand." Enyo steps under the ember archway.

The full moon shines directly down over Kaly's statue. Enyo turns back to check that Leon didn't follow and panics. *The castle is gone.* A few sharp inhalations. She recalls the veil is working. She laughs quietly before turning back to the statue.

She shakes out her arms and bends her neck from side to side, trying to stay loose. "Show me Kaly."

Nothing.

She walks closer and touches Kaly's stone shoulder. A slight breath of air is visible in the cool night air. The mouth twists and opens several times.

"Kaly?" Enyo asks.

"Can you hear me?" Kaly whispers.

"Yes, yes, I can hear you. My name is Enyo."

"Where's Leon?"

"Just under the ember archway, he is safe."

"Iana is—" Kaly's voice breaks, "gone."

"Yes."

"Danae and Itra?"

"Safe inside the castle. We're still attempting to locate the Medusa Shield."

"Medusa!" Kaly cries out, and her face pulls back in a tight frown.

"Stone inside the castle."

A twig snaps. Enyo shifts her position to stand beside the statue. She draws her dagger with her hand still on Kaly's shoulder.

"Step into the light and out of the shadows!" Enyo yells.

Another twig snaps and a man steps into view from around the boulder with his hands raised.

"It's only me, Ermal."

"I don't know who you are, but you shouldn't be here."

"I'm friends with Itra, and that statue you are talking to is Kaly, Leon's wife. I was present when she was turned to stone."

Enyo scowls at him. "Why are you here?"

"I'm a detective with the police department here. I was camping out to deter any remaining people from attempting to gain access to the castle per Itra's instructions."

"He said nothing about you being here."

"Sorry!" Itra exclaims, sprinting under the archway with Leon. "I totally forgot that he was here with everything else going on. He's a friend, Enyo. He's the one that actually killed Poseidon and protected Kaly."

Ermal flinches and looks down.

"That's great," Enyo says, frowning. "I was finally able to hear something. Go away and let me try to get some answers from Kaly."

"She's alive?" Leon starts towards Enyo.

"I can't hear her with all of you around."

Leon hesitates.

"Go!" Enyo commands.

Itra pulls on Leon to follow Ermal down the path away from her.

Enyo moans, trying to clear her mind and reach back out to Kaly. "Men!"

"Ha, but they're probably three of my favorites."

"You could hear that entire exchange?"

"Loud and clear. I think I've been in a comatose state this whole time. The last thing I remember before you spoke to me was Anton lunging towards Iana."

"Can you recall your time with Poseidon?"

"I don't know if it is all in the right order, but I think so. Ask me a question."

"Did you see the Medusa Shield with Poseidon or Medusa?"

"No, but they did discuss it. Um—something about the perfect place to hide it requiring a stone to unlock it."

"What stone?"

"Not sure. Poseidon tried to argue with Medusa on taking the shield to the future, but she cut him off."

"Ok, not the future but—" Enyo trails off in thought before continuing. "Did either of them mention a fort or the word Kelmend?"

"Fort Kelmend with Father Time, I know that legend. But I don't recall Medusa mentioning either during the exchange with Poseidon. What does the fort have to do with the shield?"

Enyo explains the recovery mission to the cave across from Fort Kelmend, finding a bronze shield, the cavern, and the passages of time opening to the hedge maze in the castle.

"Wow. When you went through the passage was there a gooey slime on your skin."

"No, why?"

"When I ran from Poseidon, we were in a cave, but nothing like you described. We were in the future. The year was 2284."

"2284?"

"Yes, I don't know if the year was significant, but I found an exit near a stream in the cave. There was a gooey crack in the wall. I came out in the present into a clearing where I encountered Ermal. He was waiting for dawn with Anton, Iana, and Elis."

"I'll take this information back to the group, but I should let you speak to Leon." Enyo cups her mouth with her free hand and shouts. "I can hear him lurking."

Leon pokes his head around the boulder in the path. She waves him forward. He jogs up.

"She can hear you now, speak freely."

Leon coughs and looks at Enyo.

"What?" Enyo asks.

"Can we get some privacy?" Leon asks.

"No," says Enyo. "It works with my connection to her."

Leon shifts his focus to his wife. "Kaly, I will fix this. Are you in pain?"

"No pain. Just focus on recovering the shield. I'm not going anywhere."

Enyo laughs at the sarcasm.

Leon frowns at Enyo, then shifts side to side. "We found your pack in a bunker in the Ottoman dimension. Are there any notes or books we should focus on that could help?"

"You found the bunker?"

"Noel, my doppelganger, and Danae did. It was crawling with Ottoman soldiers."

"In my pack, there is a journal with a list of questions concerning the Protectors of Time and research about Medusa's history pre-curse with Athena."

"You knew about the Protectors of Time?" Enyo asks before Leon can respond. "How?"

"I've dedicated my research to this area, people, society, and history. An old fable of the Protectors of Time written in ancient Greek had links back to Phorcys."

"Speaking of Greek," Leon says with a smile, "your aunt Xena is here."

"That was my Xena on the recovery mission for the shield?"

"Yes," Enyo laughs. "She was the only one not scared of heights. Can we circle back to Athena?"

"Medusa was a priestess under Athena. Athena was obsessed with finding and obtaining the Chronos Stone."

Leon and Enyo bounce up and down in excitement.

"Is that the connection?" Kaly asks.

"My word, if I could kiss you right now, I would!" Leon says. He blows out a breath. "Babe, what do you know about the Chronos Stone?"

"It was most recently represented in a few films about Hercules. But as far as my research on Athena goes, she found the stone and hid it deep underground. Check my notes in the margins of that book. I believe I wrote some references to check out once we were allowed inside the castle."

"Do you think the cave you came out of while fleeing Poseidon could fit the description?" Enyo asks.

"It's very possible, but check my notes. Ermal can show you approximately where I came out. I don't know if it works in reverse, but it's a start."

"Thank you!" Leon leans forward and kisses Kaly's stone nose. "I love you and please don't go stir crazy."

"I love you too."

Enyo removes her hand from Kaly's shoulder. "Kaly, can you hear us?"

Silence.

"Good," Enyo sighs. "I was hoping she wouldn't have to suffer awake in there. I believe she is only conscious when I'm in contact with her."

Leon nods and sucks in his bottom lip to fight back tears. Enyo pats him on the shoulder and walks back under the ember archway.

"Hey, Ermal, are you still there?" says Leon.

Itra and Ermal walk around the boulder and wave to Leon. "Ermal, we may need you soon. Can you stick around for an hour?"

"I'll be camping here all night," Ermal calls back.

"Great, see you soon." Leon takes Itra by the arm and they walk under the ember archway. They emerge just as Enyo takes flight. She lands gracefully near the front entrance to the castle and waits.

"I see you've found comfort in your wings," Leon teases as they walk back to the war room together.

"It was less terrifying then flying over the mountains this morning."

29

They enter the war room to silence. Each person has their head bent over a book.

"Good news," Enyo says. All of them look up at once. "Kaly can speak to us and she may have figured out a lead to the Medusa Shield."

Xena's eyes water. "Is she ok?"

Enyo places a hand on Xena's shoulder. "She confirms she is not in pain—I think she is only aware of her stone state when I am in contact with her."

"Good, good." Xena wipes away a fallen tear.

Enyo and Leon explain the conversation with Kaly about the cave, Poseidon and the possible link with the Chronos Stone.

Noel clears his throat. "We may have figured out another anomaly within our families." He stands after Avi nods. "Ten years ago, Xena's daughter, Pemphredo, was killed in a car accident. On the same day, my sister died of cancer and Avi's aunt went missing."

"Our lines were targeted over a decade ago?" Leon asks.

Noel nods. "It's possible."

"Did they ever find your aunt?" Itra asks.

"No," says Avi. "It is still an open cold case with the local police. She was seen hanging laundry out in the morning. When she didn't show up for a scheduled hair appointment or answer her phone, the salon owner came by to check on her. The door to the house was open, but nothing inside looked disturbed. Her keys, purse, and phone were all accounted for—there was no evidence of foul play leaving the police with no leads." She shakes her head. "At least that is what I was told by my parents about her disappearance."

Vincent holds up his book. "I have been reading over anything related to Chronos while you were out with Kaly. According to this text, a stone was stolen from Zeus by an eagle with two heads and hidden in the center of time." Itra crosses his hands and thumbs and wiggles his fingers to mimic wings. Vincent laughs and nods. "A symbolism for the double-headed eagle on the Albanian flag has more meaning now, right?"

Enyo laughs. "Pemphredo saw this happen in real time four days ago. Hermes chased the eagle over her when she was returning from the market."

"Is this the same stone in question?" Danae asks.

"Yes, according to this," Vincent says, pointing to the book. "The original catalyst for the passages of time was the Chronos Stone. It makes sense, considering the location of the cavern can only be accessed by flight."

"Does it say who was behind the eagle?" Avi asks. "Or when the bronze shield replaced the Chronos Stone?"

"Still reading," Vincent says.

"Vincent helped me with the translation of the book we found the first night back," Danae says, showing Leon a black book with a gold spine. He steps closer. "The book details the snake charm. A reversal of the curse is possible with a shield." Leon rolls to his toes. "Before you bounce out of here, we don't know which shield. We're still trying to figure out the cryptic text."

170

Leon vanishes and returns with the snake charm. Danae recoils away from Leon in her chair. "I hid it in the wardrobe in my room. Does it say anything about trial or error?"

"Still reading, please just give us time to be sure before you try every shield in the vault." She lowers her brows. "Agree?"

"Fine."

Three hours later, Vincent yawns and stretches. "Can you show me where I might lie down for a few hours?"

Leon nods, fighting a yawn in return. "We should all get a few hours of sleep. It's almost midnight and most of us barely slept last night and had a long day."

"Mmm, an understatement," Enyo mumbles.

The group rises from the table and shuffles towards the stairs. "Danae, can you show Vincent the second suite to the left of yours?"

"Sure," Danae responds, eying him with suspicion. "Where are you going?"

"To check in with Ermal and have him show me where he originally found Kaly before—"

"You promise to wait until morning to try to gain access to the cave?"

"Scout's honor." Leon holds up three fingers.

"Ha," Danae barks. "You were never a scout."

"Fine, I promise."

"Take Ermal some food and coffee."

Leon crosses under the ember archway carrying a bag of food and thermos of coffee. "Ermal?"

Silence.

He glances over at Kaly. "Soon," he whispers.

He jogs down the path and around the large boulder. The embers of a fire are still smoking in a small pit near a pack leaning against a log. He sets down the bag and the thermos.

Leon cups his mouth and tilts his chin up. "Ermal!"

The quiet chirp of a radio breaks the silence.

Leon calls his staff. He keeps his steps light, moving quickly down the path. A figure is pacing under the shadows of an old fig tree. He jogs forward.

Ermal whirls with a gun raised.

"Dude!" Leon yells and stops with his hands raised. "It's me!"

"Dammit, Leon, after the last two days, my nerves are on edge. You can't sneak up on a guy like that."

"I called your name twice!"

Ermal holsters his side arm and pockets his phone. "I was getting an earful from the chief. Unis's death has brought all kinds of red tape and unwanted snooping into our department. And then there's the extra traffic from the crazy people attempting to climb the hill."

"Sorry man."

"I'm not looking for sympathy from you, especially now." He glances up the path. "Are you going to sleep anytime soon? You look rough."

"Ha, soon, hopefully." Leon fights a yawn. "Can you show me where you found Kaly?" He nods towards the rocky boulders.

"Sure," Ermal responds and leads Leon. "It was dark, much like tonight, but I can show you in the general area."

"General area is fine. We'll be back in the morning to investigate it further."

Ermal nods. "Who was the woman with Kaly earlier?"

"Enyo, an original grey sister," Leon says.

Ermal trips and stumbles. "Sorry, an original? Like thousands of years old?"

"From thousands of years ago, but yep."

"Damn, she was kind of—"

172

"Bossy, mean, weird?" Leon mocks.

"Stunning, hot, remarkable."

Leon shoves Ermal's shoulder. "Crushing on an ancient lady."

"Ha, ha." Ermal slows and veers to the right. "Kaly was standing here when I found her. But I think she came from a few meters over that way." He points back to the left.

Leon walks past him and holds his staff closer to the rocky boulders jutting out. He drags his free hand along the rocks as he inspects the surface. His hand vanishes into a crevice. He lowers his staff towards the crack. The ember glow sputters, going dim, and then grows brighter. "Bingo!"

Ermal hands him a piece of white chalk from his pocket.

Leon stares at the chalk. "You just carry this around in your pocket?"

"I'm a detective. It has come in handy more times than I can count."

Leon marks the opening with an eight.

Ermal pockets the chalk after he tosses it back. "Is eight your favorite number?"

"Nope, just wanted it big enough to see in the morning."

They walk back up the path.

"Do I smell fried chicken?" Ermal quickens his step.

"Danae thought you might be hungry. There is coffee too."

Ermal's grin fills every inch of his face. "Please send my thanks! I haven't had a hot meal in days."

"Will do!" Leon salutes. "See you at dawn."

Leon closes and locks the large arched entry to the castle with a thought. Despite the exhaustion, he skips up the first set of stairs to the landing and inspects the hedge maze from the window. The mirror shield is still in place.

"Leon."

He whirls, calling his staff. The stairs and landing are empty. "Who's there?"

"Ember."

"The Ember?"

"Yes. To volunteer as my messenger requires great sacrifice and dedication, which I applaud. But you should know the commitment is permanent. Do you fully understand the responsibility?"

"No, but I'll learn as I go."

"Start with this." A book hovers in front of Leon. He takes the book. "Illyria, ember of mine, recover the shield or yield the line to end all time. Illyria, ember of mine, the new stone will shatter at night and breathe with light when all is right, Illyria, ember of time."

"What does that mean?" Leon begs.

Silence.

Leon grumbles, wanting nothing more than a hot shower. He vanishes. He appears standing in the bathroom of his suite. He places the book on the counter. He takes off his jacket and starts to pull his shirt off, but an urgent knock on the suite door makes him hesitate.

"Leon, are you back?" Avi calls through the door in a panic.

He opens the door.

"I accidentally manifested a woman. I've never seen her before." Avi looks over her shoulder. A tall woman with dark wavy hair and a single grey streak near her temple dressed in a red silk gown is walking towards them.

"Who are you?" Leon pushes Avi behind him.

"Hi, Leon," the woman answers.

"Nope." He shoves Avi into his suite, closing and locking the door. Alone in the corridor with this woman, he calls his staff.

"Leon!" Avi shouts through the door.

Two doors open up in the corridor.

Enyo steps out of one. The woman turns away from him, back to the sound of the door. Xena is standing a few doors down from Enyo.

"Enyo?" the woman asks.

"Pem?" Enyo asks in return. Xena walks to Enyo's side.

"Yes!" the woman responds.

"Leon, open the door!" Avi calls out.

Danae sticks her head out into the corridor.

"What's going on?" Danae looks down the corridor at the three women.

"Another sister reunion?" Leon shrugs.

"Leon, who is banging on your suite door?" Danae asks.

Leon opens the door and Avi marches out, shoving him in the chest. "Never do that again!"

"Hey," he says, raising his arms. "You came to my door scared. I didn't know if this woman was a threat or not."

"I manifested her by accident. What would you do if a stranger appeared in your room?"

Leon double taps his staff. Avi frowns at him. He turns to Enyo. "Enyo, is she a threat?"

"No, this is Pemphredo, my sister Pem."

"Crisis averted," Leon states. "Everyone, get to bed before Ember puts you there!" He rolls his eyes and walks back into his suite without another glance.

"Good night, brother," Danae laughs.

Danae closes her suite door.

Itra lifts her off her feet. "Now where were we?"

She wraps her legs around his waist. She presses her lips firmly against his. "Round two?"

30

Vincent wanders down to the war room before dawn, expecting the room to be quiet. But it's nearly full, and there is a buzz of conversation.

"Did any of you sleep last night?" Vincent asks, pulling out a chair at the table.

"How do you like your coffee?" Avi asks, looking up with a small grin.

"Strong and black," Vincent responds. A warm mug appears in front of him. The table is covered with books, papers, and maps. "Did I sleep through an entire day?"

"Sorry Vincent," Danae says, serving him a plate of bacon, eggs, toast, and a side of fruit. "Avi manifested the original Pemphredo late last night, and she shared a vision about the shield. The sisters didn't wake us up until five this morning. Be thankful you got an extra hour of sleep."

"So, they haven't slept yet?" Vincent asks, pointing with his fork after swallowing his first bite.

"We tried," Xena says from across the table, "but we didn't want to wait till morning and lose momentum."

Leon and Noel enter from the far side of the room.

"We've checked the archives and the library," Leon states. "We have every text that is in the castle that is related to Athena here in this room."

"Anyone care to fill this old man in on what I missed?" Vincent asks, taking a small sip from his coffee.

Itra sits down next to Vincent. "The vision was Athena removing a stone from the cavern with the twelve passageways and replacing it with the bronze shield. The vision faded to a dark cave with a small stream. A man in a blue tunic is handing off a shield to woman in shadows." Itra takes a sip of his own coffee.

"That's it?" Vincent asks. Itra raises a brow. "Timing wise, it still doesn't add up. Ermal killed Poseidon just before the blast at dawn. Which we were led to believe is when the Medusa Shield was removed from the vault, right?"

Itra shrugs. "That's what we were told."

"If that is true, Poseidon didn't have time to meet Medusa in the bunker and then take and hide the shield." Danae and Itra exchange a glance.

"How certain are you the man in the bunker was Poseidon?" Leon asks Danae.

"One hundred percent, but the object was covered, so maybe it wasn't the Medusa Shield."

Noel nods. "It was round like the bronze shield we recovered, but she's right, you couldn't actually see it. All of these questions are what dragged us back down here in the middle of the night." He fights a yawn. "Once you're done eating, we have a pile of books waiting for translation." He places a hand on top of six books at the end of the table. "We marked the pages."

"Yes, sir." Vincent salutes with his fork.

"When is your flight back to the states?" Danae asks Vincent.

"I never booked one," he says, pushing his plate away. "When Itra called, I left home and was on a plane in three hours. I just took the first available flight out. I never spoke to Kaly's neighbors that were watching Duke."

Danae waves Leon over. "Do you have your neighbor's number memorized, the ones watching Duke?"

Leon scrunches his nose. "I think so. I'll call them from Ermal's phone and check in."

Vincent nods. "Thanks!" He drains his coffee, pats down his pockets, and pulls out his reading glasses. He pushes back his chair and walks down to the end of the table. When he picks up the first book, the lights dim.

A silver image hovers above the table and slowly pans out from a blade to a man with wavy dark hair and a sharp nose.

"Poseidon," Itra and Danae say in unison.

The image continues to pan out to a large cavern with tiered levels and an empty center stage.

"The cavern," Noel mumbles.

The view continues to pan out, and a woman comes in to focus. She is dressed in a formal gown with gold jewels and is lounging on the highest tier.

"That's Athena." Enyo states.

"Is her hair grey or blonde?" Xena squints at the image.

"White," Enyo responds.

"Her face looks too young to have white hair," Avi says.

"She was born with white hair," Enyo says, pointing to a charm around her neck. "Leon, is that the same charm Kaly was wearing?"

Leon stands behind Enyo. His knuckles go white as he grips the side of her chair. "Yes."

The image fades and another fills the entire room.

"Did we just portal?" Itra asks, looking around. He reaches out to touch a rock near his head and finds only air. "No, it's just a very real simulation."

A man walks out of the darkness of a cave holding a round, covered object.

"Did she give you what I asked for?" a woman asks.

The group turns, looking for another person, but no one new appears.

Leon runs over and stands behind the man to try to see who he is speaking to.

The room fades back to black, and the lights come back on.

"Did you see who he was talking to?" Danae asks.

"It was just a crack in the cavern wall." Leon runs a hand through his hair. "It looks like what Kaly described." He takes a sip of coffee. "Enyo, can you try to pry any new information from Medusa armed with what we've learned in the last twelve hours?"

"Is there something specific you're looking for?" she asks, looking over the clutter on the table.

"Start with Athena and Poseidon," Xena suggests, "see if she mentions anything about a stone, shields, or passages in the cavern. And describe the cave scene and repeat his words you heard here. Maybe she'll slip up."

"And keep us on a live feed," Avi adds. The group's focus turns to her. "Think what she responds."

Enyo nods.

Vincent laughs. "Itra and I are out of that loop, so we'll need a play-by-play."

Enyo heads for the door, but Leon steps in her path.

"Do you mind to portal down?" Leon asks with a grin.

She frowns. "Fine, if it will save time."

He grins. "Tani."

She vanishes.

Enyo curses when her feet find contact with the present cavern floor. Her eyes are drawn to the opening and the lake below. The veil of darkness fading to dawn.

She removes her long sword before walking over to Medusa's now semi broken statue. Enyo shakes out her arms and bends her neck from side to side.

"Show me Medusa."

She waits. Silence.

"Do you need a little incentive to talk?" She taps the edge of her blade to Medusa's chest.

"Were you always this violent?" Medusa hisses. Her veil flutters.

"No," Enyo says and shrugs. "Well maybe."

"What do you want?"

Enyo smiles. "We found the shield."

"Impossible," Medusa says, her confidence a little shaken.

"The stream was a nice touch."

"So, you were bluffing!" Medusa exclaims. "I knew I could trust him."

"The veil around the castle has been restored. No intruders were able to enter while it was down. You failed."

"If all is well," Medusa says. "Why are you here? Is this your final goodbye?"

"I'll give you two guesses."

"Games?" Medusa complains. "The snake charm?"

"Very good."

Medusa laughs. "I'm the only one who can undo that charm."

"I don't believe you." She taps the tip of her sword to Medusa's stone chest. "Athena would never leave you something she couldn't undo herself."

"Athena!" Medusa shouts, giving her the confirmation.

"You trusted Athena and Poseidon," Enyo says in a sad tone, "but they were never really on your side."

"I've never trusted Athena."

"But you trusted Poseidon with a shield?"

Silence.

She taps her sword to Medusa's forehead. "Here's a scenario to consider. Poseidon offers Athena the Medusa Shield in exchange for the snake charm under the guise that he would place the snake charm around your neck. She agrees, and that is how you ended up with the snake charm for Kaly."

Medusa laughs.

"According to Leon, Poseidon was killed seconds before the vault triggered the alarm, creating the blast in the clearing." She drags the tip of her blade up to Medusa's chin.

Silence.

"This isn't going anywhere useful!" Enyo states.

Xena answers. *"Ask her if she's ever been to Fort Kelmend?"*

"Did you ever inspect Fort Kelmend? Or did you just blindly trust him?" Enyo asks, pacing away from the statue.

"Of course, I inspected the fort. We've been planning this for over a decade."

Enyo marches back to the statue. "Does that planning include murder?"

"Are you talking about the other descendants of your line we took care of? Old news!"

"Who are we in this scenario?"

"It wasn't really we, more like him. It was Poseidon's idea for tidying up possible loose ends."

Enyo brings up her sword to swing, but hesitates.

Ding, ding

She looks over her shoulder. Leon's face is red, his neck veins are bulging. She hands him the sword.

"Not now," Leon says in a low menacing tone, "but soon."

31

Leon and Enyo walk back into the war room to somber silence.

"I didn't kill her, yet." Leon walks over to the wardrobe in the corner. "Noel, can you put on a cloak and join Danae outside? We need to inspect the opening Kaly came through."

"If Danae goes," Itra says, "I go."

"Look bro, I plan on her being a lookout with Ermal, not actually going inside. I would prefer to have you here with Vincent and the ladies."

Xena looks up from the table and wipes her eyes. "We'll continue our research. Go, but come back soon!"

"Maybe we will find the shield," Noel says. He stands and turns his back to Danae and Leon, extending his arms. Danae takes the cloak from Leon and drapes it over Noel's outstretched arms. He looks over his shoulder and winks. "We can settle all of this before noon."

Leon vanishes without a word or warning.

"Rude," Danae scoffs. She takes his exit as their cue to meet him outside. She kisses Itra. "See you in a few. I love you."

"No risks, deal?" Itra leans his nose to hers.

"Deal," Danae says, patting Vincent on the shoulder. "Keep an eye on them. I'm leaving you in charge."

Leon appears beside Danae as she clears the bottom step. She is carrying a bag of food for Ermal.

Noel lands beside him with a grin.

"Thought you were scared of heights?" Danae laughs.

"I think I feel safer when the wings are attached." He pushes off and flies over the clearing, landing at the ember archways. Danae and Leon jog over to the communist archway.

"Leon." Danae tugs on his elbow just before they reach Noel. "Are you ok?"

"Mission ready and focused." He doesn't turn to make eye contact with her and marches under the ember archway.

"Hey Ermal, it's just us!" Danae shouts, as she clears the archway.

Noel catches up to Leon. "You good, man?"

Leon only grunts in response.

Noel looks back to Danae. She shakes her head and frowns.

They find Ermal's campsite, but not Ermal. They continue down the path and enter the clearing. The grass is tall and thick, slick with morning dew. The trees shadow the path.

A chill runs down Danae's spine, and her amulet shimmers to life.

Ermal is standing near the edge of the hill with a cup of coffee. The thermos is on the ground turned over. He is facing the eastern mountains, back lit by the rising sun. He doesn't turn to greet them.

Leon reaches him first and stands beside him, taking in the changing colors and the rise of light over the lowest peaks.

Danae and Noel watch in silence as the sun fully crests the ridge and bathes the valley with fresh light.

Her eyes wander to the forest below. "What's happening?"

At the sound of her voice, Ermal falls to his knees.

Danae and Leon slowly turn to look at each other. Noel bends to check on Ermal.

"He's breathing, but he's in a state of shock." He repositions Ermal to a seated position with his head between his knees. "Just take long, deep breaths." Noel stands and looks at Danae and Leon's color drained faces. "I don't understand? What's going on here?"

Leon points over Danae's shoulder, back towards the castle. It's clearly visible in the morning light.

Danae turns. "Oh, no!" She drops the bag of food.

"Still waiting," Noel says, his voice shaking.

"It's expanding," Leon whispers.

"What is?" Noel asks, looking from Danae to Leon.

"The veil," Danae whispers. "It's supposed to stop at the ember archways, not the entire town." She kneels next to Ermal. "Do you know when this started?"

Ermal lifts his head. "I don't know. I came down to enjoy the sunrise, but the trees and clearing looked different, thicker than normal."

Leon turns to survey the area. He nods to Noel. "I need to go, now. We can't leave the shield in the hedge maze." Leon starts back towards the castle. "Stay with them."

"Wait!" Noel calls out, but Leon vanishes. He turns to Danae. "Won't that leave the castle exposed again to all dimensions?"

"It's a risk we have to take. We can't shield an entire town and who knows what kind of trouble this is causing in the other dimensions."

32

Leon lands in the center of the hedge maze but knows in an instant he isn't alone.

"Ladies! Go to the landing windows overlooking the hedge maze, now!"

Enyo, Avi, and Xena jump up and run from the war room without warning. Vincent and Itra don't hesitate for a second and follow them. After they reach the conservatory, they split up. Enyo and Xena go right, Avi goes left. Vincent and Itra nod and split as well.

Leon looks around. The sun is not high enough to light the space—there are too many shadows. He calls his staff and double taps. The glow from his scythe only illuminates him. He digs in his pocket. He finds and activates a light stone.

Enyo is the first to reach the window.

Leon looks up and points two fingers at his eyes and turns his fingers to her before whirling his hand in a circle. She presses closer to the glass, looking for any movement in the maze.

"Do you see anyone?" Leon asks, just as Itra and Avi reach the other window.

"What's happening?" Vincent asks Xena, huffing for a breath.

"Why is Leon back?" Itra asks Avi. He presses against the window, searching the maze for Danae. "Where's Danae?"

"Three o'clock, a head just poked out of an opening and back in." Enyo points.

Leon whirls back to the shield and starts to lift it out of the arms of the statue.

"Wait," Avi stammers, *"there is one more person in the maze. At your six. Sending back-up."* Avi closes her eyes.

Enyo appears next to Leon. He looks up to the window. Enyo shrugs. He looks back to Enyo standing next to him.

Leon shakes his head. *"You can just split apart?"*

"Avi is manifesting me for backup."

"It just gets weirder." Leon whispers.

The first intruder clears the maze at a run towards the shield. Enyo throws her dagger at the invader's feet. He stops short. She draws her sword and holds the tip to his chest.

"We know there are two of you," Enyo shouts. "Answer our questions and you can leave breathing."

A second person dressed in a purple-hooded cape draped over a gold and red empire gown comes out of the maze with her hands raised in the air.

"He's only fourteen and he is here because of me," the woman says, pushing her hood back to reveal her white hair. She tilts her head towards the young man, who is glaring at Enyo.

"Athena?" Enyo asks, glancing down at the young man's gold winged shoes, tight pants, and loose red top. "Hermes?"

He nods. Enyo starts to lower her sword. Hermes takes a step forward. She raises her sword again and shakes her head.

"Pem wasn't lying?" Athena asks. "Medusa is here."

"Medusa is stone," Enyo says, nodding to Leon. "The Zeus line has been restored."

Leon raises his scythe.

"Hear them out before you do something you might regret?" Enyo meets Leon's scowl.

186

"This is Leon, a descendant of Zeus. Leon, this is Athena."

"It was your snake charm that turned my wife to stone," Leon says, taking a step towards her.

"And it's reversible with that shield," Athena says. Her posture is straight, and her face is unreadable, no smile or frown.

"How?" Leon says, raising his scythe.

"Hang the charm around the statue and whisper breathe when you place the mirror in front of her."

Leon considers her response. Her face remains blank. He takes a small step back to the shield. "Why are you here?"

"We're here to protect and serve," Hermes answers before Athena can respond.

Athena's face breaks into a wide, sinister grin.

"Isn't that right, sister?" Hermes says.

Athena tilts her head but nods.

A shiver of unease ripples down Leon's back.

Enyo disappears.

Avi inhales and coughs. "Oh, holy hell, what have I done?"

Itra doesn't turn from the window. "You have so much explaining to do."

"He called for our help. We came up here to be his eyes. I had no idea she was coming, but I'm guessing Enyo and Pem may have known and didn't share with us."

"Where is Danae?" Itra repeats.

"Here!" Danae says, breathlessly jogging up the stairs when he turns. He hugs her tightly. "What's going on? Where's Leon?"

"We have company," Avi whispers. "Hermes and Athena."

"Alone with Leon?" Danae says and pushes past Itra. She pounds her fist on the window. Leon looks up and nods. She vanishes from the window and appears next to him in the maze.

Hermes takes a step back and bows. "Queen Danae?"

Danae smirks and nods to Leon. *"Just roll with it."*

Leon clears his throat to fight a bark of laughter. "This is Athena and Hermes."

She feels the ember amulet rise from her chest. She reaches under her collar and pulls the amulet out.

Athena takes a step forward. "You! No!"

"No what?" Danae responds and takes a step back.

"Who gave you that?" Athena asks, points at the pulsing ember amulet. Her frown deepens, and the color drains from her face.

"Ember." Danae states with a smile. "Where is the Medusa Shield?"

Athena smirks. "You're clever."

She squares her chest to Athena. "Last chance, where did you hide the Medusa Shield?"

Athena lifts her chin towards Leon. "Did you know it was me? I was the woman in the cave that helped your wife escape Poseidon. I made sure she found her way out. I'm not your enemy."

Danae glares. "You didn't answer my question."

"No gratitude," Athena snarls, "no answer."

"We were summoned." Hermes interrupts the stare down between Athena and Danae.

"By whom?" Leon asks, his voice loud enough that Vincent and Itra can hear him.

"Teuta and Pax," Athena answers, looking up at the windows. "Are they home?"

Leon smiles. "They betrayed Ember and are no longer welcome. Therefore, your summons is now null and void. You may leave or be forced to. Your decision."

Athena laughs. "It's our blood right to be here."

"It was, until you used Ember's magic to curse Medusa," Danae says, keeping her voice smooth.

Enyo cuts in, almost shouting. *"Don't send her away! We need to know where the shield is exactly."* Danae and Leon glance at the window.

"Xena, go get your cloak and meet Noel outside," Leon says.

188

Xena nods and starts for the stairs.

"Wait," Vincent begs, "tell me what the hell is going on."

"Walk and talk," Xena says, waiting for him to join her. She fills him in on the call for help and the discussion playing out in the maze as they walk back to the war room.

"That's the original Athena and Hermes?" Vincent asks, assisting Xena with her cloak.

"Yep," Xena answers, heading for the front entrance. Vincent follows.

"You want to get back in Ember's good graces?" Danae asks. "Tell us where we will find the Medusa Shield."

"I only hid the shield to keep it from Poseidon and Medusa," Athena says, attempting to plea her defense. Hermes shifts from side to side.

"If you had any honor," Danae says, "you would have returned the shield at once."

"I thought Medusa was in charge. I wasn't about to hand it over to her."

"I'm outside, but I don't see Noel," Xena says.

"He's with Ermal defending the hill on the other side of the communist archway," Danae answers. Leon stiffens. *"That is why I returned. A mob of people are heading up the hillside."*

"Avi, tower! Enyo to the front entrance." Leon flares his nostrils. They nod and leave the windows. Leon rolls his shoulders and white knuckle grips the staff.

"Where the hell are you going?" Itra hisses at Avi as she bounds up the stairs.

"We have trouble approaching," Avi calls down.

Vincent joins Itra at the window. "This went south in a hurry."

Itra nods without taking his eyes off Danae.

189

"Where is the shield hidden, exactly?" Leon asks, a vein popping from his neck.

"I can show you," Athena smiles.

"Talk or leave," Danae says, stepping towards Athena. "We don't have time for games."

"There's a spire in the middle…," Hermes starts, but Athena's glare makes him stop.

"Go on," Leon encourages Hermes. "In the middle of where?"

"Another word, I will," Athena whispers.

"You'll what!" Danae cuts in and meets Athena's glare. Danae squares her chest towards Athena, and the amulet lifts.

"… of Fort Kelmend." Hermes gulps and winces, waiting for Athena's wrath.

Athena is riveted by the amulet and ignores Hermes.

"What dimension?" Leon asks.

"Ëndrra." He doesn't dare glance in Athena's direction when she remains silent. "There is a marked floor tile with this." He kneels and draws an eight in the dirt. "The key to unlock it is—the stone." His eyes dart over to Danae's chest.

Athena snaps out of it and her face turns red, a stark contrast with her white hair. "You fool!" she screams.

"Tani!" Leon yells at Athena and she vanishes.

Hermes blinks and his mouth falls open. "Where did she go?"

"Your confession will save you from her fate," Leon approaches him.

"She lied about the shield with the mirror," Hermes says. "Do not place the charm around the victim's neck, otherwise, she will be cursed for life again. Just position the mirror to reflect the statue and speak the word breathe."

"If this works," Danae says, "we'll be in your debt."

Hermes bows.

"You may leave," Leon says. "We'll send a message once we've cleared you for duty to protect and serve Ember and the Castle of Teskom."

Hermes turns into the maze without a word and walks through a passage.

Leon releases his staff and lifts the shield from the fairy statue with ease. The twelve entrances close immediately. The ground rumbles under their feet. He nearly loses his grip on the shield. Danae helps him recover and adjust his grip.

"Take my arm," Leon says to Danae.

"Do you think we should test the shield on the fairy statue before taking it to Kaly?"

Bang, bang

The noise makes Leon look up. Vincent and Itra are pounding on the window and waving frantically.

"Times up!" Leon says. Danae takes his arm, and they vanish out of the maze.

They appear next to Vincent and Itra.

Itra grabs her and hugs her tightly. "She was armed!"

"What do you mean?" Danae pushes back from him to look up at his face.

"Just before Athena vanished, she pulled a large glowing charm from her gown. Vincent thinks it was infused with ember."

"Where did you send her?" Vincent asks Leon.

Leon points down and says, "To keep Medusa company." He smiles. "I wanted insurance in case they're lying about the location of the shield and if Kaly isn't Kaly in the next ten minutes."

"What do you mean, 'keep her company'?" Danae asks, using air quotes.

"She's a stone statue standing in front of Medusa in the present cavern."

"Do you think the object she was holding is concerned?" Danae asks Vincent.

He shrugs. "I couldn't make it out, I just saw the glow."

33

"We could use a little help outside," Avi says, watching Xena and Noel argue with Enyo near the archways.

"On our way," Leon responds. "Avi needs our help outside," he relays to Itra and Vincent. He hands them the shield, vanishing and reappearing with two cloaks.

Danae turns and extends her arms.

"Can you and Vincent confirm there are two statues down in the present cavern?" Danae asks, facing Itra's frown. "And please check on Elis while you're down there."

"Can you fill us in on where and what the plan is?" Itra asks.

Leon nods. "We have a location for the Medusa Shield at Fort Kelmend in the ëndrra dimension." He turns, extending his arms. Danae drapes his cloak over him. "Which one was that?"

"Dream, you know it as revolutionary," Vincent answers.

"Hermes suggested that the ember amulet is the key to unlocking the shield." Leon takes the shield back. "And that this mirror will supposedly help Kaly."

Vincent smiles. "That's great!"

Itra cups Danae's face, pushing his nose to hers. "Come back in one piece." He kisses her softly and then tugs her in for a full kiss. Vincent clears his throat.

Danae, breathless and grinning, blushes at Vincent and Leon who are adverting their eyes.

"Kaly first," Leon says, heading out the front entrance with the shield. "Then we'll head to the fort."

Danae follows him, looking back at Itra. He mouths 'be careful'. She nods.

They can hear shouting from the last step of the castle.

"What in the hell are they arguing about?" Leon growls.

"My guess, Pem talking to Athena." Danae looks up at the tower. Avi is pacing in the glass box. *Avi, what are we walking up to?*

"An argument about who is going with you to the fort."

"Xena and Danae, come with me," Leon states, ignoring their shouts as they get closer. "Enyo and Noel, we'll be back in a few." Enyo opens her mouth to protest, but his intense glare makes her pause. She nods.

They follow him under the communist archway, and the three of them stand together in front of Kaly's stone figure.

Leon turns the mirror side towards the statue. He takes in a long inhale and holds it. "Breathe," he says with loud exhale.

Nothing happens.

Danae looks down at the shield to see the reflection. It's just the statue. Xena touches his shoulder in consolation.

The reflection ripples.

Danae gasps. "It's Kaly!"

Leon cranes his neck over and nearly drops the shield, meeting his wife's eyes.

"Breathe," he says again.

A crack of falling rock and burst of wind forces them to cover their faces and step away. When the air settles, Kaly appears, brushing dust and dirt from her face and shoulders.

"Finally!" Kaly smirks.

Leon tosses the shield without thinking and takes two long strides to Kaly. Danae and Xena dive forward to save the shield, barely softening the fall to the ground.

"Careful," Kaly says as he picks her up and kisses her neck.

He grunts in return.

"Seriously, can't breathe," Kaly struggles to say.

"Let her up for air," Xena teases.

He loosens his grip but doesn't let her go. "You're never leaving my sight again," he says. Kaly laughs.

Xena and Danae make eye contact, smile, and wipe away their tears.

"Danae?" a man calls.

Danae turns around and waves Ermal forward.

He hesitates a second before walking up the path. "Am I seeing things or is she really back?"

"I'm really back," Kaly laughs. "Have you been here this whole time?"

"Not quite," Ermal says, "but I'm happy to hear you talk again."

Kaly turns to Danae. "Anton and Elis?"

"Safe at home. We buried Iana yesterday." Danae's mouth quivers. Kaly frowns. "But Xena found her way to us."

Kaly's frown becomes a smile as she turns to Xena. "How did you find your way here?"

"My niece is very clever and left me just enough information." Xena smiles, giving her a long, tight hug. "Your dad would be proud." Kaly hugs her tighter.

"Ermal, is the town back, or is it still a forest?" Danae asks, looking down the path.

"After the earthquake, the valley returned to normal, but we still have a few people climbing the hill."

Danae looks up at the sky. "The sky appears intact. Maybe the shield in the tower caused the rip?"

"Maybe." Leon shrugs. "But we have a lead on the shield that will actually fix the veil," Leon says, looking from Kaly to Danae. "Danae, Noel, and Enyo will leave in a few to try to retrieve it. We can take over the watch. Ermal, do you want a quick return home, or do you want to hike down?"

Ermal looks from Leon to Danae. "Is he serious?" She nods. "Quick!"

Leon nods and says, "Tani!"

Ermal vanishes. Kaly lets out a small scream.

"Oh, sorry babe, I'm the messenger now." Kaly falls back into Xena. "Kaly?" He goes to her side. "Kaly! Come back."

"I think she just fainted," Xena says, checking her pulse. "She's likely dehydrated and needs to eat. Take her inside, I'll keep watch here."

He hesitates. His skin prickles with a message.

"Leon, go!" Xena insists.

Leon stands. "Xena, since you're naturally gifted with intuition, Ember's gift to you is intuitive applied learning, the ability to retain and apply any skill you've seen or read about with or without magic."

Xena's scalp tingle. She rises from Kaly's side. "That's overwhelming," she whispers.

"Do you want to try it out before we leave you here alone?" Danae asks, coming to her side.

Xena's eyes go wide, and she grins, lifting her hands over her head. She exhales and completes a standing tuck backflip with perfect precision. She laughs.

Danae claps. "What made you try that first?"

"I was my daughter's spotter while she learned that skill in gymnastics." Xena giggles. "I always secretly wanted to try it."

"Brilliant." Danae says and smiles. "Be creative and use your wings to retreat if necessary. Avi will be watching."

Leon bends and scoops up Kaly. Xena leans over and kisses her niece's cheek. Danae hands Leon the shield. He nods and vanishes with Kaly in his arms.

Xena turns to Danae. "How sure are you of the information Athena and Hermes told you?"

"I wish I could give you a confident two-thumbs-up, but something still feels off." She chews on the inside of her cheek. "It's something to go on and better than the research guessing game."

Xena laughs. "Once Kaly is well, good luck getting her out of that library."

Danae grins. "Leon, would complain about how lost she would get when she found something that drew her in. He would wake to an empty bed and find coffee cups and notepads littering every surface between the kitchen and the home office."

"Like father, like daughter." Xena says, smiling with a sigh. "Be safe. And fair warning, Enyo and Noel are not fond of heights."

"Good to know, see you soon."

34

"Anxious?" Danae asks, walking under the revolutionary archway.

Enyo shakes her head.

Noel bounces from foot to foot. "Wired! Avi conjured up an energy drink. Fairly sure there were at least three shots of espresso in it."

"I already miss caffeine," Danae says, and frowns.

They push off and fly up over the hills, crossing the valley north to the Albanian Alps.

Danae flies closer to Noel. "Did Vincent or Itra confirm that there are two statues in the present cavern and that Elis is safe?"

"Yes, and yes." Noel refuses to look down as they gain altitude. "He mentioned Elis was playing cards with Nada and winning."

She smiles and risks a look down. The trees and plants are full and healthy, surrounding beautiful small homesteads. *No half-demolished old buildings.* Several small vineyards and orchards dot the landscapes as they continue further north. She sucks in a breath as they fly over the canyon, and she focuses her attention up, admiring the peaks of the Accursed Mountains.

Enyo takes the lead and follows the river east when it splits. The valley is long and narrow. The elevation rises quickly to a small farming village.

Noel points over to his left. "There's the cave just under the waterfall."

Danae's eyes follow the flow of water down the side of the mountain until she spots a small dark opening about midway down. "How did you even find that?"

"Luck." He slows down and flies in a circle. "Where's Enyo?"

"Over here!" Enyo shouts.

Danae scans the rocky hillside to her right. Solid rock walls with small, evenly spaced openings for look out or defense. She flies towards Enyo, who is waving from a perimeter wall. Danae pauses before landing. She feels the presence of a few others.

Noel flies back up. "What's wrong?"

"There are two, maybe three people in the fort."

He nods and helps her land away from the edge. She pulls the ember amulet out from under her top. He calls and double taps his staff.

"Problem?" Enyo whispers.

Danae nods. "We're not alone."

Noel takes the lead. Enyo unsheathes her dagger and sword. She motions for Danae to stay in the middle.

They inch away from the edge, and the walls grow in height. Noel pushes off to fly up and looks over. He makes it halfway up the wall before he crashes back down. He rubs his head and looks up. "There's a barrier or something."

"Then we're likely in the right spot." Danae looks up. "We just have to find an entrance." Her amulet taps at her chest. "I believe Ember will guide our way."

They quietly maneuver along the perimeter until they find natural stone steps descending further down in a small gap in the wall. Noel looks back at Danae. She nods. They carefully navigate the narrow passage as the steps end at a small opening, only chest high.

Noel wedges himself under.

"Um, clear," he whispers.

Enyo and Danae exchange a worried glance.

They crawl under and stand by him. He slowly moves the ember glow from his staff right to left.

"Did you feel a crackle of energy as you walked under?" Noel asks.

"Yes!" Enyo adjusts her coat. "It's the same sensation as when we walked into the cavern with the passages of time."

Danae nods and nudges his staff back to the wall on the right. "Have you ever seen anything like this?" She traces the stones. "The stones are cut into triangles." She moves further down. "And set in a spiral pattern, starting here and expanding out."

Noel admires the pattern, but shivers.

Danae continues to trace the circle from the center of the wall. Her eyes continue up and she staggers back, bumping into Enyo. "There's no end."

"What?" Enyo asks, following Danae's shaking hand pointing straight up. The wall continues in an infinite abyss. "No end."

Noel raises the staff. He turns to inspect the wall on the left and finds a matching design but counterclockwise to the center of the wall on the right.

"An illusion or mirror?" Noel suggests.

"Maybe," Enyo whispers.

Noel cautiously moves forward. "Stay close and don't split up, we need to keep moving."

They slowly walk ahead and find a sunken courtyard with six different paths. Noel turns back to Danae for guidance. She nods to the right, feeling a familiar tug from the amulet. They take several paths with narrow corridors. They descend stairs at one turn and then ascend stairs at the next turn. They continue finding small courtyards that lead to various other openings.

Danae takes the lead, using the amulet to navigate what is working out to be a labyrinth of corridors. They walk up a long flight of stairs and enter a large, sun-filled courtyard. At the center is an odd structure with a single visible door.

The foundation is wide but narrows at each level before widening back out again near the middle, soaring maybe twenty stories high. The effect gives the whole structure a smooth figure eight shape.

"Is this construction even possible?" Enyo asks.

"I've never seen anything like it," Noel answers. He hesitates as his eyes follow the building to the center and back out again. "Danae, do you have the old pyramids in your dimension?"

"Yes. The rise is similar, but the edges here are soft." She steps closer and looks up. "I couldn't see this from our approach. The shield is hiding the structure from the outside world." Her ember amulet lifts away from her chest. Every inch of her skin tingles with static. She rubs her arms and tries to shake the weight on her shoulders.

Enyo motions for Noel to inspect the right side of the structure. Danae stays with her as they creep around the left side.

The building shifts with the clouds. Enyo pauses, looking from the sky back to the building. "Is it moving? Or are the clouds?"

Noel comes from around the opposite corner.

"You made it all the way around?" Danae asks.

He nods. "The only visible entry is that one." He points up to an open arched door. "Is it just me, or is this thing reflecting the sky?"

Danae smirks. "My thoughts exactly."

Noel, Danae, and Enyo proceed up the three steps to a dark opening. They can see nothing beyond the darkness.

Danae activates and throws in a light stone in, but it vanishes. She looks from Enyo to Noel. "Did it go so far in that we can't see it?"

"Only one way to know for sure is in," Enyo says, raising both weapons and charges into the opening. She vanishes in the darkness. Noel runs in after her, leaving Danae alone.

His head sticks back out a second later. "You've got to see this."

Danae sucks in a deep breath and marches forward. The darkness fades to a space she can't quite comprehend. A web of pulsing lights weaving from side to side. They rise endlessly and when she looks down; the pattern reflects as if they are walking on air or more mirrors. The effect makes her dizzy. She closes her eyes to steady her swirling vision. An image from a high school science class fills her mind.

"Noel, is it just me, or does this look like a DNA strand?" She risks opening her eyes to take a second look. "It's a double helix pattern."

"What's DNA?" Enyo whispers.

"A genetic code unique in every living organism," Danae answers slowly, lowering her gaze back to Enyo. "We have company at your six."

A small figure steps out of the darkness and pauses. A tall figure wielding a long sword follows.

Enyo frowns. "Teuta and Pax, no surprise."

"I see that you're clever enough to find his place, but extremely dumb for coming," Pax states.

Danae tilts her head to the side. "You knew where the Medusa Shield was all along?"

"It was his plan," Teuta starts to protest, but Pax raises the blade to her throat.

"Is that how you treat family?" Danae asks, raising her hands.

"Family that betrays you," Pax draws out with sadness, "leaving you with nothing for centuries?" He shrugs before laughing.

Enyo lifts a brow but doesn't react.

"Are you even related?" Noel asks.

"Patrick Alexander, her only blood relative and brother, but I go by Pax." His smug grin falls when Teuta transforms from fairy height to her queenly regal height with a purple hooded cloak and red gown.

She takes his sword in one swift move and levels the blade to his neck. "You're an insolent child." She looks over at Danae. "He was working with Medusa and Poseidon."

"Explain!" Enyo shouts.

Pax glares in Enyo's direction.

"Pax searched for Teuta's treasure for years," the cloaked queen says. She circles him so he is now in the middle of the four of them. "He never found a trace. However, he did discover one of the gold cubes infused with embers magic." Pax rolls his eyes. "And eventually the blood oath. He used the cube and oath as bait for Medusa. All to try to find the treasure. How am I doing so far?"

He cocks his right hip out and looks at his nails. "Bored, oh, but do continue."

"He found one unlucky soul from the Kelmend line crossing back under the ember archway. Pax got him to confess all the details he knew about the castle and a fairy named Teuta."

He smiles and adds, "With a promise of gold and by inflicting some painful tricks I learned from my dear old big sister, the pirate." Pax fake yawns. "Isn't it fascinating?"

"It would be if you were actually with the real Teuta," Danae says, letting this comment sink in with the others. "You see, the bronze shield reflects true identity, including the identity of a tiny stone statue in a hedge maze."

Pax's face flushes red. He turns to face the woman holding his sword. She tilts her head and smiles.

"We think she is playing both sides." Danae shifts to make eye contact with the imposter over Pax's shoulder.

Pax slowly turns to face Danae. "You're joking, right?"

"New, news?" Enyo mocks hearing his doubt and panic slowly escalating.

Pax attempts to keep his face free from any reaction. He fails and snarls a lip in Enyo's direction and glances over her head.

Enyo smiles. "Play your next card very wisely."

"Do I look like a man that would ever listen to a woman?"

Hermes steps out of the shadows.

Danae turns. The amulet lifts with a thought, and an invisible force pins Hermes to the wall. "It's a good thing Leon let him go," Danae says. "How else would you have gotten here?"

With everyone's attention focused on Hermes, Noel disarms the imposter. He rests the blade of his scythe next to her neck. Enyo has the tip of her dagger near the pulsing vein of Pax's neck.

"The Medusa Shield, now!" Enyo pricks his neck, releasing a small trickle of blood.

"The mark is directly below him," Hermes says, nodding to the floor. Pax bucks in response, slamming his head into Enyo's nose. She tightens her grip on him and holds her nose to stop the bleeding.

Danae inspects the floor and finds a single tile with a figure eight. There is a small dip in the center the size of her amulet. "Illyria, ember of mine, recover the shield." She kneels and leans closer. The chain around her neck lengthens automatically. The amulet connects to the tile with a click.

Pax screams. "The beginning and the end!" He looks up.

A humming and whirl of light shifts over their heads. A shield floats down from above and hovers in midair. The painting on the Medusa Shield appears in three dimensions. The snakes slither and hiss while the face writhes and twists in agony.

Noel recoils from the sight. The others appear to be transfixed and pay no notice to Danae as she disconnects the ember amulet and stands. She slices her finger as she attempts to take the shield's grip.

"Ouch!" Danae mumbles and shakes her hand. She inspects the cut, it's small, just a few drops of blood fall.

This snaps the others back to reality.

Danae releases her invisible hold on Hermes. He remains against the wall but sighs in relief.

"Who is she?" Pax jerks his head to the imposter with Noel.

"Pemphredo." Danae states with confidence. She turns to her and raises an eyebrow. "A pawn for Medusa or Athena, but I'm still working out what side you're on and what dimension you're from."

Enyo frowns and turns towards the imposter.

The woman lowers her hood, revealing a white patch of hair near her temple. It falls in contrast with her loose brown waves. She unhooks the cloak and reveals an oval mirror charm around her neck.

Pax groans. "You've got to be kidding me!"

"You impersonated Kaly and Medusa!" Danae says. "But Itra and I saw you get forced out of the present cavern." Danae's eyes go from Pemphredo to Hermes. "My guess is that this young man saved your life."

Hermes blushes and looks down, scuffing the floor with his winged shoes.

"This gave you a chance at revenge?" Danae asks.

She nods. "My curse for the last ten years." She taps the charm around her neck. "After I was kidnapped by Poseidon."

"Who is your mother?" Noel asks, gripping his staff.

"Rexena, but she goes by Xena."

He lowers his staff.

"I'm able to transform into any female after close observation." She blinks and transforms into Enyo.

"Hell no!" Enyo shouts.

Pemphredo snaps back to herself. "Sorry." She bows her head towards Enyo. "I wasn't sure how I could help at first, but Hermes was tracking Athena when he caught me."

Hermes grins. "Athena was desperate to recover the Chronos Stone. She left it hidden in a passage near the castle's vault during the time we served Ember. She agreed to hide the shield for

Poseidon and gave him the snake charm so he could use it to snare Medusa. Athena thought she could play him against Medusa."

"Wait, what?" Danae responds. She shakes her head. "Timing wise, this still doesn't add up."

Pemphredo raises her hand. "I was their decoy. Poseidon and Medusa used a hidden entrance in the archives to the vault to steal the Medusa Shield. We used the gold cubes to get in and out."

Danae shakes her head and paces. "And to get it here?"

Hermes raises a hand. "I was the other pawn. Athena wanted the shield locked somewhere that would require the Chronos Stone as the key to unlock the shield. She was the only one who knew where the stone was hidden, and this was her key advantage to control Medusa if Poseidon betrayed her." He frowns. "I flew Athena and the shields here just after the battle at dawn."

"This is a Chronos Stone?" Danae looks down at the amulet.

Hermes nods.

"And the bronze shield?" Noel asks. "Who took it?"

"Athena did, during the mass chaos of the battle at dawn."

Danae flares her nostrils. "The blast that killed Iana was actually Athena's fault."

"But why was there no alarm when that was taken?" Enyo asks, pointing to the shield.

Danae smacks her forehead. "There was an alarm after the incident with Leon and I in the archives, just not as big as the blast in the morning."

"And Pax," Noel suggests with a coy grin, "was the devil offering the apple?"

Hermes grins. "Pax dangled the blood oath as the keys to the castle to Medusa. She turned to Poseidon, who then turned to Athena."

Pax slow claps three times facing Hermes. "And you, my dear, played my doting boy toy and faithful confidant," Pax says, spying the smug expression plastered on the face of Hermes.

Hermes bows with such grandeur that the group laughs to near tears.

Danae regains enough air between giggles. "So back to the fool that started it all. Pax, any last words?"

"You're going to kill me?"

"Your greed led to the actions that killed my sister-in-law. I believe my actions are legal in this part of the country where blood feuds are still honored. I believe a life for life is just punishment or I can let Ember decide. Your choice."

"Ember," Pax says. His feet immediately leave the floor.

Enyo steps away.

He wiggles his legs, looking around. "What's happening?"

"Ember," Danae says. She watches her amulet pulse.

The ground rumbles under their feet.

Noel gestures towards the exit. "It's closing, we need to go now."

"Danae?" Enyo asks.

"Go!" Danae starts to move for the door, keeping her eyes on Pax hovering in the air.

Hermes, Noel, Pemphredo, and Enyo clear the threshold.

An ember light fills the space, engulfing Danae.

"Danae!" Enyo yells, reaching for her. Enyo only finds air. The entry closes and expels Enyo back. "No!"

Noel touches Enyo's shoulder to help her up, but she jumps up and draws her dagger. He holds up his hand and uses one finger to point behind him.

Danae waves.

Enyo exhales. "How did you manage that?"

Danae holds up the amulet and the shield. "I'm guessing these?" She shrugs. "Hermes, can you fly with Pemphredo?" He nods and takes Pemphredo's hand. "Noel, I think two hands are better than one carrying this thing back."

He grips the shield and starts to push off.

"Wait!" Enyo shouts. "How do we know what happened to Pax?"

"We don't," Danae says. "We trust Ember." She smiles and pushes off with Noel.

Enyo paces back and forth. She double checks the entrance to the structure is sealed. Satisfied, she pushes off to follow, but a chill runs down her spine. When she looks back, the building is gone. In its place is a stone monument of a man with a scythe on one knee and a hand held up with a round object in his palm.

35

Itra and Leon are standing in the front entrance admiring the changes to the entry's mural. The mural added three additional people in the last few hours, and twelve red dots are painted in a purple sky. A different dot glows every five minutes, moving clockwise.

"Incoming from the east, at least five!" Avi shouts.

Leon spins around and scans the clearing. It's empty.

Itra turns and looks up.

"It's Danae!" Itra shouts. He leaps down the four giant steps as the group lands in the clearing. Leon follows a few strides behind.

Hermes and Pemphredo hover overhead. Danae notices their hesitation. She nods to Hermes.

"Leon, you've met Hermes and Pemphredo," Danae says. Leon frowns. "Give her a chance. She's spent the last decade being forced to assist Medusa and Poseidon." Her stern tone stops Leon from protesting. "They're both welcome here, and they played a huge role in recovering the shield."

Leon studies Pemphredo's face before taking in the shield. The snakes hiss at him. He recoils. "Is that thing alive?"

"Something like that," Noel says happily, handing him the shield.

Leon holds it out, away from his body. *"Avi, let me know what you see in a minute."* He vanishes with the shield.

Pemphredo stumbles back, pointing to the spot where Leon had been standing.

"It's alright," Noel teases, "he comes with a bell."

Itra hugs Danae. "Are you alright?"

"I will be if this is the right shield, and we finally get some rest." She examines Itra's frown. "What's happened?"

"One thing at a time." He looks up and lifts a hand to his brow to shade the evening sun. "Is it working?"

"I can't see the castle!" Xena shouts.

"By the panic in Xena's tone, I'm guessing yes," Danae answers, nudging Itra. "Is she still on the other side?"

Itra nods.

"Avi, what do you see?" Leon asks.

"An untouched valley. No homes, cars, or roads," Avi answers.

"It's working. The veil is back!" Danae kisses Itra.

"You're all back?" Xena shouts after coming under the ember archway. "It worked?"

"Yes!" Avi answers.

Pemphredo turns at the sound of Xena's voice. "Mom?"

The sun is behind Xena, making her features dark and hard to see.

Xena starts to walk across the clearing but stops when she sees her daughter's face. "Pem?" She pushes off and glides through the sky, landing in front of the group. Her eyes are solely focused on the single strand of white wavy hair framing a familiar face. "Are you my Pem?"

Pem's knees buckle. "Mom!"

Xena takes her in her arms. "It's ok, I've got you now. You 're safe."

Pem's sobbing draws Avi down from the tower. Kaly and Vincent come out of the conservatory, and the group come up the four giant steps, giving Pem and Xena some space.

Leon appears with a small jingle.

Danae starts introductions. "Hermes, this is my husband, Itra, and his uncle Vincent. You've met my brother Leon; this is his wife, Kaly."

Hermes rolls up to his toes and bounces back down. "It worked?"

Leon smiles. "Yes."

"And this is Noel, Avi, and Enyo," Danae continues.

"I recognize Avi," he says, tilting his head towards her.

"How?" Enyo's posture goes rigid.

"I followed Perseus that night." Hermes smirks. "I was his eyes in the sky."

"You were spying?" Enyo asks, her tone level but stern.

"No, we knew that once we left the safety of our lands that we could get ambushed. It was a layered defense strategy only. One of your sisters spotted me during the exchange. We locked eyes for a solid minute, neither making a move."

Enyo furrows her brows. "Which one?"

"The one that looks like her." Hermes points to Avi. "She placed a finger over her mouth and chin. I nodded in return and flew higher out of sight before I could be detected by any others."

"You knew that the blood oath was forged?" Enyo asks.

"Where do you think Pax got his intel?"

"What game are you playing?" Enyo pulls her dagger. "And whose side are you on?"

210

"Ember's," he says. "My duty has always been to protect and serve."

"If that's the case," Itra says, stepping forward. "Why did you keep the blood oath a secret?"

"Keep your friends close but your enemies closer." Hermes shrugs. "I'm a kid. I can be in the room and people speak freely, like I don't exist. I gathered the intel and waited until I knew I could leverage enough information to get back in the good graces of Ember."

"Why didn't you bring us back the shield, then?" Itra asks.

"One of Athena's plans, once the passages opened in the hedge maze, was to retrieve the Chronos Stone from her hiding spot. The shield was locked away, and the only key is around Danae's neck."

"And the attacks?" Itra asks.

"I knew pieces of Athena's betrayal to Medusa, but not the entire plan. And I'm fourteen, I couldn't stop an army."

Itra shakes his head. "Vincent found a book describing an encounter with Ember and Chronos. A proposal to unite." He points the amulet. "This was his engagement gift to Ember."

All color drains from Danae's face.

"Danae, are you ok?" Xena asks, keeping an arm around Pem as they clear the last step and join the group.

"She needs a moment to digest the news about the stone," Kaly suggests.

Pem raises an eyebrow. "Kaly? You're ok?"

"All good, cousin," Kaly says, "but if you ever impersonate me again, I will unleash a wrath of hell on you." Kaly fails to keep her expression stern for long and breaks into a wide smile. She walks over and hugs Pem tightly.

Pem stiffens in her embrace, but eventually relaxes and hugs her back. "I'm so sorry, Kaly, really, I had no choice."

"I know," Kaly whispers.

The sun falls behind the mountains on the far side of the lake, and the temperature drops almost instantly. A small shiver runs through the group.

"Xena," Leon says, turning to her. "Were there any more people climbing the hill when you came back through?"

"Two kids with full packs and camping gear," Xena answers, looking back towards the archways.

"They can't see any sign of the castle now, right?"

"No sign at all."

"We can check back in the morning. I think this group needs a hot meal, showers, and sleep."

Noel wastes no time turning towards the conservatory.

"You two are very similar," Kaly says, winking at Leon. "Motivation food, check one for Leon and Noel."

Hermes pauses to admire the mural as the rest of the family joins him.

"Looks like the new arrivals were blessed by Ember," Danae says.

Kaly, Pem, and Hermes stand together looking at the various faces matching each one to each family member.

"Why are Vincent and Itra missing?" Hermes asks.

"We are descendants of Mui and only here on invitation."

Hermes gasps. His pupils double, filling his hazel eyes. "The alliance! You two are the alliance?"

Danae nods.

"You aren't the Queen?"

"No, why?" Danae laughs.

"When you appeared next to Leon in the hedge maze, the reflection in the mirror shield showed you with a crown and regal gown."

Leon laughs. "All hail, Queen Danae."

Hermes bows.

Vincent snorts in surprise. This causes a spontaneous ripple of laughter around the group. Danae shakes her head and ushers them inside. Leon closes and secures the large entry doors.

The smell of food wafts out of the dining hall door as Itra holds it open. The giant table is full of various meat and pasta dishes and fruit and vegetable platters. Dishes cover every surface between each of the formal place settings.

"Thanks, Ember," Leon murmurs as the last of the family files in and picks a seat. He sits next to Kaly and raises a glass of wine. "To family."

They each take a glass and repeat in unison. "To family."

Xena takes Hermes's glass before he can sip it and replaces it with juice.

"Hey!" Hermes frowns.

"Fourteen," Xena chides him. "Is that true?"

"Yes, but I'm allowed a glass of wine with dinner."

"Fine," she replaces the juice with wine but only fills it halfway.

Hermes glares at her.

Xena smiles.

"Rexena!" Pemphredo scolds.

Xena frowns at Pem. "Fine." She fills his glass a little more.

36

An hour later, the group exhausts their curiosity after a rapid exchange, including Vincent's twenty questions about Fort Kelmend and the new monument. A battle of yawns spreads around the table.

Noel is the first to raise his napkin in surrender. He pushes back from the table. "I'm done. I plan to shower and then sleep. Only wake me if my bed is on fire!"

"Same!" Enyo yawns. She stands and follows Noel.

"Leon," Danae says, leaning forward. "Do you think we should try to get Teuta back tonight?"

He doesn't remove his eyes from Kaly to answer. "It can wait." He vanishes with his wife.

Pem chokes on her wine.

Itra and Danae exchange a knowing look.

Vincent clears his throat. "I'll show Pem and Hermes their suites, away from the couples." He winks in Xena's direction. She laughs and stands, nodding for Avi and the others to follow.

Danae and Itra stand but don't follow. Itra takes her hand and leads her out of the dining hall to the conservatory. Alone at last, he softly kisses her forehead and her small button nose. Their eyes meet.

"We're safe?" Itra asks.

The warm air of the conservatory goes chilly. Danae stiffens. "I hope so. What else are you not telling me?"

"I can't shake a feeling," he says, "like we unlocked something."

"The same phrase from the riddles is on instant replay," Danae says. "The new stone will shatter at night?"

"Do you think the new stone is the monument Enyo described?" Itra asks.

Danae's eyes widen, and she grabs Itra's arm. "Elis, we need to talk to him."

They jog through the conservatory to the back foyer and descend to the present cavern. She hesitates at the threshold. The presence of Medusa and Athena ring through every nerve, making it hard to move.

"Are you ok?" He comes back to look her over. "Do you feel them?" She nods and takes a deep breath.

"I think I'll be fine." She takes his offered hand and enters the cavern. "There is no light tonight." She lifts her chin to the wide opening.

"The shield is definitely working. I can't see the border crossing or headlights over to the north."

Danae shivers and focuses on the interior wall. "Show us Elis."

A light grows, and then Elis fills the cavern. She sighs at the sight of her nephew's face. He is coloring at a coffee table. Anton is on the couch asleep with his laptop still open on his chest.

"Hey buddy, can you hear me?" Itra whispers.

"Hi, Uncle Itra!" He holds up a paper. It's a drawing of twelve red dots in a dark purple sky with clock hands pointing to twelve and six. "He's coming."

"What do you mean?" Danae fails to hide the panic in her tone.

"Father Time." He holds up a second drawing of a man with a long beard on one knee wielding a scythe.

"Hey buddy," Itra asks, squeezing Danae's hand. "Is he Ember's friend?"

Elis nods. Anton stirs. Elis moves to catch his laptop. "I need to go put dad to bed."

The cavern goes dark.

Itra curses, but another door opens in the cavern. They exchange a worried glance. The last time they entered this door, Teuta led them to the future cavern before the rogue descendants started their assault.

"I suppose the future has a message," Itra says.

Danae takes in a deep breath and walks past the statues of Medusa and Athena. She leads Itra through the door and down the small passage until they enter another cavern.

"We are here. We are open. We are present," Itra says.

A bright light fills the entire cavern. They blink several times to try to get their eyes to adjust as the image zooms in on the ember amulet. It appears with a small crack down the center until it splits in two. As it divides, twelve red dots appear in a circle. The dots at twelve and six pulse just before the image fades.

Danae lifts her amulet to inspect the stone. There are no cracks or damage.

Itra nudges her as the image of a single crib appears.

She sucks in a breath. The view rolls forward directly over the crib. There are two babies swaddled in red and blue blankets. She exhales and cradles her stomach. Itra puts his arm around her as the image zooms out and the entire room is visible.

"It's the nursery in the archives," she whispers.

The image fades into a dark forest. Three people run through it.

"The sisters." Itra tightens his arm, drawing her closer to his side.

The cavern falls dark and the door to the stairwell opens.

216

"Shows over, but the adventure is not," Itra mumbles.

They climb the stairs in silence. Danae yawns twice on the way up. She stops to catch her breath in the front foyer. Itra loops his arm around her as they head towards their suites.

"If six o'clock is in the morning," Danae says as they reach the steps to the suites. "Do we need to wake the family now?"

"But if he is a friend and not an enemy," Itra argues as they climb, "who's saying there is a threat?"

When they reach the landing, a small snore rumbles out from the first door. This quiets their discussion until they close their own suite door.

"Ember will wake Leon if there is a threat," Itra says. Danae turns to look at him. "We read the messenger book while you were out today."

"Do you think he will listen to her?" Danae asks. "You saw the primal look on his face before he vanished with Kaly."

Itra smirks. "It's not a command. She compels the messenger. Like the time we were shoved out of the suite when the bell rang with Teuta during our first visit. We couldn't stop the invisible force at our backs."

"But—"

He interrupts her thought with a kiss and picks her up. He moves her to the shower.

She bites his lip as the water falls over her head.

"Old move," she teases.

He grins before swinging her out of the shower and plunging her into a full, warm bath.

She comes up for air and wipes the water from her eyes to find him facing her, lounging in the tub.

"New move?" Itra teases with a smile.

She splashes him in the face before sinking back under.

37

At five, there is a light knock on the bedroom door. Danae stirs. She untangles from Itra and slips out of bed. Walking to the door, she dresses for action, complete with a jacket and shoes, anticipating Leon on the other side.

Leon raises his hand to knock again as she opens the door and slides out, closing it softly behind her.

"Hey, sorry to wake you, but we may have a problem?"

"What's happened?" she asks.

"I overheard a discussion between Enyo and Noel when I came up with Kaly. They mentioned flying back to the fort."

"Did they go?"

"They just left. Ember woke me when the front door opened. And two cloaks are missing."

"Do you want to wake the others just in case?" she asks.

Leon shakes his head. "What happened after dinner?" he asks.

As they walk down to the war room, Danae shares the conversation with Elis, his drawing, and the images they saw in the future cavern.

"Is your amulet still intact?"

The amulet rises from her chest to eye level. She inspects both sides. "It looks the same."

"If the riddle about a new stone is relevant to Chronos." He rakes a hand through his hair. "Are they in danger?"

"We need to check the archives or," Danae says facing Leon, "better yet, get Teuta back out of the maze."

Leon frowns, vanishes and reappears with the bronze shield. He takes her hand, and they land with a practiced ease in the center of the hedge maze.

"She was right," Danae says.

"Who was right?" Leon asks.

"Teuta. She said portaling from one area to another becomes easier."

Leon recalls his first ride to the archives via portal. "I'll be damned, you're right." They shift the mirror until they can see Teuta's face.

"Breathe," they say in unison.

The statue of the fairy remains, but the reflection of Teuta ripples and vanishes from the mirror.

Ding, ding

They turn to find Teuta holding up her brass bell. She smiles. "Ember said have patience, they'll figure it out. But when you saw my reflection and then left, I questioned her logic. As always, she's right."

"Sorry we left you here for so long," Danae apologizes. "The Medusa Shield is back, and Athena is in stone with Medusa down below."

"And Pax?" Teuta snarls, just saying his name.

"You knew he was bad news?" Danae asks.

"He has always been trouble. I knew he was involved in this scheme, but had no evidence or indication from Ember. What did you discover?"

Danae sighs. "He is the one that kicked off the events that led to the rogue descendant's attack. He found a gold cube and the blood oath. He used these to get Medusa on board to take you down and find your treasures."

Teuta holds up a hand. "How did he know the oath was forged?"

"Hermes."

Teuta nods. "And where is Pax now?"

"We left him at Fort Kelmend."

"Alive?"

"I'm not really sure." Danae frowns. She explains their encounter with Pax and Pem.

"You actually saw the helix?" Teuta asks, bouncing up and down.

Danae nods. "You've heard of it?"

"Heard of it? Are you kidding?" Teuta twirls in a circle. "The threads of life, time, and space woven in light to fill the night."

Leon and Danae glance at each other and shrug.

Teuta stops twirling and goes completely still. "Was there any fighting inside? Did anyone spill any blood inside?"

Danae nods. "Enyo and Pax got into a little scuffle. She scratched Pax's throat with her blade, and he gave her a bloody nose. I only sliced my finger on the shield's grip." She holds up her ring finger to show Teuta the small cut. "Why do you ask?"

"Oh, no!" Teuta vanishes for a second, then returns. She takes their hands and the three of them land in the archives. Five books fly towards them at once. Teuta holds her hand up and the books fall to the table and open as the pages turn and settle. She dances from one foot to the other and mumbles.

Leon and Danae stand back and watch. Teuta's energy and frustration escalate.

"What's going on?" Danae whispers to Leon.

"This!" Teuta turns, holding up a book. "This is what's going on!"

The page shows an illustration of a family tree with roots tied into one infinite loop.

220

The caption is faded, but Danae tries to read it aloud. "The lines of life are woven here."

"What does this have to do with a weird building in an old fort?" Leon says, staring at the page as he looks for any other text.

"It's Chronos, not a building. You just gave Father Time our genetic material."

"What do you mean?" Leon says, looking up from the illustration.

"He is a weaver of life, time, and space. A weaver can only be as good as the materials. And our materials, like our blood, hold the key to this castle."

Danae backs up to a chair and sits down.

"Enyo and Noel left to inspect the monument that appeared in the place of the building," Leon says.

"When?" Teuta asks, her face draining of all color.

"Right before we got you out of the maze," Leon says, bending to her level. "Why do you look like you could vomit? Are they in danger?"

Teuta frowns and vanishes, leaving them alone in the archives.

Leon sits in the chair next to Danae.

"What epic can of worms did we just open?" Danae asks.

"If Teuta is frightened," Leon mutters, "a big ol'can of fuckery."

Danae sighs.

"Leon, is Danae with you?" Xena asks.

"Yep, we are in the archives," Leon answers.

"And Enyo and Noel?" Xena asks.

"That's another story. Gather whoever is up and meet us in the war room."

"Time to go." Leon takes Danae's hand and attempts to portal her out, but nothing happens. "I guess my messenger status has been revoked."

"Teuta!" Danae calls.

Teuta appears with her hair frazzled and a vacant look of horror on her face. "A little busy."

"I see that," Leon says, pointing to her hair, "but you left us stranded down here."

"Tani!" Teuta says.

The floor vanishes beneath Leon and Danae and they appear in the war room just as Xena, Kaly, Hermes, Itra, and Vincent enter.

"Are Avi and Pem up yet?" Leon asks.

"We're coming!" Avi says from the stairwell. "What's on fire now?"

"First," Leon says, "around five this morning, Enyo and Noel took two of the cloaks and set out to investigate the monument at the fort." Leon holds up a hand as the questions start to fly. "Second, Danae and I freed Teuta from her statue holding cell using the bronze shield. As such, I'm no longer the castle messenger."

Kaly pushes out a long exhale. She grins as eyes turn towards her. "I love research, but a life sentence was a little hard to swallow."

"Last," Leon continues, "retrieving the Medusa Shield may have set a few things in motion yesterday."

"Last night, Itra and I spoke to Elis, Iana's son," Danae says. "He gave a message that Father Time is coming."

"On top of all that," Leon says. "Teuta is frazzled about blood left inside the building she refers to it as the helix."

Vincent stiffens.

"What blood?" Avi asks.

Danae explains the details of the altercation between Pax and Enyo and her tiny injury.

"Three lines," Vincent whispers. He barely has time to pull out a chair to sit before his knees give way. "The threads of life, time, and space woven in light to fill the night."

Leon and Danae glance at each other and sit across from Vincent. The rest of the group sits down and waits.

"Vincent, you know why she is so freaked out?" Leon softly asks.

Vincent nods. "The helix is written as a legend."

A book appears in the room and lands on the table with a loud thud.

Kaly yelps in surprise.

The cover is an infinite loop.

Avi unconsciously touches her amulet.

Vincent nods, noticing Avi's movement. "The Protectors of Time symbol was fashioned after the infinite loop of time itself. Particles binding and weaving together, creating the fabric of life, time, and space." Vincent pauses to look directly at Avi, then Kaly and Xena.

The book falls open to an illustration of three figures standing in a circle holding hands. Beside them are another three figures in the same pose.

"We just gave Chronos three powerful bloodlines to compete with the Protectors of Time."

38

"Noel, survey to the right," Enyo says as they fly past the waterfall and cave opening. "I'll go left."

He nods and banks to his right. The maze of stone walls and steps can be seen without the veil hiding the interior of the fort. The monument is at least ten meters high and five meters wide. It seems massive in comparison to Enyo's description.

Enyo slows as she takes in the number of passages and stairs. She finds only one entrance from the maze to the center. No movement below. She slowly descends, taking a closer look between the stone walls and empty stairwells.

Noel follows her lead. They meet in the middle, but they remain hovering above.

"What are you looking for?" Noel asks, inspecting the monument with a closer look.

Enyo doesn't answer, just points to the open palm of the monument. She flies over and hovers directly above the giant hand. "There was something in the palm yesterday and now it's missing. Something round."

Noel flies to her side. "Was it stone or reflective?"

Enyo frowns. "Stone, but the shape was smooth like the exterior of the building. Or maybe it was a mirror reflecting the stone of the palm?"

"We flew through some pretty wet clouds on the way here. Do you think the rain overnight may have washed it away?" Noel ascends, looking over the ground directly under the palm. He circles, looking for any round objects.

"Not likely," Teuta says, appearing next to Enyo.

Enyo spins in surprise, losing altitude. She corrects and draws her dagger. "How?"

"How what?" Teuta asks, tilting her head to the side to shake the water from her ear.

"How did you find us?" Noel asks, coming back to Enyo's side.

"Leon knew where you were headed," Teuta states. "Leon and Danae released me this morning."

"And just like that, we are supposed to trust you?" Enyo glares at her, drawing back for an attack.

Teuta nods. "I can tell you the object you are looking for is gone, and I'm pretty sure I can help us locate it before it is too late."

"Too late for what?" Noel asks.

"I have no time to explain at the moment. They need us back."

Enyo starts to object, but they fall hard on the floor back in the war room.

Leon and Itra stand and assist Enyo and Noel to their feet.

"That stupid fairy," Enyo mumbles.

"Welcome back," Xena laughs. Enyo scowls in her direction. "Good morning to you too."

Enyo steps behind the red screen in the corner and wishes her clothes warm and dry. The feather cloak floats over to the wardrobe in the corner. Her hair uncoils from all three braids at once. The sheer volume of her hair extends up beyond the screen before she steps out. She sits at the table and a steaming mug of coffee appears.

Noel takes Enyo's lead and steps behind the screen. He swaps his clothes for dry and warmer layers. His feather cloak releases and shakes.

Kaly and Pem watch the cloak glide back into the open wardrobe. It shuts automatically. Their wide grins are nearly identical.

"Do you want to start, or shall we?" Leon asks Noel.

Enyo and Noel share a look of indifference.

"We just went back to check on the fort and to make sure Pax was still gone," Noel explains, sitting down and picks up his warm mug of coffee. "We could see the labyrinth of walls and stairs leading to the center where the building once stood." He takes a sip before continuing. "The monument is massive, and the description Enyo gave over dinner was accurate, minus one missing object."

"Missing?" Hermes asks. The group turns in his direction. He blushes at the attention.

Enyo nods. "When I looked back and saw the monument yesterday, there was something round in the palm of the statue," she says. "Now the palm is empty, with no trace of anything below or beside."

Teuta appears between Leon and Danae. Danae smirks when Leon jumps in surprise.

Ding, ding

Teuta draws the attention of the room to her and places her handheld brass bell on the table. Leon removes the bell around his neck and drapes it around hers. It falls to her waist. She frowns and shortens the chain with a thought.

"Ember appreciates the dedication and sacrifice the family has made to recover the shield over these few chaotic days." Teuta straightens. "However, the intrusion of Athena and Medusa, along with their help from Pem and Hermes, are issues we need to address." Pem and Hermes shift in their seats. "The events of yesterday have unleashed an unforetold danger to our lines and the castle."

A few others shift in their seats, and the others dart a glance of concern around the table.

Teuta transforms into her queen form. "The helix is the connection of life, time, and space and has been dormant for thousands of years since Ember's rejection of Chronos. The blood of our lines spilled inside the helix has awakened him and his broken heart. His first path of destruction will be to bring Ember to her knees and all those who serve her."

"Is this the part where you start the pep talk and cheer us on," Leon mocks. "Or do you have more bad news?"

Teuta looks down and gives Leon a look of contempt that makes him squirm in his chair. She continues. "The powers of Chronos are documented here in the castle, so we will study and be prepared. Securing and protecting all catalysts will be crucial and our first priority."

Vincent holds up a finger. "The bronze shield, the Medusa shield, the gold cubes, and the amulets?"

Avi and Danae cover their amulets.

"Yes," Teuta says, "but also the staffs that Noel and Leon possess."

Both men tug their sleeves down to cover the ink.

"And the round object in the palm of that statue was what?" Enyo asks, leaning forward to meet Teuta's eyes.

"Urtar."

Enyo's face falls.

"What is urtar?" Leon asks, looking from Enyo to Teuta.

"In Albanian," Vincent says, "it means a northern Albanian man that is an advisor or judge. In Illyrian, it is a stone of judgement."

Teuta nods. "In this case, the latter translation is unfortunately correct, the stone of judgement."

"If this stone was as big as the palm of the statue," Noel argues, shaking his head. "How would a person just walk away with it overnight?"

Enyo clears her throat. "The stone is like our cloaks, it will blend in with a person's essence."

"You've seen this in action?" Xena asks.

"My sisters and I shared a vision less than a month ago. A person touched a stone and a glowing gold scale appeared. The person stacked a pile of glowing red rocks on one side and three ember rocks on the other. The scale balanced. It did not tip in one direction or another until a baby cried."

"So we're good until I deliver?" Danae asks, looking from Itra down to her waist.

"Wait, what?" Hermes asks, finally taking in the room. "You're pregnant?"

Danae nods.

"Are you carrying time, as the alliance foretold?" Hermes asks.

"Yes," Teuta confirms. "We have several months to plan and prepare for a major attack. The catalysts are still at risk, regardless of Enyo's vision. We have to be vigilant."

Kaly holds up a hand. "Who is the person from the vision?"

Enyo shrugs. "It wasn't that clear."

Teuta sighs. "Pax. We'll likely see him again, although as a slightly modified version of himself."

"Are we talking a clone or immaculate conception?" Itra asks.

"Chronos is a god like Ember is a goddess they require a vessel," Teuta explains. "We gave him Pax."

Danae shakes her head. "Why would Ember let this happen? I gave the decision of punishment to her."

Teuta shakes her head. "Chronos took control. Ember has little to no control or power in his domain, minus the ember objects you possess."

228

39

The heavy burden Teuta laid on the family before vanishing leaves the room quiet for several minutes.

A growl from Itra's stomach breaks the silence. He smirks.

"Breakfast, anyone?" Danae says, too cheerfully.

The family exchange looks and nod.

Itra gives Danae a small peck on her cheek. She squeezes his knee.

As the table fills with various breakfast dishes. Noel and Leon don't hesitate to fill their plates.

"Junior," Vincent whispers.

"What was that?" Leon asks with a mouth full of bacon. Kaly frowns at him, but he just shrugs.

Vincent swallows a sip of coffee. "Do you think the shield will work on Junior?"

"It's worth trying," Danae says between bites.

"Who is Junior?" Hermes asks.

"Mui's son," Itra and Vincent answer in unison.

Hermes nods. "If Medusa unveiled her eyes to turn him, the shield should work."

The room falls quiet of chatter with only a chorus of forks against plates for several minutes.

Kaly is the first to push back from the table. "I need to stand, or I'll slip into a food coma."

Leon nods. "Library or archives?"

"Archives," Kaly says.

Teuta arrives. Leon and Kaly vanish.

Danae frowns. "You can at least warn them before yanking them from place to place."

Teuta shrugs. "Anything else?"

"Yes," Itra says, holding up a hand. "Vincent and I need the bronze shield and access to the landing near Junior."

Teuta tilts her head to the side. "Vincent and Itra, will you please come with me?"

They nod and vanish.

Noel and Hermes are in a whispered conversation at the end of the table.

"What are you two debating?" Danae asks.

Noel looks in her direction. "The castle security and how to improve it."

"Ok, good," Danae says and nods. "Ladies, what is your plan of action for the day?"

"All things Chronos," Xena answers as a parade of books floats into the room and land with care on the table. "You?"

"Time," Danae says, pushing back from the table. "I need to understand what I'm growing."

Xena nods. "Mother to mother, it's a challenge at every stage." Xena pats Pem's cheek.

"Mom, really?"

"Yes, Pem, really," Xena says.

Danae and Kaly laugh.

230

Danae walks into the dining hall. The door swings open from the conservatory and a man fills the threshold.

"Junior!" she gasps.

He laughs. "In the flesh." His smile fades after taking in the design changes made during his absence.

Itra and Vincent enter behind him and tiptoe around to face him.

"So, the good news," Vincent says, holding up his hands. "The Medusa Shield is back." Junior folds his hands into fists and looks down at him. "But we technically failed to protect and serve."

Junior starts cracking each of his knuckles.

"The Zeus line has been restored through Danae and Leon," Itra says. "When Danae gives birth, our bloodlines can unite as allies to protect and serve Ember and the castle."

Junior snaps one last knuckle. "You need to walk me through everything that happened after I saw Medusa."

Danae pulls out the end chair at the dining table for Junior.

He shakes his head. "Let's do this in Ivan's study."

Danae shrugs. "We can try. I haven't had a chance to check that area after everything changed."

They follow Junior as he attempts to open the first of three doors on the opposite wall from the conservatory. It's locked.

He steps back. "Open says me." The door remains locked. He curses under his breath.

"We don't have a study per se," Danae says, "but we do have a war room."

She shows Junior the farthest door on the right. He nods and follows her into the crowded space. Kaly and Leon are back at the table with a map and a spread of books. They are deep in discussion with Hermes.

Junior stops at the threshold and stares down at each face.

Leon stands and smiles. "Junior, welcome."

Danae notices Leon's fake smile.

"Is this ok or would you prefer to go back to the dining hall?" she asks, but he holds up a hand.

"How long have I been stone?"

"Four days," Itra says after counting back.

Junior's face falls at this new reality.

"Would you like me to introduce you to the family?" Danae asks, feeling his discomfort.

"Later."

He stalks back to the dining hall and sits in his former seat at the head of the table. "Why is the table empty?"

"The thought provoked abilities are disabled for your line," Danae says. Vincent and Itra join him at the table.

Danae sits next to Itra. "Can I get you anything?"

Junior opens his mouth, but no words escape. He closes his mouth and swallows hard. "A hot meal and wine."

Two full plates of food and two bottles of red and white wine arrive on the table. He nods in appreciation. He pours a full glass of red wine and drains it before filling it again. "Itra, will you start? I promise not to interrupt until you've all finished."

Three hours later, Danae and Itra have recounted every moment since their last encounter with Junior.

"You're done?" Junior asks, placing another empty wine bottle back on the table. He had given up on the glass after the first hour.

Itra and Danae glance at each other and nod.

"First, let me offer my condolences for your loss," says Junior. "Our family trust will provide for Elis. Iana's sacrifice, like many others over the centuries, is not forgotten." Itra nods in response. "The actions and events over the last four days were unexpected. We apologize for not preparing either of you for the weight this responsibility can have on a family."

Danae's eyes well with tears. "Thank you," she says, "but Junior, please don't apologize for something no one had any control over. We're managing so far." She attempts a full smile but falls short.

"What punishment has been administered to Athena and Medusa for their actions?"

"A lifetime of stone for the moment," Teuta says, joining the table. "Do you have a suggestion or thoughts on a better alternative?"

"A few ancient options come to mind," Junior snarls.

Teuta laughs. "We'll have a family meeting this evening to discuss proper punishment. If you would like to stay for the night, you are welcome." Junior raises an eyebrow. "Ember welcomes all input for securing a plan to shield the catalysts and delay Chronos for as long as possible."

40

Junior enters the war room. The room is quiet. Nearly every head is lowered over books, papers, and empty mugs.

Kaly looks up from her notes. "Hi Junior, my name is Kaly."

"You know the wife you barred me from saving," Leon says.

"Leon!" Danae says, cutting him a look.

"Truth hurts," he mumbles.

"Junior, what he really means is that you are welcome here. Please join us," Kaly says, giving her husband a firm look. He meets her eyes and nods once with a frown.

"I understand his frustration with my decision," Junior says. "Our decisions were not perfect and cost this family a great deal. For this, I apologize. As the senior member of the Mui line, we failed Ember and we failed to protect one of our own." He glances at Itra and Vincent.

They nod in return.

Teuta arrives, breaking the tension in the room. "Junior is here to provide any insight into things that we may have overlooked during today's planning," she says, twirling from side to side.

Itra holds out a chair for Danae before sitting. The others make room at the table as Vincent and Junior sit down.

A fresh round of coffee with mugs appears on the table, and Vincent fills his mug and lifts it in appreciation towards Danae.

She smiles and nods.

"Noel and Hermes," says Danae, "what did you figure out about the castle and its security flaws?"

Noel nods to Hermes. "We need to find a way to disable all gold cubes," Noel says.

Junior leans forward.

"They can be used to enter the castle without tripping the alarm," says Hermes. "I know of at least five in my dimension alone."

Junior leans back. "I knew there were more cubes than what we had stored in the vault."

"But Ember knew the cubes recovered from the morning battle were fake, right?" Itra asks.

"True, we confirmed all but one cube was fake," Junior says. "We believed the attack that morning was a cover for Medusa while she stole the Medusa Shield. But I understand it was taken earlier, and we missed the alarm."

"Half true," Hermes adds. "The bronze shield was also taken by Athena during the siege at dawn."

"How?" Junior asks.

"She was in the first crowd when the veil of time slowed everyone down," Hermes explains. "She was apprehended and taken inside the castle for questioning and escaped." The group turns towards him, and he holds up his hands. "She found the shield and fled without my help. I tracked her back to Poseidon's cavern. She promised Poseidon to hide the Medusa Shield in exchange for access to the castle once they were back in charge."

"We know that she was in the future cavern before the morning siege." Leon turns to face Kaly. "Athena mentioned that it was her that helped you find the opening in the cavern and escape."

"A woman did help me, although she was startled by my appearance, almost as if she recognized me. I had no idea who she was."

Teuta flicks her wrist and several images of Athena hover above the table. "Do you recognize her now?"

Kaly points to an image of a slim oval face and framed by white wavy hair. "That is the face and hair I remember."

"Do we know how Athena accessed a secure vault and fled unnoticed?" Xena asks, looking between Junior and Hermes.

"The escape part is easy," Hermes explains. "She can morph into any woman nearby and blend right in. It's her gift from ember that enchanted the charm Pem is wearing." Pemphredo blushes as all eyes fall on her. Hermes continues. "And the blast threw everyone off. She shuffled out among the chaos."

"How could she conceal an object that big and go unnoticed?" Kaly asks.

"Several of the units were carrying swords and shields," Hermes states.

"How did she enter the vault?" Junior asks.

"The catacombs," Hermes says. "Below the castle floor is a labyrinth of tunnels and trap doors. She played in all of them as a child."

"But the tunnels are armed with various traps and triggers," Itra interrupts. "I've seen them in action."

"True," Hermes says, "most are, but there is a drainage pipe large enough for a person below the elephant fountain in the conservatory. It ends in a small stream next to the vault. Athena would hide trinkets down there as a kid."

Junior pounds the table with his fist. The mugs jump and spill. Kaly stands up to clear the books and notes away from the mess, but the liquid vanishes as quickly as it is spilled.

Vincent looks to Junior before speaking. "Ok, so we know her way in," Vincent says, gesturing a hand to Hermes to continue. "How did she get out of the vault?"

"She crawled back to the tunnel and used the gold cube with the coordinates to that stairwell." Hermes points to the stairs leading to the Zeus wing of suites. "Dressed like the guards, she walked out with the others to check on the wounded and corral the rest of the intruders. She walked out virtually unnoticed." Hermes looks to Noel. He nods. "That is why our first suggestion is to disable all gold cubes from so we can prevent entries and exits."

"I agree." Leon states.

"I, second." Itra and Xena state in unison.

"Great!" Avi says and smiles, "but how do we disable something in three dimensions and in different times?"

"We don't," Teuta answers. "Ember does."

"If we do this," Danae says, holding up a hand. "Will it change the past and therefore change the future somehow?"

"What do you mean?" Xena asks.

"Enyo and Avi arrived here using the gold cubes," Danae says. She looks between the ladies as they shift in their seats. She then points towards Noel. "Plus, Noel and I used one to escape from possibly fatal gunfire as well as a capture situation in the bunkers."

Itra blows out a long breath. "Any chance we can disable the rest and collect and destroy the ones Danae mentioned?"

A pile of gold cubes appears in the center of the table. A soft voice fills the war room.

"Illyria, ember of mine, the new stone will shatter at night and breathe with light when all is right, Illyria, ember of time."

The lights in the room dim as the gold cubes float, moving and fitting together, forming a perfect circle. The circle splits in two perfect gold arcs. One arc hovers above the Xena and Enyo. The other half hovers between Danae and Leon.

"Protect time, unite to fight. Ember of mine."

The group twists around, looking for who is speaking, but the lights come back on.

Enyo reaches up to touch it, but she pulls back when the arc brightens. Xena and Enyo join hands and pull the arc down as one.

237

Danae and Leon take their lead and join hands before pulling the other arc down.

The arcs vanish. A gold ring appears around the left thumb of each person that touched and pulled down the arcs. They hold up their thumbs and inspect the new accessory.

"Was that Ember?" Kaly asks, rubbing her arms to shake a chill.

"What do we do with this?" Leon asks, tapping the gold ring on the table.

"Repeat the phrase," Teuta explains. "Protect time, unite to fight. Ember of mine." The gold arcs reform and the rings disappear.

"Then what?" Noel asks.

"The gold arcs are portals," Teuta says. She flicks her hand, and a scene appears between the arcs. A figure waves the arc standing in a room with stone walls, and a dark round spot appears. The figure steps through the darkness and enters a forest.

"How do you control the location, like where and when?" Danae asks.

"Thought provoked," Teuta says. "Each descendant blessed by Ember reach up and take back the arcs." Everyone but Mui, Vincent, and Itra joins hands and pulls the arcs back down. "Now that the gold cubes are secure with each of you. I believe we can move on to the other matters at hand."

The family tears their eyes away from the newly forged rings and returns their focus on Teuta. "The security of the castle. Are there any additional flaws we need to address?"

Noel looks down at his notes. "Outside knowledge of the castle's existence is a risk. The exposure over the last four days may increase outsiders' attempts to breach the castle."

"Any memories of the castle or the clearing will fade from any witnesses like it does when the family returns home," Teuta says.

Vincent nods. "I had to dodge Communist patrols on this hill when I entered and exited," he says. "If they never found and entrance or way to make the archways work, I think with the veil in place, it should be ok."

"Any other concerns?" Teuta asks.

"We need to secure any other hidden entries, like the one Hermes described," Leon says.

A paper map lands next to Leon. He unfolds the aged paper and finds detailed drawings of the catacombs.

Vincent puts on his glasses and leans over his shoulder. "This is Gjeto's handwriting here in the corner. Itra's grandfather was a master engineer from Mui's line."

A three-dimensional image of the castle appears above the table. A small legend is in the corner.

Kaly leans closer. "Markers in blue indicate expected air movement in a space. Red indicates a leak."

Itra stands and turns the image. "There are at least ten leaks on the first floor alone."

Junior clears his throat. "Pardon me," he says. He takes a sip of coffee and swallows. "An area poorly overlooked by my line. We checked the exterior on a regular basis but never questioned the interior."

"It's ok, we can divide the workload to repair each of these," Danae says.

"Actually, we may not have to divide the workload," Kaly says. She pulls a book from the stacks in front of her. "The castle will automatically repair itself if given proper instructions. In my research about the catalysts, I found an entire catalog of books about protection mechanisms built into the castle. Did you know there is an entire section devoted to mechanical engineering in the archives?"

"I found several volumes of blueprints during my first visit to the library," Itra says.

Kaly nods. "Pretty much any innovation done in the last two thousand years is documented and stored here," Kaly explains. Leon smirks at her. "Sorry I know, I know. Get to the point, Kaly," she says to herself. "The castle has an interior mechanism to rebuild. An auto-correct feature. Much like the auto reset you described when the new line takes over."

She flips through the book and stops at a page with a single line of text. "Repair the old, fix and fold to renew the castle to new and bold," she recites.

A whirl of air and light flashes through the war room. The family dives under the table as the air picks up their notes and books. The table and chairs shake before the air blows through the room and out towards the dining hall. A loud clatter of noise echoes from all sides and settles to a dull hum after several moments.

Itra takes Danae's hand as they crawl out from under the table.

"Is everyone ok?" Danae takes in the room as heads pop up over the table and they return to their seats.

Nothing looks wrong or out of place. Even the previous mess of notes and books looks the same, just in cleaner and tidier piles with less chaos.

"Sorry, I didn't realize the power of the phrase," Kaly apologizes. Leon helps her back up.

"No harm done, it appears," Xena says. "Does anyone see Teuta?"

The group looks around and under the table.

"Odd," Danae says. "Teuta?" Teuta does not appear. Danae shrugs. "Leon, can you check the map now?"

"No red marks," Leon says. He rotates the image to check the rest of the floors.

"No prisoner statues either!" Teuta says, appearing next to Leon.

"Where are they?" Junior growls. The group cowers in response.

"Good question," Teuta says, dancing back and forth. "I've checked the present and future caverns, the vault, archives, and even Athena's old suite."

Noel turns to Danae. "Can you feel their presence using your gift?"

Danae counts thirteen souls in the room before she closes her eyes and breathes in. A crackle of energy runs up her spine, and she forces her body to remain still.

"There is a faint presence of something up in or near the towers," Danae says, standing. "Leon and I will check the west tower off the rear foyer. Enyo and Noel head to the east tower." Itra attempts to protest. Danae shakes her head. "Hermes, fly the perimeter. Teuta, please check the hedge maze. The rest of you, please complete a full sweep of the suites. Make sure you check every door."

The family nods. Leon and Noel call their staffs at a run across the dining hall to the conservatory. Enyo unsheathes her dagger and follows close on their heels.

Danae trails behind them, feeling the amulet—no warning of danger. She slows at the rear landing window.

Teuta is laughing, staring at two stone heads balanced in each of the fairy statue's extended hands.

"Teuta, is that what I think it is?" Danae asks, tapping on the glass. Teuta looks up and nods, not even trying to hide her amusement.

"What is it?" Enyo asks.

"Teuta located their heads. They're no longer attached to their stone figures."

"And we just found the headless statues up here," Leon says.

"Up where?" Xena asks.

"Picture a gold, headless gargoyle perched on the tips of the glass domes over the dining hall and conservatory."

Teuta is still laughing when they all return to the war room. The family gawks at her amusement.

"Teuta?" Danae asks.

"I've had a century-long running joke with Ember." Teuta giggles. "I suggested we add new bold figures to the domes." She chokes down a laugh. "I thought it would be a nice update to the plain old exterior."

The family tries and fails to hide their amusement and are still snickering when Hermes returns.

"What did I miss?" Hermes asks, looking at Enyo, who is only smiling.

Enyo fills him in on Teuta's joke. The retelling lands the family in another round of contagious laughter.

"My sister is dead?" he asks. His question immediately silences the room.

"I'm so sorry, Hermes," Enyo says and straightens. "Forgive us, we weren't thinking of your relationship with her."

"No, it's ok," he says. "Is it bad that I am kind of relieved?"

The family collectively exhales.

"No, not at all," says Xena. "If that is how you feel. Grief over the death of family comes in many forms."

He sucks in a deep breath and looks up from the floor. "I spotted a man pacing outside one of the archways. I think he has a weapon."

Junior starts for the door, but Itra blocks his path. "It's likely Ermal, you met him before the battle."

Junior's scowl relaxes to a grin.

Itra looks around Junior to the others. "A friend. Danae, can you walk with me?"

"Yes, of course," Danae answers. She pats Hermes on the shoulder as she follows Itra out of the war room.

41

"You good?" Itra asks.

"Getting pretty tired of the swing of action," Danae says, brushing her hair away from her eyes. "But otherwise, good." She laces her fingers through his and they walk towards the main entrance.

The afternoon has officially faded to evening. Warm pink and yellow streaks of light fill the skyline as they make their way down the steps.

Itra helps her down the last giant step. He drapes his arm around her as they cross the clearing.

"What are you going to tell Ermal?" she asks, tugging him closers as a cool breeze drifts over her neck.

Itra smirks. "Your bloodline, your problem," he says. She pinches his side, and he twists away, laughing. "What? Not as funny when the tables are turned?"

She pats her belly. "Our bloodline, our problem."

"Ok, fine," he says. "We've always told Ermal the truth. Why change it up now?"

"True." She hesitates at the ember archway. "Hermes is right, I only sense one person on the other side."

Danae takes Itra's hand, and they walk under the archway. They encounter a very pale and sweaty Ermal.

"Hey, Ermal," Itra says. "Are you ok?"

"Not exactly!" he says. "You know the crack Kaly came through?" They nod. "Leon marked it the other night and was planning to explore it for the shield thing you guys were trying to find."

"What's happened?" Itra asks.

"Two missing teens. Locals. I found their packs near the marked opening."

"I'm so sorry," Danae apologizes. "Xena spotted two hikers yesterday evening. We didn't run them off because we got the shield back and the castle was hidden again. I didn't think about the other cavern."

"There is a search party starting down at the lake. I haven't called to report the discovery of the bags because I don't want anyone else to go in."

Itra nods. "Give us thirty minutes, tops. We'll get them back. Do you know their names?"

"It's Franc and Mira's nephew, Mateo, and his friend Ricio."

"Our neighbors?" Danae asks, the panic rising in her voice.

Ermal nods.

"Oh, dear!" Danae whirls around and steps back under the ember archway. *"Leon, Kaly, and Hermes cloak up and bring one for me. Run, don't walk!"*

"Danae, what's happening?" Xena asks.

"The hikers you saw yesterday are local teens. They found the opening Leon marked where Kaly came through. We need to try to get them back."

Leon lands. Danae turns, and he drapes the cloak over her. Kaly and Hermes land a few seconds behind him.

"Hermes, do you know if there is a way to control the time as you enter the opening?" Danae asks as the four of them emerge under the archway.

244

Ermal steps back in alarm. "Hey!"

"Ermal, this is Hermes," Danae says, nodding at Hermes. "He's been in that passage before. Let's hope with Kaly's memory and with Hermes this will be a quick in and out."

Danae turns to Itra. "Stay here with Ermal." She kisses him quickly and turns to jog after the others.

"Wait!" Itra tugs on her arm. "You can't risk getting stuck in another time right now."

"Ember will keep us safe." Danae states with confidence. She pushes off and flies to catch up with the others.

Ermal stammers out a string of curses before finally pointing up. "She flies?"

Itra's still frowning when he looks at him. "Sometimes."

Danae lands beside Leon and Kaly. "Where's Hermes?"

Leon nods to the opening.

"He went in first?" Danae asks. "Why?"

"He didn't give us a chance to argue," Kaly says. "He flew over and in before we had a chance to yell."

Danae starts for the opening. Leon physically picks her up and sets her down behind Kaly.

"We go in this order," Leon says, leaning over Danae, "no arguments."

Danae glares at Leon.

Leon takes Kaly's hand and turns to the side to enter the narrow opening. She tightens her grip as she feels a ripple of energy pass through him. Kaly follows a step behind and reaches her other hand out for Danae.

Danae takes her hand as they shimmy through the tight opening.

Leon slides out and wipes a slimy film from his face before calling his staff. The warm ember glow shows a small stream in a cavern. He scans the room. Kaly and Danae wipe away the remnants of the slime.

245

Kaly points to a corner across the stream. "There."

A staircase of uneven stone steps ascends. Kaly leaps the stream after Leon. Danae follows.

"He went this way," Kaly says, pointing down at the wet shoe prints still visible on the bottom step.

Leon sprints up the stairs and stops at the top to listen. He motions for them to continue their ascent. A muffled conversation can be heard once they reach another opening. He risks a look around the corner and finds Hermes with two young men.

"Don't ever do that again!" Leon states, walking around the corner, startling the men.

"And this kind soul is Leon, his wife Kaly and his sister Danae." Hermes gestures to each of them as they walk towards the group.

"Mateo?" Danae asks.

The taller young man nods.

"I'm Itra's wife, we're Franc and Mira's neighbors."

"Oh," Mateo whispers. Some color returns to his face. "We thought it was a safe and dry place to wait out the rain. Are we in trouble?"

"No, you're not in trouble," Danae says with a smile. "Do you need any medical attention?"

"No ma'am," Ricio answers. "Do you know where we are?"

"Yes, and we'll get you home this evening."

"Sorry ma'am, but I don't believe that home exists anymore." Ricio nods towards the large opening.

Kaly and Leon share a look before checking out the opening. Danae follows a step behind. The spherical buildings in the valley below sway like seaweed.

"2284," Kaly whispers.

Leon stiffens.

Kaly turns, takes his staff, and walks over to the small cavern where Poseidon had held her hostage. The floating cots are still against the wall. She turns the cots over and starts looking behind every stone.

"What are you looking for?" Leon asks Kaly.

"If that passage works like the others you described, it could require a catalyst to keep it open. There might be something here."

The others join Leon.

Danae feels a tug from her amulet to her left. "Check over here. Bring the light."

Kaly brings over the staff. They scan the wall and find a straight line above her head, joining another straight line down to the ground.

"It's a freaking door!" says Kaly.

Danae and Kaly push together, and the door hisses as it opens to the clearing and the castle.

"Son of a—this is how he streamed in the army!" Leon yells.

Ricio takes a step back, but Mateo inches closer. "Is that the castle on the hill?"

"It's the future ember archway." Danae points to the ember stones at the base of the threshold. She walks under, spotting the past archway and the other three. She nods and steps back under. "That's the catalyst." She points at the ember stones.

"How is a cave tethered to an archway?" Kaly asks.

Danae shrugs. "Let's get these guys home first."

They retrace their steps back down to cross over the stream. Leon goes first with Kaly. Mateo and Ricio follow. Danae hesitates and turns to face Hermes.

"Did you know about the future archway?" she asks.

Hermes shakes his head. "Athena mentioned easy access before I flew the shields away. I didn't understand at the time, but now I do."

Danae turns to walk through, but stops. She asks, "Why 2284?"

"A legend of two," Hermes answers with a smile. "I'm sure there is a copy in the archives."

Danae nods and shimmies through the crack. A very anxious Itra grabs her as she comes through a second before Hermes.

"Are you hurt? What happened? Why didn't you come through with the others?"

"I'm fine, and nothing happened." Danae steps back, eying Itra. "Are you going to be a helicopter parent hovering over our children?"

Leon laughs. Kaly elbows him.

"Maybe," Itra mumbles. "I'm glad you're good."

She smiles and then frowns. "They don't look so good." Mateo and Ricio are pale and stiff. She shakes her head. "They saw some things that may be hard to explain. Do you mind walking them down with Ermal?"

Itra nods. "Ermal called it in. The medics are heading up the main path. And I'll call Franc." Itra points behind her. "We scrubbed away the remaining mark near the opening."

"Thanks," Danae says and sighs. "Please tell Mira we're sorry if they were worried."

Itra nods. He kisses her cheek.

Danae says, "I'll be waiting at the archway."

Itra and Ermal help the young men navigate the path and walk down the hillside. The others retreat to the ember archway.

"Kaly, can you look into a legend of two?" Danae asks. "Hermes stated there was some significance to the year 2284."

Kaly's eyes go wide. "I can't believe I didn't put it together."

"You know of this legend or why it is significant?" Danae asks, leaning on the archway.

Kaly nods. "It's ancient folklore. The legend of two is the balance of good and evil, new and old, man and woman, God and the Devil."

A small wave of chills runs over Danae. She trembles. The ember amulet vibrates, sending a calming sensation back over her nerves.

248

"Like the urtar stone," Leon says.

Kaly nods and paces, ticking off each thought on her fingers. "The year in numerology, 2-2-8-4, union – union – new beginning – creation."

Hermes nods to Danae. "Your union with Itra creates a new alliance and the creation of time."

"And the union of the Protectors of Time," Kaly adds.

Leon rakes a hand through his hair and blows out a long breath.

"Ok," Danae says, stepping away from the archway, "we know the meaning of the numbers, but not how a place can be connected to the future archway." Danae nods towards the archway. "Head inside. Itra should be here in a few."

Hermes goes under the archway without hesitation, but Leon and Kaly stay back.

"Danae," Kaly says, "we've been discussing another Chronos connection this afternoon and now with the creation of the gold arcs."

"Why does your expression say I should sit down to hear the rest of this?" Danae looks from Leon and Kaly.

Leon drapes an arm around Danae.

"The Protectors of Time book has an entire section related to Father Time," Kaly says. "The first few lines are significant." She pauses. "By grace, a race to create the line of Ember's time. Three souls of new and old will form the arc's divine line to free Father Time."

"Yea!" Danae's sarcasm deflates a little. She leans into Leon. "More riddles." She bites down on the inside of her cheek. "Elis has referenced Father Time several times, but he has never sounded afraid or worried."

"Leave it to you to put faith in a six-year-old boy," Leon says and ruffles her hair.

"I can't afford the darker path at the moment," Danae says as she pushes him a way.

"Darker path?" Itra asks, walking up behind them. She shakes her head and hugs him. "Mira says hello and thank you for finding her nephew and his friend."

42

When they reach the base of the giant steps, they hear shouting from inside. Danae and Leon scramble up and sprint inside, towards the shouts. Kaly and Itra follow on their heels.

They skid to a stop in the dining hall.

Junior and Teuta are nose to nose, shouting in an ancient language.

Vincent is translating the exchange to Xena as the others watch the action.

"Children, to your corners!" Danae shouts over their heated exchange.

Junior scowls in her direction but takes a few steps back.

"Do you two want to explain?" Danae asks, pointing from Junior to Teuta. "Or should I ask Vincent to give us the play-by-play translation?"

They remain silent, teeth bare, and seething mad.

Vincent is grinning ear to ear.

Silence.

Danae nods towards Vincent.

Vincent mock bows. "Short version. Hermes let the group know about the future archway connected to the cavern. At this,

Junior lost his mind, upending the table in the war room. He has made accusations towards Teuta, claiming that she is the only one capable of such a connection. She threw back her own theories, blaming his ego and oversight for the loss of the shields and the archway problem."

"Frankly, we don't have time for a blame game," Danae says calmly. "We need a solution to the problem and a way to prevent it from happening again."

Several volumes of books burst out of the library door and land on the dining table. The lights brighten in the space and a meal arrives between the stacks of books.

"Those who are able to keep a cool head and help are welcome to stay," Danae says and looks directly at Junior. "The others can go loiter and stew elsewhere."

The scuffle of chairs fills the silence of the hall as the family sits down. They start dishing out the prepared dinner and wine glasses are filled.

Leon raises his glass. "To Danae, for taking charge." He smirks. "All hail, Queen Danae."

She attempts to hold back a smile as the family smiles and repeats in unison. "All hail Queen Danae."

Teuta and Junior exchange a look of surprise. Junior sits at the table, but Teuta vanishes.

They discuss the research and references to Chronos over dinner.

"The vision Enyo explained is the same tale in an old fable," Xena says. "I found two versions of the fable in the archives. In each fable, the scale remains balanced until a baby cries. But the figure who touched the stone was a woman in one version and a man in the other."

"Could this mean Ember has also possessed the urtar stone?" Vincent asks.

Xena nods. "Possibly."

252

"Found it!" Avi shouts louder than she meant to and blushes. "The future and past archways can be anchored to a specific time and location if the space has a window to the present."

"Great, now we know how it is anchored," Leon says, leaning forward. "How do we cut the chain?"

Avi looks up from the page. "Destroy the window?"

"Is that a question or an answer?" Itra asks.

Avi shrugs. "A guess." Another book flies over her head and lands open in front of Itra.

He reads the page and looks up at Leon. "Have you researched what your staff can actually do?" Noel and Leon exchange a look and shrug. "Well, the ember glow you use as a flashlight is a wee bit more lethal."

Leon takes the book from Itra and Noel moves to Leon's side to read over his shoulder. "The ember staff can open and close any passage with a single command and can create enough light to burn an entire village with a thought. The scythe can cut a hole in time, creating a window to another world."

"Teuta!" Danae yells and stands, knocking over her chair. Teuta arrives in a flash. "The next time you drop a weapon of mass destruction without instructions, I will end you myself."

"It was Ember's gift," Teuta says.

Danae points a finger in her face. "And you're her damn mark maker."

"What's a mark maker?" Pemphredo asks.

"Great question," Danae says. "A mark maker teaches a new mark about their gift." She bends down to Teuta's level. "Your exact words, right?"

"Yes, you're right," she says, holding her chin up. "I failed."

"Anything else that you want to admit?" Leon asks.

Junior leans forward and grins.

Teuta glares at Danae and vanishes.

"Coward!" Danae yells into the vacant space.

Xena brings over a warm mug and hands it to Danae. "Chamomile tea with lavender. Take a breath, we've got this."

"I'm mad, but I'm fine." Danae says, lifting her mug.

"We know how to close the present window," Kaly says. "And how to open it again if ever necessary." Kaly looks over at Danae.

Danae nods. "Leon, I would like to sleep in my own bed someday soon," she says. "Do you mind taking Hermes and whoever you feel can be helpful to close the window tonight?"

Leon nods. Noel rises and heads for the war room. "I volunteer. How many cloaks will we need?"

"Three is fine," Leon says, leaning over and kisses Kaly on the cheek. "Be right back."

Vincent yawns before standing from the table. "This tired old man has had enough fun and adventure for one day. See you in the morning."

"Thanks for all your help today," Danae calls out as he leaves the dining hall. "I'm heading up to the tower to be sure nothing goes boom." Itra stands with Danae and they walk out, following Hermes, Leon, and Noel with their cloaks.

"Ladies, good night," Junior says as he stands and heads for the war room. The ladies nod but remain seated.

When the door closes to the war room. Enyo walks over and closes the door to the conservatory. She gestures for the other ladies to stand. They join Enyo under the glass dome.

"I think this may be our only chance to properly welcome Kaly and Pem," Enyo whispers to the ladies.

Enyo stands between Pem and Kaly, grasping their hands. Avi takes Kaly's other hand and grasps Xena's free hand, who is joined with Pem's other hand, completing the circle.

They chant in unison. "We summon thee to unite the three, with these two souls ever fold, into our hold. Bring us light to guide the night. To protect the ember in time, Illyria of mine." A whirl of air gathers around their ankles and blows straight up, lifting the loose hair of Kaly and Pem. "Unravel the weave and hear us breathe." They continue as Enyo's braids release and her hair lifts and connects with Kaly and Pem. "Bind our line to protect time, our legacy thine." A red and purple light swirls around the five. "A blessing of two, you can't undo."

The dining hall abruptly falls into total darkness.

Danae enters the tower and searches the clearing. She watches Leon, Noel, and Hermes jog under the communist ember archway. "Be safe," she whispers as Itra joins her.

He wraps his arms around her. "As you said before, Ember will keep them safe."

She flinches. "I realize now how ridiculous that is, considering—"

"Iana," Itra whispers into her hair.

"I'm sorry," Danae apologizes. She leans back against him.

A vibration against her back makes her look up at him. He's not laughing out loud, but he's still laughing.

"What has you tickled?" she asks.

"I really thought you were going to deck Teuta." He smiles and coughs before laughing out loud.

"I thought about it, but what kind of queen gets in a fistfight?"

"Ha!" He laughs, releasing her, and bows dramatically. "Did you catch the exchange between Teuta and Junior when we saluted you?"

Danae nods. "I'm pretty sure that is why Teuta didn't stick around."

He nods to the clearing. "Someone just poked their head through the future archway."

A small rumble shakes the tower.

"Who was it?" Danae asks, moving closer to the glass of the tower.

"Leon, maybe?"

Noel steadies himself, feeling the rumble subside. "Leon?"

"Here!" Leon calls out. He slides out of the narrow opening. "It's closed and clear. Ready?"

Noel nods. Leon looks up and signals Hermes. Hermes nods and flies back under the ember archway.

Leon calls his staff and lowers the glow inside the crack in the cave wall. "Close says me!"

The sound of rocks plopping in water starts and then a thunder and crack sends debris flying towards Noel and Leon.

They stumble back and cover their heads. When the roar of falling rocks stops, they cough and wipe dust from their eyes.

"I'm guessing it worked?" Noel coughs and spits the remaining dust out of his mouth.

Hermes lands between them. "The future archway is clear of the cavern," he says, "but you permanently changed the landscape here." He grins and points up to the sky. "It looks worse from up there."

Leon shrugs. "Bold and new, right?"

Noel laughs.

They walk back under the ember archway. Leon spots Danae pacing in the tower. Itra points out their return and she waves. He gives her a thumbs up.

Danae sags against Itra.

"Time for bed?" Itra whispers.

"Beyond," Danae yawns.

On their descent, they pause at the landing window overlooking the hedge maze.

"The moonlight appears to be a spotlight for their heads," Itra says, feeling a chill up his spine. "That will give me nightmares."

"You and me both!" Danae frowns. They wait at the entrance for the guys to return.

"All good, sis," Leon says. He ruffles her hair. "You look rough. Go to bed, brother's orders."

"Ha, ha!" She closes and secures the door with a thought. "Any issues?"

"Other than a landscape redesign," Hermes says, "no issues." He laughs. "From the sky rocky hillside now looks like a ring with twelve jagged points."

His words freeze everyone in place.

"You mean like a clock?" Itra asks.

Hermes nods and shrugs.

"Is that a bad thing?" Noel asks.

"To be determined," Leon and Danae answer in unison.

43

The sun streaming in from the bedroom window stirs Itra. He rolls over, feeling Danae's side of the bed. It's vacant. He sits up and looks around.

"We're home!" He hops out of bed and throws on a pair of shorts. "Danae?"

"On the porch!"

"Good morning, beautiful," he says, walking over to Danae. He kisses her lips, tasting a hint of ginger. She hands him a steaming mug of coffee. "Did we get back last night or this morning?"

"Pretty sure we went to bed there and woke up here," Danae says, taking a small sip of tea.

"Does that mean we're no longer needed?" Itra asks, raising one eyebrow.

"For now," she says, looking up at the hills. "I wish we had a chance to discuss an actual plan with the family."

"Maybe we're the only ones who were sent home," he suggests, scooting in closer to her.

She shakes her head. "I received an email from Kaly and Leon. The ladies returned home last night, and a few hours later Leon appeared next to Kaly. And she also had a new message from Vincent asking about Duke."

Itra shakes his head. "After the last month of chaos," he says with a sigh. "I'm ready for a day at home with you and no fires to put out for a change."

"That's good because our garden isn't going to weed itself," she says with a grin at his immediate frown. He slides an arm around her and takes a few long sips of his coffee.

"We also had a message from Anton," Danae says as she scoots in closer. "Elis returned to school, and the teacher sent home a note."

Itra lowers his mug and turns to see her face.

"The students gave him cards to help cheer him up, but one of the cards caused Elis to make a big scene in class." She frowns. "Anton scanned the card."

Danae picks up the tablet and swipes to open the message.

A detailed drawing of the five ember archways fills the screen.

"How?" Itra whispers.

"The student said this is how her grandma describes the gates to heaven."

Itra sets down his mug and takes the tablet from her. He zooms in and out several times. "Incredible. Who was the student?"

"That was my first question after I ask if Elis was ok after the incident." She pauses a beat. "Elis is fine, but Anton says the student was fairly new. Their family recently moved to the city from Nikç."

"Nikç?" Itra's eyes widen. "As in Kelmend?"

Danae nods. "My assumption too, but we don't know for sure."

He hands her the tablet. "Are you still wearing the amulet?"

She reaches up and tugs on the chain. "Yes," she answers, and holds up her left thumb to show him the gold ring. "And this. Why?"

"Do you think this means we may remember our time at the castle? Or will it fade again?"

"If it does fade, will that be so bad?" She turns to face him completely. "We could use a few months of peace."

His frown slowly fades into a smile. He kisses her on the forehead and pulls her in for a hug. "Peace would be great."

Acknowledgments

This book and the inspiration for this series came from Art, my husband, and his desire to explore Albania, his home country. I've enjoyed being along—sometimes far behind—for the ride. He provided a stress-free environment to create and write. Thank you for the support and encouragement, and for making sure I always come down the mountain.

My thanks also to my faithful friend and lifesaver for this project, my editor, Jenny Leonard. Her wisdom transformed the manuscript. You're a beautiful new mom, an amazing friend, and the best editor a new author could ever dream of—THANK YOU!

About the Author

Kim Malaj lives on a vineyard and homestead in northern Albania with her husband, Arti, author of Northern Albanian Folk Tales, Myths and Legends. Although she is a Show Me State (Missouri) lady at heart (Go KC Chiefs and Royals!), she loves her life at Homestead Albania.

When she's not writing, she tends to the garden, orchard, vineyard, and livestock. She's also been known to brew up batches of raki and wine, and other sweet and savory treats made from the fruits and veggies produced in the garden. She is an avid photographer, an active blogger about the homestead, and a hobbyist drone pilot, learning the art of aerial photography and filming.

Visit the blog: www.HomesteadAlbania.com
For publishing news: www.KimMalaj.com